FOLLOW THE WHITE DOG

JOSIE HARJO BOOK FOUR

CATHERINE SEQUEIRA

FOLLOW THE WHITE DOG

Published by Barcelos Publishing, LLC, Sacramento, CA, USA

The Library of Congress Cataloging-in-Publication Data is available upon request.

ISBN 9798990323063 (trade paperback)

ISBN 9798990323070 (hardback)

ISBN 9798990323056 (ebook)

Our books may be purchased in bulk for promotional, educational, or business use. Please contact your local bookseller for more information.

First Edition: March 2026

Printed in the United States of America

Novels by Catherine Sequeira

<u>Josie Harjo Series</u>
If You Hear Hoofbeats
The Lady or the Tiger
When Pigs Fly
Follow the White Dog

<u>Stand-alone Novels</u>
The Before and The After

To all of the beginnings and endings in life.

CHAPTER
ONE

The comfortable crooning of Hank Williams was interrupted by the *shick, shick, shick* of the six-inch blade against the honing steel. Cutting open a body was easier with a fresh edge, and I was mighty fussy about keeping my knife in pristine condition. I had a job to do, and I didn't want to mess around with a dull blade.

After several swipes against the metal rod, I gently ran the base of my thumb sideways across the blade, grazing it against the sharp edge. The grooves of my fingerprint caught ever-so-slightly against the steel, like brushing against Velcro.

Perfect.

I dropped the honing steel through the slot on the butcher's block and gripped the handle of my knife. The bright lights of the necropsy floor bounced off the blade. The grip of the black plastic handle felt just right as it settled in my palm, like slipping on a favorite pair of shoes. My fingers curled around the white letters that spelled out "HARJO."

A few feet away, Dustin snapped on a pair of gloves. "How you wanna do this, Doc?" he drawled in a thick Oklahoman accent.

He moved to stand next to me, his tall, wiry frame putting him a few inches above me. His gloved thumbs were looped in the pockets of his coveralls. His lower lip folded over his mustache, and his beard bobbed slightly as he took stock of today's work.

I pursed my lips, considering. It was busy this afternoon, and three bodies were laid out across the room. If we didn't divide and concur, we'd be up to our elbows in blood until well after five.

I surveyed the lineup.

The necropsy floor was cavernous, and the tracks for the hoist laced the high ceiling. At the far end, a thoroughbred horse lay stiffly on a large, hydraulic table, left side down and legs extended in partial rigor. To one side, there were three stationary metal tables for the smaller animals. A goat graced one, and a cat lay on the other.

My eyes circled back to the horse. Even from across the room, it was obvious what had happened. The lower left rear leg was bent at an odd angle, and I was pretty sure I could even see some bone poking through the skin. Without reading the history on the submittal form, I knew the horse had been training for the races, had broken its leg, and had been euthanized. There'd be a lot of heavy lifting with that case, but it wouldn't be challenging. We just had to document the injury, take some samples for drug testing, and write the report for the insurance claim.

Seeing the direction of my gaze, Dustin offered, "Want me to knock the horse out?"

Dustin was the best necropsy technician I'd ever worked with and could get that horse done lickety-split. Usually, an animal that big was a two-person job, but Dustin was a magician with the hoist. Using the large metal chains, hooks, and the whirring electric strength, he'd have the legs reflected and the cavities opened in less than twenty minutes, all on his lonesome. I couldn't imagine my life at the lab without him.

As the pathologist on duty, I'd still have to do a once-over after he got everything open, but if he tackled the horse, it would free me up to get started on the other two bodies. I trusted him implicitly.

"Sounds good." I nodded over to the closest of the smaller critters. "I'll get started on the goat."

"Want some help settin' up?" he asked.

The goat had a history of diarrhea, and I'd be shocked if it wasn't infectious. I'd have to collect samples to send off to various departments for ancillary testing to look for whatever bug might be causing it. As the necropsy tech, Dustin usually prepped everything and labelled the containers.

"Nah," I replied, not unkindly. "I got it. It should be easy enough. That one, however...." I nodded my chin to the cat. "We'll save that one for last."

The cat had died unexpectedly, and the owners had found the body on the front lawn. "I'm sure it was a hit and run," the elderly man had grumbled when he'd dropped the cat off for necropsy. "Belinda—that old crow next door—she's had it out for 'im from day one. Says he pisses on her flowers and kills her gardenias." This had been followed by an angry huff.

I was pretty sure Belinda hadn't done squat to the cat lying on the second table down. I just hoped I could prove it and prevent any neighborly fisticuffs.

"Welp, best get 'er done," Dustin said nonchalantly.

He moved over to the large animal table and turned the hose on. He soaked the floor and positioned the running water below the table drain to keep the workspace tidy. Once blood dried, it was a bitch to wash up.

The goat waited for me, so I made my way over and snapped on a pair of purple nitrile gloves. The carcass was an adult Nubian, and its left floppy ear rested against the table. The legs stuck stiffly out from the edge. Stinky, unformed feces matted the hair on its rump. It was a far cry from the usual pelleted feces and further evidence of diarrhea.

I flicked the rounded belly with my gloved fingers. I couldn't hear the *thud* over the music, but the tautness did not bode well.

Sigh.

Just one look at that round, yoga-ball of a stomach, and I knew I'd be coming home smelling like ass. I'd already tied my dark hair back into a ponytail to avoid ensnaring any dead animal bits, and my coveralls would protect me from the worst of the blood splashes. But the smell—there wasn't anything I could do to protect myself from that. I knew it'd hang around me like a death glow.

And, of course, Armand was coming over tonight.

Even though I would be self-conscious about the stank, Armand never seemed to baulk at the *parfum de bœf mort* that occasionally clung to my hair and skin.

Giddiness tingled in my stomach at the thought of seeing him tonight. My best friend Laila had introduced us last summer when he'd been in Stillwater on sabbatical from Romania. Our relationship had been a whirlwind, and when his visa ended three months later, it had practically crushed me. But with Laila's help, he'd secured a small grant and another six-month visa. He'd been back for about five glorious months. I tried to soak up as much of him as I possibly could. Thus, our scheduled dinner tonight, during which I hoped to not smell like the ass-end of a goat.

In an attempt to reduce the smell-penetrating surface area, I turned my body sideways and extended my knife like a rapier. I took a deep breath and held it. The tip of the blade pierced the stomach, and I took a step back.

There was a slight, underwhelming wheeze, and the stomach dipped slightly.

My shoulders sagged. That half-ass-deflate meant most of the gas was trapped in the intestines. The whole thing was going to be a giant, soupy mess. Any thoughts of a stank-free evening were hopelessly dashed.

I glanced over to Dustin, feeling a hint of remorse. The horse looked mighty fresh, and I knew Dustin wouldn't go home smelling like a bucket of shit. He already had the front limb reflected and was working on the back. There was blood on his gloves, but his coveralls were squeaky clean. And I knew that no fleck dared drop into his immaculately groomed, graying beard.

He caught my look, glanced at the goat, and gave me a friendly smirk. He knew what was what.

"Just taking one for the team over here," I called out playfully over the music.

He barked a short laugh. He turned back to the horse and began disarticulating the hip joint.

I turned my attention back to the goat and stabbed into the axilla, extending the incision forward and then back as I reflected the front leg to the other side of the table. I repeated the same motion in the inguinal region. There was a smacking *pop* as I cut through the round ligament of the hip joint, and the back leg flopped to the other side of the table. Pinching an edge of skin between gloved fingers, I skinned the hide back.

The belly of my knife slid gently over the abdominal muscles, careful not to nick anything below the thin layer, and the tissue snapped back. Sausage-like intestinal loops filled with gas popped through the opening like a balloon animal. I extended the incision, and the loops spilled onto the table, finally released from the confines of the abdominal wall. I quickly grabbed a loop that was trying to sneak off the edge and tugged as much of it as I could toward the end of the table.

After getting the intestines situated, I stabbed the diaphragm. Burying my hand in the carcass, I dug past the liver and cut the muscle of the diaphragm away from the chest wall.

It was time to open the thorax.

I stuck my knife into the rear leg of the doe; a meat-sheath was one of the safest places to stash a blade when not in use. Taking the loppers, I crunched through the ribs, first down the edge of the sternum and then along the vertebral column. With a few swipes of the knife, I snipped through the remaining soft tissue attachments and pulled the rib cage away from the body.

Both cavities were open, and I took a step back to take it all in. The thoracic organs looked squeaky clean. The lungs were fluffy pink, and the heart, which was still tucked into the pericardium, didn't look half bad.

The abdomen was a whole other bag of beans. The liver looked normal. But the intestines, in all of their gassy, ropey glory, looked downright pissed. Thin strands of fibrin coated the bright surfaces like cobwebs. Even though this goat had been dead a day or two before they'd decided to bring it in, rot couldn't magic up a lesion like that. This goat had a rip-roaring enteritis before it died, and a bacterial infection sat at the top of my list.

Regardless of the sour, sewer smell, it was a fairly easy necropsy from there. A few snips of the intestine would go to PCR, where I was certain they'd ID the nasty bug that had laid waste to this poor doe's gut. I'd still collect nibbles for the formalin jar, but I bet dollars to donuts I wouldn't have to look at anything under the microscope. I could save some money and time if the PCR lab could hit a home run for me.

I pressed my lips together and tried not to breathe deeply as I went through the motions of dissecting the intestinal tract. We'd all had the occasional slurp of rumen contents or blood splash into our mouths as we yapped away. The last thing I wanted was to take a sip of whatever bacteria raged in this poopy soup. Based on the hint of partially digested blood and dying tissue that tainted the smell, I was pretty sure my good friend *Salmonella* had a rager of a gut-party in those ropey loops.

The sound of wheels rattling across the epoxied floor echoed through the room and pulled me out of the rhythm.

Dustin pushed two wheeled offal bins, one in each hand. He passed one of the fifty-gallon barrels over to me with a nod.

I smiled. "Thanks."

The edges of his mustache tilted down in a grimace. "Boy, that one's ripe." He wasn't exaggerating; this one was definitely a stinker.

"Yup." I frowned at the loops of angry bowel.

"I'll leave you to it." He wore a playful smirk as he trailed the other offal bin behind him over to the horse.

We were both used to bad smells; cutting up dead animals was our job after all. But there was something about a *Salmonella* gut that made me recoil. I figured it was an evolutionary response, like getting goosebumps when a lion roars.

Keeping my mouth firmly closed, I collected a section of slurpy intestine for testing. After dropping it in a petri dish and closing the lid, I paused to consider.

I could just send one section off to the PCR lab and call it quits. I knew Dr. Manuel Rodriguez and his team would screen for the common causes of diarrhea in goats, something would ping positive—most certainly *Salmonella*—and I could wrap this case up in a tidy bow.

But whether I liked it or not, I needed to consider Gerald.

Dr. Gerald Richter ran the microbiology department and always had a bone to pick with the PCR team. Both labs could identify bacteria in samples, but they went about it in different ways. Ever since the PCR test had missed pseudorabies in some pig samples back in December, Gerald had been quick to tout the benefits of traditional testing methods wherever and whenever he could. I wasn't sure I wanted to deal with his bullshit over something so petty.

He's gotten a lot better, though, a magnanimous voice whispered in my head.

Reluctantly, I admitted that the little voice was right. For years, Gerald had been a relentless work troll, bullying just about everyone in the lab in one way or another. But a series of events, most notably the stuff with the tiger, had changed him. He was still weird as fuck—some things simply couldn't be changed—but he wasn't a complete shitass anymore.

Plus, he apologized to Dustin.

When I'd overheard that little nugget of a conversation, I'd just about shit myself with the shock of it. I figured there might be hope for him after all, even if he hadn't gone so far as to apologize to anyone else.

I chewed my cheek.

A diarrhea screen, which included PCR, microbiology, and parasitology, was heavily subsidized by the state. It would cost the owner roughly the same amount as the PCR alone, which was important in an industry with such thin margins. Plus, running all of those tests would offer a more comprehensive result for the owner. Sometimes, when animals got the trots, there'd be what we not-so-affectionately called a "two-fer." In those cases, there'd be more than one infectious organism at play.

Decision made, I grabbed another petri dish for microbiology. I cut a section of the angry small intestine, and it slurped into the plate. Brown-tinged, opaque fluid oozed from the open ends of the loops. Finally, I milked some of the soupy feces from the colon into a specimen cup for parasitology testing.

Easy peasy.

With the important part of the necropsy finished, I went through the motions with the rest of the organs. I took sections for histology on the off-chance that I might need to go back and look at anything under the microscope. Once I was finished and the goat had gone through the biodigester, there'd be no going back.

With the dissection done, I dropped all of the remaining bits and bobs into the offal bin. I scrubbed the table, using extra disinfectant, and lathered up the stainless steel. The fresh chemical smell washed over me, chasing away the *Salmonella* stink.

Just as I finished up, the whir of the hoist grumbled across the room. Dustin had wrapped things up with the horse and was lifting the gutted carcass off the table. Using the controller, he navigated the body back into the large animal cooler.

I rinsed the table once last time and watched the suds swirl down the drain. Once I felt confident that any residual bacteria had been pulverized with the lemony cheer of the disinfectant, I swapped out my gloves for a fresh pair and made my way over to peruse the bits and bobs from the horse. Dustin had removed all of the organs, sectioned them, and saved the relevant lesions for me.

He stood beside me with thumbs looped in his pockets. "Nothin' much other than a broken leg. Just a few bot larvae in the stomach."

Sure enough, rows of brown cocoon-shaped larvae were anchored on the gastric mucosa. It was an incidental finding and wouldn't have hurt the horse at all. But the presence of bots was still a lesion. I made a mental note to add it to the report.

I looked over the other organs, pinching a section of liver between my fingers, making sure the texture was right. My gloved hands squeezed the lungs, palpating the normal foam-like bouncy texture.

Last but not least, I examined the broken leg. Dustin had disarticulated the joint and removed the limb at the knee. He'd skinned it to reveal a nasty compound fracture of the lower cannon bone. I examined it closely, making sure to capture the details for the report.

"Pictures are on the digital camera if you need 'em," he said. "I'll send the joint fluid along to the tox lab as soon as we finish up."

I bobbed my chin in appreciation. "Thanks."

It was routine to take pictures of racehorses, mainly for insurance purposes. Most of the horses that competed in racing, dressage, or one of the other million competitive equine sports in Oklahoma were usually worth a pretty penny.

Submission of joint fluid for drug testing was also part of normal procedure. It probably wouldn't have anything to do with how the horse had fractured its leg, but the racing association tightly monitored any and all drug use. Some of the shadier trainers injected prohibited drugs into the horses' joints so they could train or race even if they were a bit lame. Testing would ensure that the team working with this horse was on the up and up. Joint fluid was an easy enough thing to collect, and the money the lab made running equine drug tests kept Sandy's department afloat.

Dustin itched his chin with his shoulder since his arms were still bloody up to his elbows. "Anything else before I tidy up?"

"No, sir," I replied. "It's good to go."

We worked in tandem, schlepping the horse parts into the offal bin.

When I reached past him for the liver, he teased, "You got an air of *Salmonella* 'round yerself, Doc." He lifted an eyebrow, and a grin twitched the edge of his mustache.

I huffed a laugh. "I couldn't help but notice how you jumped on the racehorse, leaving me to dive into a diarrhea case all on my own." I threw my arm dramatically across my forehead like a damsel in distress. "Now, I'll smell like the Bog of Eternal Stench *forever*. Armand will leave me, and it'll be all your fault."

"He'll get used to it. Dolores don't even notice no more."

I waved a hand. "Psht. You guys have been together—what—thirty years-ish? I'm sure my olfactory bulbs would be dead after all that time, too."

"Somethin' to look forward to in ol' age," he said with a wink.

With the hydraulic table cleared and the gutted horse carcass stowed in the large animal cooler, I turned my attention to the cat. The necropsy would be easy enough, and would smell like roses compared to the goat.

Dustin and I put on a fresh pair of gloves.

He nodded his chin toward the cat. "What's the deal with this one?"

I smirked. "Found dead. They think the neighbor ran it over."

"They always do." He shook his head. "Welp, now's as good a time as any."

I carefully examined the outside of the body first, checking for any scrapes, wounds, blood, or anything else to suggest trauma, of which there was none. I splayed the cat's toes, pressing my thumb on the little toe beans to extend the claws. Each nail was perfectly sharp with no evidence of the split, ragged edges typically seen in animals that had been hit by a car.

I guess Belinda is cleared of hit-and-run charges.

Dustin put a blade on a scalpel handle and passed it over to me. The cat was small enough that my knife would be taking a well-deserved break. I was pretty sure it was still recovering from its adventures in the Land of Stank.

In less than ten minutes, the cat's abdominal and thoracic cavities were open. My shoulders sagged. Everything was utterly unremarkable.

"Well, that's not very excitin', is it?" Dustin commented, echoing my own thoughts.

I shrugged. "Let's collect urine for toxicology just in case."

My gut said the neighbor hadn't run over the cat, poisoned it, or done anything else to cause its death. I could count on one hand how many intentional poisonings had crossed beneath my blade in my seven years at the lab. But in a predictable lack of faith in their fellow human beings, folks often thought everything was their neighbor's fault.

If this cat died from a toxin, it was more likely to have lapped up a tasty puddle of bright green coolant in the owner's garage. When a poisoning did happen, it was almost always unintentional, as tragic and oftentimes preventable as it was. But, no matter how the chips fell in this case, collecting samples for toxicology covered my ass should the owner come back accusing Belinda of slipping rat bait into a can of cat food or some such nonsense.

Dustin passed me a syringe, and I pulled as much of the urine out of the thick-walled bladder as I could. I squirted the fluid into a red-top tube and passed it back to Dustin before dropping the syringe in the sharps bin.

I slowly worked my way through the organs. I'd done so many necropsies that my body flowed from one step to the next on muscle memory alone.

At the liver, I paused. A very faint, alternating light and dark pattern peppered the surface, like the shaved edge of a whole nutmeg. Other than that, the abdominal organs weren't that exciting. I took a section of everything for histology and saved a chunk of liver and the kidney to the side in case I needed it for toxicology.

I moved to the thoracic cavity, removing the pluck from tongue to lungs. The lungs were light and fluffy, and a small section bobbed in the formalin jar, floating at the top just like it should.

"Heart looks a little big," I murmured to myself.

Dustin grunted in agreement.

I slid my hands back up the trachea to check the thyroids. They sat like two small leeches on either side of the cartilage rings, looking fine and dandy. Big hearts in cats with hyperthyroidism were a thing, but I couldn't blame those two itty-bitty organs this time.

"Hmm," I murmured and turned my attention back to the rest of the pluck.

I removed the heart and weighed it. Sure enough, the organ was two grams over what I would expect for a cat that size. Dustin went in search of a ruler, knowing I'd be measuring wall thicknesses and valve circumferences next.

I opened up the right side of the heart and felt a flitter of excitement. A white, threadlike worm about five to six inches long was coiled inside. I practically bounced on the balls of my feet with the rush of solving a case so quickly,

I held the heart out for Dustin to see and grinned. "All in a day's work."

Dustin let out a low whistle. "Don't see that very often. Most cats are on Revolution nowadays."

I nodded, folding my lips in, sad that the cat had died from a preventable disease.

Oklahoma was a den of parasites, and heartworm was only one of a million little buggers that might set up shop in an otherwise healthy mammal. Dogs were much more likely to get heartworm than cats, but a hundred adult worms could throw a party in a canine heart, and the dog would only show a hint of exercise intolerance. Cats were a different story; in most cases, one worm was enough to kill them.

"At least the neighbor has been cleared," I mused. "We don't need the tox samples anymore."

"Yup," Dustin said, plunking the red-top tube with the urine sample into the sharps bin.

With the diagnosis in the bag, it was smooth sailing from there. To be thorough, I took measurements of the heart and snipped a couple of sections for the formalin jar. Soon enough, the cat's remains had been bagged for cremation, and we were scrubbing down the table.

All of the cases this afternoon had been slam dunks. I thanked my lucky stars for an easy day. I enjoyed times like this: just enough cases to keep us busy and all of them walking away with a diagnosis.

"Thanks for the help," I said, slipping off my gloves and tossing them in the trash. "I'm going to write these up and head out. If anything else comes in, it can chill in the cooler overnight."

Dustin tossed me a friendly salute and replied, "Sounds good, Doc. Have a good evening. And don't skip the shower. You still got your friend Sally ridin' with you."

I pulled my ponytail forward and took a whiff. My lips tipped into a disgusted frown. He hadn't been lying. The smell of *Salmonella* hung around me like a rotten sewer rat.

"That's what I get for taking one for the team," I teased back with a smile.

With a wave, I stomped through the footbaths, eager to get the reports released and jump in the shower.

Armand was coming over, and I didn't want any guests along for the ride.

CHAPTER

TWO

I tumbled through the front door of my house about thirty minutes before Armand was supposed to arrive. I dumped my purse and keys on the side table and tried not to trip over Yersi as he circled around my legs.

The nasty smell of goat shit swirled around me, and nothing could stand between me and a shower. To Yersi's dismay, I headed straight for the bathroom, peeling clothes off as I went, ignoring his pitiful meows for dinner. With the slight chonk he packed, the Great Slayer of Canned Food, third of his name, ruler of Casa Harjo, could wait a hot second.

I zipped in and out of the shower, spending a few extra seconds to really suds up the shampoo. The coconut smell filled the steamy room. I knew my hair wouldn't dry before Armand arrived, but at least I didn't smell like a dead sewer rat anymore.

The possibility existed that my nose was too fried to pick up on some residual stank, but I knew Armand would just roll with it. He was remarkably unfazed by the gruesome details—and smells—I invariably brought home. I guess showing up to our first date with dried horse blood on the back of my elbow set the tone for our relationship. He understood that people in my profession might bring a bit of work home, and sometimes, that meant I'd crawl into bed smelling like a bag of ass. It couldn't be helped; some smells simply took two or three washes to fully chase away.

I dug through my drawers, trying to find the sexiest bra and panties I could find. We'd been together long enough that I could probably sport a pair of granny panties and still be cool, but I was feeling frisky and wanted to look cute. I slipped the lacy black panties over my curvy hips, hoisted my sails with the matching bra, and pulled on one of my nicer embroidered dresses. It hugged in all of the right places and flared at my hips. Plus, the black would hide the many Yersi hairs that always seemed to find a way to cling permanently to my clothes.

Yersi cried from the hallway, positioning himself in just the right spot such that his plaintive meows echoed through the house. I had to give it to him; the bugger knew a thing or two about optimizing acoustics.

Another loud yowl wailed through the house. According to him, he would waste away into nothingness unless I fed him immediately. If he could speak Human, he'd be telling everyone how I was the Evil Withholder of Food and that his living situation was untenable. He'd sing that tune until I fed him and worshiped at the altar of the Black Death.

Trying to ignore him, I toweled my hair one more time and combed it out, letting it hang past my shoulders. I skipped the make-up and added a set of dangly, beaded earrings. They weren't practical, but I liked the comforting feel of them brushing against my shoulders.

Yersi's meows turned plaintive, like I had crushed his soul.

"Okay. Okay," I huffed. "Your turn, bud."

He let out a *merf* that could only be interpreted as "Finally!" and scurried to the kitchen to wait. I followed close behind, pulled a can out of the fridge, and spooned his dinner into his bowl.

He buried his face with another relieved *merf* and began snarfing everything down. Just as I dropped the can into the recycle bin, a light knock sounded at the door, and my heart lurched. Yersi looked up for all of a millisecond, licked his lips, and went back to gobbling his food.

"Coming," I called out, trying not to speed to the door. It had only been two days since I'd last seen Armand, but I couldn't get enough of the guy.

When the door opened, I practically melted on the spot.

Armand's chin was slightly tilted down, and faint wrinkles of happiness danced around his soft brown eyes. The cute dark curl that always seemed to escape had spilled over his forehead. His lips turned up in a soft smile that barely pulled at the dimple in his cheek.

A goofy grin spread across my face. "Hey."

"Hey," he echoed, voice husky.

He put a foot on the threshold and pulled me into a hug. I took a deep breath, inhaling the rich, spicy smell of his aftershave. I nuzzled his neck over the collar of his polo and then pulled away just enough to give him a long kiss.

With a gentle sigh, I stepped back to let him all the way in.

"I come bearing gifts," he said, his Romanian accent slipping through, and lifted the takeout bag, which I hadn't even noticed until that moment.

Only Armand could distract me from delicious food.

I took another deep breath, and finally caught the smell of Indian curry. "Thank you," I sighed. "I'm starved."

And for more than just Indian food.

The thought brought warmth to my cheeks, and I couldn't help but feel like a schoolgirl waiting for a first kiss behind the bleachers.

Having finished his meal, Yersi emerged with a slightly judgy *merf*. Completely ignoring me, he sashayed by. Given the delay in feeding his imminence, I would be on his do-not-snuggle list for at least five minutes. He swirled around Armand's legs, rubbing his cheeks against his slacks.

Armand smiled and bent over to give him a scratch. "Hello, Yersi. Is she treating you well?"

Yersi's tail flicked like he understood, and he responded with a judgy *meow*.

Is the cat actually giving me the side eye?

In the moment, it sure felt like it.

My stomach grumbled. "Shall we?"

Armand nodded with a smile and followed me into the kitchen, Yersi hot on his heels.

"How was your day?" he asked casually as he set the takeout bag on the counter.

I couldn't take my eyes off his hands as his strong fingers worked the knot at the top of the bag. I felt myself flush again. Mortified, I licked my lips and turned so he couldn't see my cheeks go red.

"The usual," I replied with a shrug. "A goat with diarrhea, a horse with a broken leg, and a cat with heartworm. Bread-and-butter type of cases. It keeps the lights on."

I pulled two bowls from the cabinet and set them on the counter as he removed the containers.

"I'm glad you had a good day," he replied. "Even though you had three cases, I bet it went fast without the students. Do you miss having them out there?"

During the school year, small groups of senior veterinary students would cycle through the pathology floor as part of their mandatory clinical rotations. With graduation just around the corner, the pathology rotations had wrapped up, and we didn't have any students on with us this week.

I noodled over Armand's question. "I like having the students around, but it's nice to have a mellow day every once in a while. You know: easy cases, no students to worry about, that kinda thing. Dustin and I can just knock everything out and move on. Like a vacation without a vacation."

He nodded as he spooned rice into his bowl. "I understand. I feel the same."

His "real" job was as a professor in the plant biology department at a university back in Romania. He taught a handful of courses along with mentoring graduate students and running his lab. While on his second stint at Oklahoma State, he had no regular teaching duties and only had to deliver the one-off guest lecture. He was enjoying the break and the opportunity to focus on his research.

"How about you? How was your day?" I asked.

"Strikes and gutters," he said, frowning slightly as he shared our favorite movie quote.

I lifted an eyebrow as I spooned curry over my rice.

"I was really hopeful about G624, but the pattern of root growth isn't optimal," he started.

We moved to the table, bowls of curry in hand, as he continued to explain the finer details of the strain of drought-resistant wheat he was working on. I loved that nerdy part of him and listened with interest as I asked questions between bites of food.

The conversation drifted, and we both went back for seconds. I knew the food would hit hard, and I'd be sleepy soon. But it was just too delicious not to eat a bit more when the food was still nice and fresh.

Everything was so relaxed and easy with Armand. I didn't have to worry about saying the wrong thing, or being fake, or pretending to be happy all the time. We could easily fill up the evening with idle chit chat or sit in comfortable silence. I loved every moment with him.

Dishes cleared and bellies full, we snuggled onto the couch and turned a show on for background noise.

Feeling relaxed from a tasty meal and a bit love-drunk, I asked, "Want to come to Aunty's this weekend? Tessa will be coming. She hasn't been in forever because of weekend rotations. But with graduation coming up and all, she has this weekend off. Might be the last time for a while with her new job. I'm sure she'd like to see you."

Every Sunday, I'd make the trek down to Ada to have brunch with my favorite person on the planet: Aunty Molly. She was my rock, and I'd weathered many a storm over brunches at her house. I couldn't imagine life without those wonderfully simple moments: good food, excellent company, and all within the peaceful setting of her cozy home. I hoarded those Sunday bunches like Sméagol with his Precious, and was a bit stingy when it came to asking others to come along. Tessa joined us when she could, but otherwise, it was just Aunty and me.

Respectful of our Sunday brunches, Armand had never pushed it. He'd only been to brunch with us a couple of times. He'd worked out the perfect balance of joining just often enough to share that intimate part of who I was while also giving Aunty and me enough space for one-on-one time. Something felt right about him joining us for brunch this weekend.

He made a *hmm* sound. "I'd love to join you. I'd planned on playing football on Sunday, but I'll ask if we can move it. It's just a pick-up game."

I grinned and lifted an eyebrow. "You mean soccer," I teased.

He rolled his eyes. "No, I mean *football*."

We shared a snicker.

"I don't want you to miss your time with the guys," I said truthfully. "We can always catch up another day."

He hugged me closer. "It'll be fine. I'll be there." After a beat, he asked, "Did Tessa get the job with Dr. Anderson?"

I felt a flutter of happiness in my chest. "Yep. I'm super excited for her. I know working in rural medicine wasn't her first choice, but they really clicked over the winter holidays. Plus, it's a great way for her to get all of her debt paid off."

Dr. Anderson was one of the best mixed-animal vets in Oklahoma. He was well past retirement age, but worried too much about his clients to hang up his hat just yet. Tessa had been a perfect fit and an excellent choice as heir to the throne. I couldn't help but feel a bit smug about having been the one to make the introductions.

"That's good news," he replied. "I'm happy for her."

"She'll start right after graduation," I added. "I think she's picking up his weekend on-call hours, so we won't be able to see her much. Senior rotations have kept her busy, and I suspect this job will be about the same. It's good money, though."

I snuggled closer to his chest. He kissed the top of my head and ran his fingers through my hair.

It felt wonderful to be close to him, and every muscle in my body relaxed against his chest. If I held my hand just right beneath my cheek, I could feel the slow thudding of his heart. I breathed deeply, enjoying the smell of his aftershave and the faint undertone of his own unique scent. Every part of me enjoyed the moment and never wanted it to end.

I silently kicked myself for not asking him to bring Ileana. Even though she was sweet as pie, Yersi had little patience for the bouncy, ditzy dog, and Armand never brought her unless we had planned a sleepover. Being a work night, this was supposed to be a simple dinner and a cuddle. But I couldn't help but want more. I wanted to fall asleep to the soft sounds of him breathing and wake up feeling his strong body next to mine.

I wrapped an arm around his waist, hugging him tightly. "I wish you'd brought Ileana. I want you to stay and never leave."

He ran his fingers through my hair again. "I don't want to go, either. I want to stay right here with you in my arms."

I tilted my chin up and practically fell into his eyes.

"But I do need to let Ileana out once more tonight," he said in a resigned sort of way. He reached down for a long, soft kiss. "I'll stay until you fall asleep."

I uncurled from his arms and clasped his fingers loosely in mine. I pulled him slowly up from the couch. He brushed the hair from my neck with his free hand and kissed it softly. My skin tingled. Turning toward the hall, fingers still loosely intertwined, I led him to my room.

CHAPTER

THREE

The next morning, I woke before the alarm, feeling alone and empty in my bed.

Having sensed the change in my breathing, Yersi hit the floor with a light *thump*. It would be mere seconds before he began his plaintive meowing for breakfast.

"I'm coming. I'm coming," I grumbled, knowing my meager attempts at consolation would be brushed aside by his mighty paw. Until food graced his bowl, he wouldn't quit with the nagging.

I shuffled into the kitchen and took care of His Royal Highness. As I reached to start the kettle, I noticed a small handwritten note.

Good morning, iubita mea. I wish I could be there to have break-fast with you. Love, Armand.

My heart swelled with affection. These little hidden notes were a thing he'd started doing when he'd come back. They were old-fashioned, but I couldn't help but swoon a little every time I found one.

I clicked the kettle on, eager to get my tea brewing.

For the millionth time, I wished he were here with me this morning. We hadn't talked about moving in together. His work situation was a huge elephant in the room that didn't leave space for anything else. His visa's expiration date was just around the corner, and those discussions were uncomfortable. Instead, we tended to avoid the topic like an armadillo with leprosy.

Even though Armand and I didn't live together, I missed him when he was gone. I wanted to curl up on the couch with him every night and wake up next to him every morning. Instead of getting more time together, I might never be able to wake up next to him again. The thought crushed me.

The kettle clicked off, pulling me from my thoughts. I poured the hot water over the steeper, and the smell of the rich, black tea washed over me. I dipped the steeper a couple of times and set it to rest while I checked on the chickens.

The heavy humidity hit me as soon as I opened the back door. The sun had started to peek over the horizon, but the bright rays did nothing to cut through the gloom. Low, dark clouds hung threateningly in the southwest.

I wrapped my arms around myself, pulling my robe tightly around my body, and shuffled over to the chickens. They were still perched in their nesting box. When I refreshed their food, they slowly shifted and stretched before coming out to peck at the feed, clucking softly.

Normally, I'd take a few moments to enjoy the vibrant flowers in the yard and smell the deep, heady notes of blooming jasmine. Today, the clouds looked angry, and I couldn't help but feel like they were trying to chase me back into the house.

I shook off the chill with a quick shiver, grabbed my mug and a yogurt, and sat at the counter. Yersi had finished his meal and joined me in the adjacent chair, swiping his paw across his black whiskers.

My phone confirmed what my gut had told me. There was a high chance of intermittent thunderstorms. Unfortunately, they were also the kind that liked to throw down the occasional tornado.

"Great," I grumbled.

I'd grown up in Oklahoma, and tornadoes were just a thing that happened in late spring. They were as common as leaves turning colors in the fall or ice storms in the winter. *The Wizard of Oz* had tainted the world's view of tornadoes; Kansas couldn't hold a candle to Oklahoma when it came to the number of twisters that would touch down each season. The whirling spirals of doom were just part of living here.

Though a tornado was par for the course this time of year, I couldn't help but be grumbly. The heavy rain, winds, and hail would beat the crap out of my garden. The raised beds overflowed with veggies, and some young okra plants had finally started to get going. I didn't want everything to get trashed in a storm.

Feeling mildly perturbed at the universe, I finished getting ready and headed into work. Yesterday had been the usual level of busy: just enough to keep things interesting but not so crazy that I'd had to stay late or have mountains of glass to look at under the microscope. I hoped for more of the same today. But with swift changes in the barometer, who knew what to expect? Dramatic weather had a tendency to throw everything out of whack and pluck off the sickest of the animals.

I parked my car and killed the engine, cutting off the tunes mid-song. As soon as my hand touched the driver's-side door handle, a large gray truck pulled in next to me. My heart reflexively sank.

"Fuck," I muttered under my breath.

No matter when I pulled into work, Gerald always seemed to swoop in right behind me. I'd even varied my arrival times, hoping to shake him off, but he just kept rolling in at the same damn time as me.

Every. Single. Day.

It was kinda creepy when I sat down and really thought about it.

I waited for him to pull all the way up before opening my car door. There wasn't much space between his behemoth vehicle and my tiny Prius, so I had to twist my body sideways or risk dinging his truck with my door. A frown of annoyance swept across my features before I could tuck it away. I was grateful he couldn't see my face.

Even though Gerald had been half-decent lately, I still wasn't up for one of our usual stilted conversations. I hunched my shoulders and sidled between the two cars, hoping to beat him inside. The door of his truck slammed shut just as I reached the tailgate. I kept an even pace, eyes cast down.

"Good morning, Dr. Harjo," Gerald said.

His sharp, nasally voice made me cringe inwardly, but the Oklahoma-polite in me couldn't ignore him.

"Good morning, Dr. Richter," I replied cautiously, sneaking a peek.

As per usual, he was immaculately groomed. His thin, brown hair was parted perfectly, and every strand was held neatly in place with pomade. The morning's shave was so close that his skin shone like a baby's bum. His expensive button-up shirt and slacks were crisp and had iron-pressed creases. The outfit was topped off with a bland tie and a pair of shiny loafers. Despite everything we'd been through, I still couldn't shake the *American Psycho* vibes.

There was an awkward silence as we made our way across the parking lot. I shifted my purse and cleared my throat uncomfortably.

If we'd met like this less than a year ago, he would have already said something nasty and possibly body-blocked me. Maybe he would've added a "Pocahontas" at the end like a shit-cherry on top. But ever since the thing with the tiger last fall, things had been different.

Better. But not perfect.

Dare I say he's turning into a halfway decent person?

When we reached the top of the stairs into the lab, he held the door for me and said matter-of-factly, "Have a nice day." His tone was weird, and the words felt forced, but I had to give him credit for trying.

I met his eye. "You too, Gerald."

After sweeping through the door, I made a beeline for my office before the moment could be ruined. I knew I'd never be best friends with the guy. Hell, I didn't even think I'd be comfortable with him joining our group at lunch. But things were getting to the point where we could be in the same space without me wanting to throttle him.

Baby steps.

I dropped my stuff off in my office. After grabbing a fresh cup of tea from the breakroom, I went in search of Dustin, clenching the mug of caffeinated bliss. I found him sitting at his desk, plunking away at his keyboard with his two pointer fingers. A full cup of coffee sat steaming beside him.

I rapped the knuckles of my free hand lightly on the door frame and said, "Morning, Dustin."

He looked up and smiled, the edges of his mustache tilting up. "Mornin', Doc." He leaned back and gestured across from him. "Wanna sit?"

I moved into the cramped office and took the small chair. "Anything come in overnight?"

"No, ma'am," he said, rocking in his chair a bit. "But I expect it'll pick up."

My thoughts exactly.

Every once in a while, someone would bring in a dead animal after closing, and Josh would then put them in the cooler for storage. But it was more common for dead bodies to roll in as soon as the lab opened. The vet clinics, including the vet school across the street, would simply hold the bodies in their own refrigeration units until they could bring them over.

I took a sip of my tea and cradled it in my hands.

Knowing we had some time for idle chit chat, I asked, "Going fishing this weekend?"

"Yes, ma'am," he said with a grin.

I listened with a smile as he talked about which lake he planned on going to, what he was fishing for, and even *oohed* and *aahed* over a couple of pictures of fancy flies he'd bought just for the occasion. I didn't fish, but Dustin was my buddy. He was a great coworker, maybe even the best I'd ever had. He just had a way of making things better. What made him happy made me happy.

After putting his phone away, he asked, "How 'bout you? What are y'all up to this weekend?"

"Meh," I said. "The usual. Chores on Saturday and Aunty's on Sunday."

"How's Tessa doin'?" he asked, genuine concern in his voice.

To this day, I was the only one in the lab who knew with certainty that Tessa had stolen the tiger parts; I'd even gone with her to the police station to sign the plea deal. That being said, Dustin was smart enough to put two and two together; the cops had stopped harassing him just as I'd taken a depressed, suicidal veterinary student under my wing. I was sure he'd sussed it out, but it wasn't my business to confirm or deny anything, and he'd never asked.

As hard as the whole situation had been, it was pretty damn magnanimous of him to be asking about her. He'd been the main suspect for a fair amount of time, and half the lab had turned on him; he still carried those scars. Despite all that, he didn't seem to hold a grudge against Tessa. He knew she'd been in a tight spot and had been forced into doing something desperate. There was an understanding there.

That's not to say Dustin didn't hold grudges against others. He'd been guarded around certain people around the lab since the fiasco, and I wasn't sure that'd ever change. Even after Gerald had apologized for accusing him—an act which had shocked all of us—Dustin was still a bit cautious. Once bitten, twice shy, and all that.

I looked down at my cup thoughtfully. "Tessa's doing good. Really good, actually." I paused to take a sip. "Charlie Anderson offered her a job. She starts the Monday after graduation."

Dustin gave a slight nod of approval. "Good for her. Dr. Anderson is a solid fella."

I felt a flitter of happiness and pride. "It's great for both of them. She worked there over Christmas, and they clicked. He'll stay on a year or two to show her the ropes before he officially retires. But I'm pretty sure he's going to pass the practice on to her eventually."

I was sad to see Charlie retire; he was a great vet. But if it had to happen, Tessa was an excellent choice to fill his shoes. She'd turned things around since the stuff with the tiger, and I was proud of her.

The ringing of Dustin's desktop phone interrupted us.

"Excuse me, Doc," he said and reached for the phone.

I pointed to the door and raised an eyebrow.

He shook his head and turned his attention back to the call. "Dustin here." After a beat, he said. "Thanks, Anna. Be right there." Another pause. "Alright. See ya later."

He hung the phone up and looked to me. "Colic horse from the vet school. Want me to lay it out?"

"No time like the present," I answered, chugging the last bit of my tea as I followed him out.

By the time I'd changed into my coveralls and rubber boots, Dustin was at the dock, using the hoist to pick up the horse from the forklift. The whir of the hoist moving along the ceiling tracks muffled the ever-present sounds of Hank Williams.

I stepped over the foamy foot bath, the fresh smell of disinfectant tingling in my nose, and snapped on a pair of gloves. I palmed my knife and waited by the hydraulic large animal table.

With a deftness only seen in a necropsy tech of his caliber, Dustin used the hoist to perfectly center the horse left side down on the necropsy table. Just as he unhooked the chains, Anna stuck her head through the necropsy room door.

"Here's the submission form," she called out over the music and dropped the form in the hanging wall holder.

I stashed my knife and headed over to read it.

"What've we got?" Dustin asked, joining me.

"Six-year-old quarter horse with colic. Died on the way to the vet school. Not insured. They want private cremation." I dropped the form back in the holder. "Should be nice and easy. Let's get going."

Dustin gave me a nod, and we dove right in. With the aid of the hoist, we removed the front and back legs within ten minutes.

I skinned the right side of the thorax and abdomen. Using the belly of my knife, I gently cut through the abdominal wall muscles. They were tight, and it didn't take much effort for everything to stretch open. Loops of gassy bowel popped through, threatening to spill out onto the floor.

"There it is," I said, feeling like I'd found a pot of gold. Even the easy cases could be satisfying.

Dustin leaned over to look at the dark red sections of the colon. "Yup," he agreed with a nod.

Though the affected bowel sang to the nerd in me like a siren, there was an order of operations to follow when doing a necropsy. As if watched by a pathology god, it was physically impossible for me to skip any steps. With only the slightest hesitation, I left the colon and started on the chest cavity.

A bead of sweat trickled down my temple as I used the loppers to chomp through the ventral ribs, drawing a line of cracked bone from the abdomen to the neck. I passed the loppers across the horse to Dustin, and he chomped through the dorsal side. My knife slid through the intercostal muscles, creating a handle to pull the rib cage back. Soon, the right side of the rib cage fell free, weighing heavily in my hand, and I dropped it into the bin marked for cremation.

As expected, the heart and lungs were squeaky clean.

I returned to the abdominal organs, palpating along the colon. I was up to my elbows in horse guts when my gloved fingers finally found the torsion. The twist felt like a tight knot.

"I'm going to get the GI tract out. Mind sorting through everything else?" I asked.

He tossed me a friendly salute, his blood-covered gloves stopping a millimeter from his forehead.

I cut the attachments and tugged the intestines out of the abdomen. They spooled out onto the ground with a *slurp-splat*. I let the weight carry everything into a pile on the floor, where it would be easier to spread the miles of intestine out.

At this point, blood streaked past my gloves and onto the bare skin of my arms. There was an annoying itch as it started to dry. I tried to ignore it. Even if I washed it off, new smears of blood and GI contents would simply replace the mess that was already there. I might as well just suck it up.

I teased out the intestinal loops, laying everything out from stem to stern. There was a clear line of demarcation where the torsion had been, and the normal tan of the healthy intestine transitioned abruptly to the dark red dead tissue.

Just as I leaned in to run the intestines with my knife, the phone on the necropsy floor rang, echoing over the soft sounds of "Lost High-way." Dustin and I both perked our heads up like meerkats responding to a sentinel's alert chirp.

"I'll get it," I called out.

He nodded in reply and went back to work on the pluck.

I snapped off my gloves and headed to the phone on the wall. As I turned, I glanced through the glass window that opened to the reception area.

A uniformed police officer stood at the reception desk with his back to us.

My heart sank into my shoes.

CHAPTER
FOUR

The phone rang again, shaking me out of the deep sense of foreboding.

"This is Dr. Harjo," I answered. The phone's handset was cool against my ear.

"Hello, Dr. Harjo. This is Anna. I've got a gent with a dog for necropsy. Would you like to interview him?"

Fuck no.

I couldn't help my knee-jerk reaction. Between the Shadowhawk and the tiger cases, I'd had enough of the cops. We didn't cross paths with the police much in my line of work. When we did, it was usually for some unpleasant reason or another. But no matter how much I didn't want to talk to them—or get within ten feet of a case they'd brought in—I needed to suck it up.

"I'll be right there," I replied, feeling proud of myself for saying it without a sigh.

I hung up the phone and glanced down at the cracked blood caked on my skin from my glove line to my forearms. The blood splatters on my coveralls were halfway between a modern art painting and a serial killer caught in the act.

The sigh I'd been holding finally escaped.

"Got another one," I called over to Dustin. "I'll be right back."

"Alright," he called over, still focused on getting the pluck out of the colic horse.

He hadn't noticed who was hunkered on the other side of the necropsy window. Part of me was glad. When everything went down with the tiger, he'd gone to a dark place, and the cops had forced him there. It had killed me to see him backed into a corner like that. I'd do everything in my power to shelter him from whatever waited on the other side of that glass.

At the sink, I lathered up my arms, making sure my skin was squeaky clean. Then, I stepped into the footbath, taking the large scrub brush to my boots. I didn't have time to change out of my Sweeney Todd look, so I threw a fresh lab coat over my messy coveralls and buttoned it up. Blood spatters and a few drops of intestinal contents peeked out beneath the hem, but I figured if that bit of gore bothered the cops, they were in the wrong profession.

I trudged to the receiving department, trying but failing to arrange my scowl into a pleasant smile. Stuffing my hands in my lab coat pockets, I threw my shoulders back with fake confidence and rounded the corner.

And I stopped dead in my tracks.

"Officer Watts," I blurted. A cool sense of dread gripped my spine.

He turned to look at me and leaned one elbow on the receiving window counter. He wore a traditional police uniform with a sidearm buckled to his side. His blond hair was speckled with gray and cropped short like he'd just stepped out of boot camp. Middle-aged wrinkles creased the skin around his sharp blue eyes.

They were *not* the wrinkles of a lifetime of laughter.

"Well, Dr. Harjo." He drew out my name with a crocodile grin. "Funny how our paths keep crossin', ain't it?"

"It is," I answered coolly.

It wasn't.

In fact, of all of the cops in Stillwater, this was positively the last person I wanted to see again. I knew there were other police officers in our small, two-Walmart town. I'd verified it with my own eyes when I'd ventured to the only police station in our fair city to support Tessa. And yet, this would be the third time Officer Watts had crossed the lab's threshold. The last time he'd been here, he was about to nail Dustin to the cross over the stolen tiger parts.

I hoped Dustin wouldn't have to see him. Dustin would roll with it, cool as a cucumber, like he always did. But I was certain this shitass would somehow dredge up all of the drama from last fall. Dustin had finally started to heal, and I didn't want this prick to knock him back a few steps.

"Please have a seat," I said, gesturing to the small room off to the side of the vestibule, trying to get him out of the line of sight of the necropsy window. "I'll be with you in a moment."

The last two times I'd shared a room with Officer Watts, he'd been interviewing me. This time, I'd be interviewing *him*. A part of me wondered how his ego would handle that, since Officer Watts had more than a dash of misogyny in his personality profile.

I stepped to the side as he moved past me to the interview room. The faint smell of pomade trailed after him. With the guy tucked firmly out of sight, I moved over to the receiving window.

Anna caught my eye, folding her lips and creasing her eyebrows.

"This is gonna suck, isn't it?" I asked quietly, hoping Officer Watts was out of range.

She nodded sadly. Her fingers sped across the keyboard, and a barcode printed out. She peeled the sticker off and placed it on the submission form before passing it through the receiving window.

She cleared her throat. "He said the handler is outside sayin' good-bye. I'll call Dustin to bring it in. Dustin should be able to get the body in before you finish up with...." She tossed her head in the direction of the interview room.

I glanced up from the submission form and caught her look. "Thanks, Anna."

She smiled sadly with an unspoken agreement to keep Officer Watts as far away from Dustin as possible.

Before I headed into the monster's den, I read through the form and tried to get my bearings. With each word, the icy hand of dread slowly clenched at my chest, and a buzzing sound filled my ears.

On today's agenda: a police dog.

Top differential: murder.

Anna hung up the phone with a *clunk*, making me jump.

Seeing my expression, she tossed me a sympathetic look. "Yeah, I know. It's going to be rough. Just think about the cookies Carol brought today and try to make it to lunch."

A smile somehow pushed its way through the stress, and I huffed a laugh. "Save me fifteen of whatever she brought. I think I'll be eating that instead of my salad."

Taking the submission form, I headed to the small room, resigned to my fate.

***

The interview room was a small, sad little thing. There was just enough space for a desk and a few chairs. The walls were the bland, scuffed, off-white typical of depressing government buildings. The fluorescent bulbs buzzed as the hum of the lights sucked the soul out of the room. Cremation pamphlets and grief counseling brochures sat limply in wall hangers, faded and dusty.

I took the seat opposite Officer Watts.

He leaned back in the chair with one ankle crossed on his knee. A hand rested casually on his sidearm, like it was no big thing. The other sat loosely in his lap, elbow leaning on the armrest.

I laid the submission form on the desk and clicked my pen, ready to take notes. My voice caught in my throat before I could even start.

During my three years in residency and seven years as faculty, I'd never once had to interview a police officer about the alleged murder of another. With any other case, I'd offer condolences of a length that varied based on social cues. This would be followed by questions about how long the animal had been sick, what the clinical signs had been, if any other animals were affected, how the animals were kept—those kinds of things.

This case wasn't a horse with a broken leg or a goat with diarrhea. Police dogs had been sworn in and were treated as human beings under the law; this was some serious shit. And I had no clue where to even start.

I cleared my throat, trying to buy some more time.

Officer Watts sat still as a statue, studying me. He was used to grilling people and seemed snug as a bug in a rug, even if he was seated on the other side of things. Me? I was a fish out of water. I just hoped I didn't flop around, gasping for air and looking like a complete dumbass.

I gave myself a mental slap on the cheek. I was being a big baby about this. This case was like any other, and the process was the same. I needed to tease out any relevant history and go cut up a dead body.

I could do this.

My eyes scanned the form again. "Nine-year-old Belgian Malinois. Found dead in the police car."

It was an annoyingly vague history, especially coming from someone whose job it was to gather and report as many details as possible.

All pathologists had done their fair share of necropsies while blind to the case history. But any details we could glean might be helpful. A good history also gave us some idea of what samples we should collect during the necropsy. Sometimes the histories would lead us down the wrong path, but if we followed the lesions, we'd almost never be led astray.

"Can you walk me through what you know so far?" I asked.

He gave a slight shrug, and the corner of his mouth turned down. "We don't have much information at this point. The victim had been working out at Will Rogers Airport. After inspecting a fairly large shipment, the victim was placed in the police vehicle. He was found dead approximately an hour later."

"That's…"

…*not at all helpful*, I finished, but thankfully didn't say out loud. That information did fuck-all to narrow down the innumerable list of differentials.

I tried again. "Any signs before he passed? Vomiting? Diarrhea? Anything?"

"I don't have that information. The handler hasn't been questioned yet."

Questioned?

"Is he a suspect?" I asked, slightly aghast. Handlers had close bonds with their dogs, and I couldn't imagine one of them hurting their partner.

"Everyone is a suspect," he said, somewhat ominously.

My lips pulled into a thin line. I knew what "everyone is a suspect" felt like. Even I'd been questioned when the tiger parts had gone missing. But Dustin had gotten the brunt of it. This shitass sitting across from me had bird-dogged him until the end.

Trying to brush away my irritation, I pulled my focus back to the case. "Any information at all would be helpful. Like how the dog behaved before he died, where the car was parked, who had access. Anything."

Even though I kept trying, I wasn't hopeful I could eek anything useful out of this gremlin.

He drummed his fingers on his thigh. "This happened outside my jurisdiction. I'm just here as the local liaison, assisting with the chain of custody and all. Detective Pollard will decide what can be shared with you."

Another cop? Fuck.

Today was turning out to be all sorts of lame.

"Detective Pollard is…?" I nudged. It was like pulling fucking teeth.

"You don't do this very often, do you?" he scoffed, his lips pulled into something between a smug expression and a sneer.

My hackles rose.

I interviewed people on the daily and dealt with all sorts of personalities. Everything from crying, grizzled cowboys to erratic, hand-wringing Shih Tzu owners. All of them had sat in that chair where Officer Watts's ass was currently planted. I was damn good at my job and could pull info out of the toughest customers. I didn't appreciate being talked down to, and it wasn't worth trying to pull facts out of a recalcitrant shitass unless I had to.

This interview needed to end.

I plastered on a patient look. "What is the best way to contact Detective Pollard?"

The submittal form listed an annoyingly vague "Oklahoma City Police Department." I knew that the general phone number would lead me into a soul-sucking phone tree where I'd be left to wander aimlessly for hours.

Officer Watts crossed his arms. "He's here. He rode down with the handler. He's making sure the dog is transferred to y'all without being tampered with." He raised an eyebrow. "I'm assuming the security has improved in this establishment since the last time I was here."

I wanted to slap the smug look off his face, but that would land my ass in jail cell.

Instead, I flashed him a syrupy smile and ignored the jab. "Well, I guess we'll just wait then." I clicked my pen and folded my hands over the submission form.

The air crackled.

Thankfully, the universe decided to rescue me, and a tall man breezed through the door.

"Dr. Harjo?" he asked in a deep voice. A smile tipped his lips that was somehow both cordial and sad.

I put him in his late fifties. The light brown skin around his dark eyes was laced with wrinkles. His salt-and-pepper hair was buzzed almost to the skin, and an inch or so graced the top. He wore a generic suit and tie that stretched tight over his broad-shouldered frame. He'd clearly been fit once, but was getting a little soft around the belly in his old age. His body posture was relaxed and open.

I instantly liked him.

Standing, I tried to keep the relief from my face at having a decent person to finally talk to. "Yes, sir. I'm Dr. Harjo." I reached out for a handshake.

He clasped my hand firmly but didn't crush it. With a nod, he said, "Nice to make your acquaintance. I'm Detective Pollard. Please call me Chuck."

His accent was all rural Oklahoman with a hint of a lilt that put me right back on the rez.

"Nice to meet you, Chuck," I replied. "Sorry we have to meet like this. Would you like to have a seat?"

"Thank you, ma'am." He said, pulling the empty chair closer to the desk, and sat down.

Officer Watts hunkered in his seat. A muscle in his cheek bobbed as he clenched his teeth. I was surprised to see him clam up around the detective and could only guess it was because Chuck outranked him. I had a feeling Officer Watts liked to be the one in control.

I returned to my chair and clicked my pen, ready to take notes.

"I'm the lead detective on the case," he started by way of introduction. "I drove up with Austin to drop Tohbi off."

"Austin?" I asked.

"Austin Carlyle. Tohbi's handler. He's mighty upset, as you can imagine. I figured I'd give him some time alone while I came in to take care of things."

Officer Watts shifted in his seat and cleared his throat.

Chuck looked unfazed and continued, "This is hittin' the department pretty hard. Austin insisted on coming along, and I didn't see anything wrong with helpin' a grieving man."

My heart warmed.

"It's always difficult losing an animal," I commented. "Handlers have a special bond with their partners. I suspect it'll be a rough go for a while."

Chuck folded his lips sadly and gave the slightest of nods.

After a respectful pause, I said, "I'll do my best to find an answer for you." I looked down at the form. "The history is pretty thin. Anything you can add?"

"We're just getting started on the case, but I can share what I know so far," Chuck answered. "Austin and Tohbi started their shift at six this morning. They were covering a fairly big shipment that came in on a cargo flight. From what I gather, Austin put Tohbi in the vehicle while they wrapped things up and then found him dead a little after."

Chuck looked at me somewhat apologetically.

Officer Watts frowned.

"Do you know if Tohbi was acting normal? Had he been sick at all? Do you know how long he had been in the car?" I couldn't help rattling off questions. There still wasn't much to go on at this stage.

Chuck shook his head. "I don't have more for you right now. I know it ain't a lot of information. I'm gonna take Austin back, get some food in him, and get more details. If I turn anything up that might be useful, I'll give you a jingle."

"Thank you, sir," I said, unable to keep the disappointment from my voice.

With what little I'd gathered so far, damn near anything could've killed the dog. I might open him up and discover he's riddled with cancer or find a bullet buried in his brain.

I glanced down at the form, trying to hide the swelling panic in my chest. I noticed with relief that the "private cremation" box was checked. That was one less tough conversation I needed to have.

"I think I've got all I need for now," I lied. "I'll do my best and try to get you the gross report by end-of-day."

"Appreciate it," Chuck replied. He leaned to the side to pull his wallet out of his back pocket. He fished out a business card and pushed it across the table. "Here's my card if you need to get a hold of me. It'll be quicker than callin' the department and trying to make your way through that godforsaken phone tree."

An appreciative smile tilted my lips at his superb mind-reading abilities.

"I don't have a card handy," I replied. "But if anything comes up, please call the lab and ask for Dr. Harjo. You'll get a Carol or James instead of a phone tree, and they'll put you right through."

Chuck huffed a laugh. "Sounds good," he replied with a tip of his head. "And thank you kindly."

The chairs scratched across the linoleum as the three of us stood. Chuck stuffed his wallet away. I slid Chuck's card into my lab coat pocket and reached for his hand again. He gave it a nice shake and pushed his chair in.

The Oklahoma-polite in me forced my hand out to Officer Watts. He gripped it firmly and smirked. I didn't know what was going through his head, but I couldn't help but feel like he was laughing at me. Part of me wanted to grip his hand, pull him in closer, and knee him in the nuts. Instead, I plastered on a fake smile and released my grip.

Officer Watts followed Chuck to the door, but stopped at the threshold to face me.

"Oh, by the way—" He tapped a finger on the left lower edge of his cheek. "You got some blood on your face right there. Might want to clean yourself up." His eyes danced with malevolent glee before turning his back to me and leaving me mortified.

***

"Well, that fucking sucked," I muttered to myself as I stomped back to the necropsy floor. I picked at the dried horse blood on my face, feeling like Lady Macbeth.

Dustin laid a large dog on the small animal table closest to the door. He stepped back and stuffed his hands in his pockets, looking somber. The thing was huge, with long, thick hair that was white as snow. He looked like Ghost from *Game of Thrones*.

I snapped a pair of gloves on and joined him.

Dead things didn't spook me; they passed through our doors on the daily. But there was something about this great beast that sent goosebumps up and down my arms. I wasn't sure if it was the look of such an unusual dog or all of the drama that had swept in with it.

Dustin looked equally unsettled.

"You good?" I asked, feeling yet another tingle of worry.

"Don't know why, but that white coat is givin' me the creeps," Dustin said, frowning slightly.

"It is unusual. Color variants are rare in purebreds. I've seen a few melanistic German shepherds. But this...."

I couldn't finish.

White was a common enough coat color in purse dogs, and I wouldn't have batted an eye if this had been a Bichon Frisé or a toy poodle. Even a bigger dog, like a Pyrenees, sure, I'd be cool with a coat like that. But there was something about seeing the shape of a Belgian Malinois in the color of fresh snow that just messed with my head. It felt like a bad omen.

"Whatta the eyes look like?" Dustin asked, pulling me out of my dark thoughts.

It was a clinically curious question, and I found myself wondering the same thing. I leaned forward, and slid one of the eyelids back with my thumb. I was met with an icy blue iris, unfocused and with the glazed appearance unique to the dead.

I flinched and took a step back, as if I'd found a nest of scorpions.

Quit being so jumpy! I berated myself for being ridiculous. I was acting like a preteen singing Bloody Mary in the mirror at a sleepover.

The color had gotten me, though. I'd expected the brown that was typical of a Belgian Malinois. Maybe even the red of a true albino. Somehow, the blue was even more off-putting than any other color I could've found.

The eyelid stayed open, the iris peeking past the nictitating membrane stretched across the corner.

"Huh," Dustin grunted, looking as discomfited as I felt.

I reached over and forced the eyelid closed.

"The owner was real upset," Dustin said, eyebrows furrowed like he was noodling over something.

"The handler?" I asked, thankful for the distraction.

"Yep, guy was crushed. Didn't want to let the little one go." Dustin's voice was gruff, a hint of sadness edging into his voice. "He took the dog's collar off and cried so hard he practically collapsed right there on the dock."

I chewed on my cheek. "Did he say anything? Give any clues as to what might've happened?"

"He kept 'pologizing 'bout not leaving the AC on." He lifted his shoulders in an unreadable shrug.

My heart thudded in my chest. In a flurry, I hustled over to the supply cabinets and dug through the drawer for a thermometer. I pressed the button to turn it on and inserted it into the dog's anus, hoping beyond hope that I wouldn't find an elevated temp. Animals that died from being locked in hot cars had elevated body temperatures, even after death, and those high temps could last for a few hours.

"Ya thinkin' heat stroke?" Dustin asked, doubt lacing his voice.

It was May in Oklahoma, and the sky had been gloomy and gray a couple of hours ago. Even the weather app had warned of heavy rain and possible tornadoes. I couldn't imagine it getting hot enough in a car to kill a dog on a day like today.

"Not really," I answered. "What was the temp when we got into work? Sixties, maybe?"

"Sounds 'bout right. With lots of cloud cover."

"It's just weird that he said that," I said, eyes locked on the thermometer. "I want to be thorough. This is a suspicious death and could be prosecuted as murder. I've never had to go to court before. But if I do, I want to be able to say I checked this."

It was a long shot, and I wasn't surprised when the thermometer beeped, measuring a body temp of 100°F.

"Below normal," I announced, jotting the time and temperature down on the form.

My mind quickly did the math. Dogs tended to run hotter than people, with expected temperatures between 100.5 and 102.5°F. Algor mortis varied based on ambient temperatures, rigor, and a gazillion other things. But as an estimate, core temps dropped one to two degrees per hour after death. Even if I added a couple of degrees to the current body temp as a fudge factor, it still wasn't anywhere near a temp that would've killed the dog.

"Was the drive from OKC long enough for the body temp to drop?" Dustin asked.

I tapped my pen on the counter, considering. "Maybe? But...I don't know. It doesn't seem likely."

Dustin sucked on his mustache, unable to take his eyes off the dog.

"Did he say anything else?" I asked.

Dustin shook his head. "Just how much he loved him. That kinda thing."

I chewed my cheek. "Let's get the horse finished up, and then we can dig into this one. We're going to need to focus."

After a beat, I added, "But let me get this damn blood off my face first."

CHAPTER

FIVE

Normally, having a bunch of dead animals lying around the room was par for the course. But the police dog really messed with my head. It sat in my peripheral vision like a large, white blot on the cool steel table. Every time I turned my back to him, light goosebumps would trace along my forearms.

The horse. Finish the horse, I kept reminding myself, trying to stay focused.

If we didn't hustle and wrap up the horse necropsy, all the tissues would get dry and tacky, and cleanup would be a bitch. Plus, there was something about the horse that was comforting. Like the routine of a simple colic case would protect me from whatever clusterfuck awaited me with the dog.

Crouched over the intestines, I ran my knife along representative segments of the endless loops of bowel, spot-checking the mucosa from stomach to distal colon. Yet no matter how hard I tried, my eyes kept dancing back to the white dog.

The hoist whirred to life as Dustin raised the empty horse carcass, steered it across the ceiling tracks, and tucked the body away in the cooler, where it would wait until it was picked up for cremation. By the time the cooler doors closed, I'd measured and documented the torsion, and my knife had made the last required slice through the bowel. Working together, we schlepped the endless loops of bowel off the floor and into the offal barrel, a back-breaking task if there ever was one. After that delightful workout, we both had splatters of gut contents along our coveralls and down our arms.

Ignoring the itch of horse juice on my skin, I moved to the hydraulic table to examine the remaining organs. After finding the torsion in the gut, there wasn't much left to see, and I was able to do a quick once-over before tossing everything in the offal bin.

After storing the bin with the horse's remains in the cooler, Dustin returned to help me wash down the large animal table and tidy up this end of the room. There was a slow, silent tension, and for once, even the ever-present Hank Williams felt *off*. We both knew how serious the next case was going to be, and we were stuck in our own heads. Too soon, the large animal table was squeaky clean and smelling of disinfectant.

I slowly rinsed the blood and gut contents off my arms, trying to enjoy the fresh, lemony smell of the necropsy floor hand soap. The warmth of the water tingled against my itchy skin. I dried my arms with paper towels and reached up to redo my ponytail, catching any loose strands that had escaped during the heavy lifting.

I looked down at my coveralls and flicked off a small dried chunk of partially digested feed. After surveying the splatter on my coveralls, I weighed my options. After a short internal debate, I figured I didn't need to change. The blood hadn't soaked through to my underwear, and I figured that was a win.

Dustin was decidedly cleaner than I was. He always knew how to stand, cut, and move things around without turning into a Jackson Pollock painting. He only had a spot or two of dried blood on his coveralls, and after he'd washed his arms, he was ready to move on to the next case.

I moved to stand next to him, hands stuffed in my pockets, and stared down at the dog.

The large dog. The police dog. The snow-white dog. The murdered dog.

The words tumbled through my head like a twisted version of *Go, Dog. Go!*

I was reluctant to get started, and I could sense that he was, too. Dustin had worked on the necropsy floor for over twenty years and had seen just about everything. But this case—this stupid fucking case—was altogether different, and we knew we were wading into some heavy shit.

Sure, legal cases would pass through our doors ever so often. But they were rarely prosecuted. And even in the most heinous of animal cruelty cases, the powers that be would just take the pathology report and negotiate a plea deal. Frankly, we spent more time documenting every detail on insured horses than we did on any case that might wind up in a courtroom.

This case was different. This was serious, and neither of us wanted to mess it up.

"Might as well start with getting some pictures." I forced the words out, breaking the heavy, brooding silence.

Dustin grunted in agreement and went to the cabinets to get the digital camera. He slung the strap around his neck and rested one hand on the grip.

I pulled fresh gloves on, pressing the fingers of one hand into the interdigital spaces of the other to get the fit just right. My hands were sweaty, and it was easier said than done.

Grabbing a label, I wrote down the date and case number before adding my signature. I placed the tag in frame, moving it as we shifted between shots. The small *beep* and *click* of the digital camera sounded with each view Dustin captured.

"Any tattoos?" Dustin asked.

When present, tattoos were the best way to confirm an animal's identity. DNA identification wasn't really a thing in veterinary medicine. There wasn't a market for it beyond the pet version of genealogy testing. Instead, valuable animals, such as racehorses and some service dogs, would have identification tattoos.

I folded back each tall ear, scanning the pale inner surface for the distinctive blue ink. Coming up short, I moved to the inner thighs, gloved hands spreading apart the white hairs, looking for anything that might resemble an identification tattoo.

I stepped back, fists on my hips, and pursed my lips. "Nothing."

It wasn't a huge deal that the dog didn't have any tattoos. I just didn't want to miss them if they were there. Missing something like that could seriously derail a court case, especially if I were the expert witness.

Stop thinking like that! I chided.

The handler had brought him in with a police escort to maintain chain of custody, and I was pretty sure no one was going to question whether or not we had the correct dog. Further, it was a white Belgian Malinois, for crying out loud. He was probably the only one in the entire state of Oklahoma.

I had a lightbulb moment. "Let's check for a microchip."

"Good idea, Doc," Dustin replied.

I dug through the supply cabinets. We had a microchip reader somewhere, but we rarely used it. Most animals were submitted by their owners or the vet who treated them, and identification was never really required. Once in a blue moon, a good Samaritan would bring in a dead animal they had found, and a reader would come in handy to find the original owner. But that was the extent of it.

My eyes landed on the small handheld reader. I grabbed it and joined Dustin back at the necropsy table. Thankfully, the batteries hadn't died, and it fired right up. I swiped it over the dog's back and received a reassuring beep.

"There we go," Dustin murmured.

He jotted the number down on the submission form as I read it out for him. Seeing those numbers on the paper made me feel oodles better. It was like the ground beneath me was a little more solid.

With the animal identification part of the necropsy completed, I ran my hands along the thick, snow-white fur, checking for any external injuries, masses, or other lesions. I leaned forward to inspect the dog's mouth just as the song changed over. When Hank crooned the first verse, goosebumps spread over my arms.

I straightened my back, hands inches away from the dog's face, and caught Dustin's eye. "Seriously?"

"'Angel of Death,'" he said with a low, forced laugh. "Of course, that song would come on,"

"Geesh," I said, looking at the goosebumps on my arms dramatically and adding my own forced snicker. "What are we, twelve?"

The nervous laughter at our misbegotten idiocy was enough to shake off the heebie jeebies and light a fire under both of our asses. Dustin released the camera from his tight grip, letting it hang from his neck. The goosebumps on my arms disappeared.

With some effort, I was able to open the stiff jaws and examine the oral cavity. Clotted blood coated the tongue. I wiped it away with a gloved thumb. There was a puncture wound in the tongue, surrounded by a fresh, deep red bruise.

"Looks like he bit his tongue right before he died," I commented. "Can you get a picture of that?"

The fact that the dog had bitten his tongue didn't mean diddly squat. Animals would occasionally bite their tongue, especially if the last moments of their life were agonal. The lesion wasn't necessarily significant, but I felt the need to document every single, itty-bitty thing I found.

Dustin adjusted the identification tag to get it in frame and clicked a couple of pictures.

I went through my mental checklist, making sure I got everything I needed before I started cutting. Once I made the first cut, there was no going back.

I clasped my knife. My hand settled perfectly between the butt and the bolster, my palm resting over the flat side of the handle and fingers lacing over the curve. The grip felt stable. Secure. Familiar.

Dustin put the camera on the counter and pulled on a pair of gloves. He moved to the opposite side of the table and held up the right front leg, face solemn.

No time like the present.

The tip of the knife pierced into the axilla, and I extended the cut forward and backward through the skin. The sharp edge of the knife took care of any remaining attachments, and Dustin reflected the leg toward the opposite side. Blood seeped through the white hair.

We repeated the same process with the right back leg, the slight *pop* of the hip joint barely audible over the music. Within a couple of minutes, the right side had been skinned, exposing the ribs and the abdominal muscles. Now that we faced muscle and bone, it was easier to slip into the routine of the necropsy.

"There's no evidence of trauma to the soft tissues," I said. "We should probably get a picture of that."

I stepped back as Dustin repositioned the tag and snapped a few more pictures. We didn't usually take pictures if there wasn't a lesion. But I had a feeling that this case could go sideways fast, and I wanted to document that there was no evidence of abuse.

Please let this be cancer. My kingdom for a splenic hemangiosarcoma.

The belly of the knife slid over the muscles of the abdominal cavity, and they stretched apart. At a glance, everything inside looked normal, and I couldn't help but feel a twinge of disappointment.

I stabbed the diaphragm, and there was a reassuring gasp of air. Using the loppers, Dustin and I took turns crunching through the rib cage. With the slab removed, I surveyed the body cavities.

"Well, damn," Dustin murmured at the sight.

There was a depressing lack of lesions in the thoracic cavity, and I couldn't help but huff. Before I could ask, Dustin moved the tag and snapped a few shots of what appeared to be normal internal organs.

Frowning, he said, "Think blastin' the AC for a couple of hours could've cooled the body enough?"

He was back to heat stroke, and I didn't blame him. I was grasping at straws, too.

I considered, then shook my head doubtfully. "Doesn't feel right for that."

Even though I had a feeling the dog didn't die from heat stroke, I had no proof. A lethal, high body temp often didn't result in any gross or histologic changes. The diagnosis of death due to heat stroke usually hinged on documenting a core temp of over 105°F after death. I just had to hope I found a lesion or something else significant enough to prove what my gut was telling me.

"Let's collect everything and our monkey's uncle for toxicology," I said.

Dustin wrinkled his eyebrows, trying to follow the hard right turn my brain had made. "Whatcha thinkin'?"

"Not sure," I said truthfully. "I just don't want to need something a week from now and not have it. Can I get a syringe for urine?"

Toxicology cases sucked. I had to know what I was looking for before I could order a test to confirm it. There wasn't a slam-dunk tox test that would miraculously discover the chemical, compound, or whatever had poisoned an animal. Those tox screens on streaming shows were predetermined panels that looked for specific poisons or drugs. Just about anything could've killed this dog, especially in Oklahoma, where toxic compounds, both natural and manufactured, lurked everywhere. For all I knew, the dog could've been stupid enough to snarf down some oleander leaves.

Dustin prepped a syringe and handed it to me. "Doesn't look like there's much in there," he mused.

"Yeah, but I gotta try," I replied.

I stuck the needle into the bladder and pulled the plunger back. Nothing came out. I repositioned the needle a couple of times, but no matter how hard I tried, there was nothing left in there to aspirate. Frustrated, I tossed the empty syringe in the sharps bin with a huff.

"Hope we don't need urine for anything," I griped.

"Want aqueous humor?" Dustin asked.

I chewed my cheek as I noodled over the question. We frequently tested the aqueous humor for nitrates in cattle. I wasn't sure what I'd need it for in a dog, and it sure as hell wouldn't be a replacement for the urine, but I figured it wouldn't hurt to collect it.

I shrugged. "Might as well."

Thankfully, Dustin took care of that chore, collecting a small amount of fluid from the spooky blue eye and sparing me the sight of those icy, cool daggers.

I looked away, focusing on the abdominal organs. The gastrointestinal tract of a carnivore was much more manageable than that of the horse, and I had it out and on the table in less than a minute. I laid it on the open space at the end. After cutting the spleen free from the stomach, I bread-loafed it, took a section, and then pushed it to the side, underwhelmed.

So much for splenic hemangiosarcoma, I huffed to myself.

A small part of me hoped the intestinal tract would be more interesting. Starting from the top, I sliced open the stomach to examine the contents.

"Hmm," I murmured.

"Find something?" Dustin asked.

He'd seen just about every lesion a million times over, and stomach contents were rarely exciting. His uncharacteristic interest in the case only underscored how unique it was, and I couldn't fight the worry building in my stomach.

I gestured to the stomach contents. "Mind taking a picture of that?"

There were chunks of minimally digested sausage wadded into a ball. The surface of the stomach was a deep red.

After the photographs were taken, I pinched through the stomach contents. I didn't see any leaves, berries, or anything that screamed toxic plants. The sharp green tinge typical of rat bait was also absent. It just looked like gray, slimy, half-eaten ground meat. I guess I wasn't really expecting a slam dunk to be hiding in there, but a person could hope.

I scooped some of the contents into a plastic container. Stomach contents could be used for toxicology testing, particularly for ingested toxins. In a case like this, I didn't know what I'd need down the road.

I took several sections of the red area in the stomach wall and dropped them in the bucket of formalin for histology. I didn't expect to see anything but a little bit of congestion or hemorrhage under the microscope, but I wanted to be thorough.

I ran the rest of the intestinal tract, making sure to check the pancreas as I went. Everything was unremarkable. The redness that tinged the stomach lining wasn't present further along in the intestines. I took some sections of small and large intestine for posterity, but I wasn't expecting to find anything.

The liver was next. I bread-loafed it, cutting thin, even slices, and pinched one between my fingers. It was also unremarkable. I collected a large fist-sized chunk to freeze for toxicology and took smaller sections for the formalin bucket.

It was rinse-and-repeat with the kidneys. When I opened them on the half shell, I felt my heart sink even further with the consistent lack of any lesions. I collected a few sections for histology and dumped the rest into a container for toxicology.

By the time I'd finished up the abdominal organs. Dustin had the pluck out. I ran my knife down the esophagus and trachea; they were both completely normal. I collected the thyroids out of habit more than anything else and plunked those in the formalin jar along with the sections of the esophagus and trachea.

I cut the heart free. After slicing open the left side, I scooped some of the semi-clotted blood into a red top tube and passed it to Dustin to label. I had no idea what test I would run on it, but I didn't want to be the dumbass who didn't collect a sample that might be needed later.

This is a possible murder, after all, I kept reminding myself.

I methodically ran through the necropsy, slowly but surely running out of locations for a lesion. My chest felt tight with worry.

When it came to the thoracic organs, only the lungs remained. One look at the pink fluffy lobes, and I knew I wouldn't find shit. I still went through the motions of cutting regular slices and palpating the organ. I collected a couple chunks for the formalin bucket, and they bobbed on the surface as they should.

I chewed on my cheek. "Guess we need to take the brain," I grumbled.

The brain was a pain in the ass to remove, and we didn't do it unless we had to. Given the lack of lesions in the other organ systems, this was definitely a "have to" moment.

"I got it, Doc," Dustin said. "Want CSF?"

I nodded.

Lifting the head, he stuck a needle through the ventral atlanto-occipital joint and tried to aspirate. Nothing came out.

"Sorry, Doc," he said. "Won't be able to get you any fluid."

I shrugged. "I probably wouldn't run any tests on it anyway."

Sometimes, it simply wasn't possible to get cerebrospinal fluid on a dead animal, but I still felt a tad salty that this carcass was being stingy. I thought it was because I was trying to cover my ass, and not having that sample prevented one "t" from being crossed. Urine would have been more useful, but still.

Dustin inserted the tip of his knife in the atlanto-occipital joint, cut the attachments, and placed the head on the table. The eyelids had slid open with the removal of the head. Seeing the white hair and the crystal blue eyes completely and totally fucked with my mind.

I had to look away.

I bagged up the parts, keeping my head down as the *buzz* of the electric bone saw cut through the music. I labelled the remaining containers and bussed them over to where we stored samples. The blood went into the fridge. The stomach contents, aqueous humor, and fresh tissues went into the freezer. I logged everything on the clipboard hanging on the fridge for chain-of-custody.

The formalin bucket with the abdominal and thoracic organs went on the counter to go to the histology lab. Since I hadn't found an obvious cause of death on necropsy, I'd have to look at the tissues under the microscope. I poured fresh formalin into a second bucket, labelled it, and brought it back over to the table for the brain.

Dustin finished opening the skull just as I arrived.

The brain was resting on the table, and he fished out the pituitary from the base of the calvarium.

"Well, shit," I huffed.

The brain was perfectly, frustratingly normal.

"I wonder if I should freeze some brain for tox, too," I hedged.

"Might as well," Dustin said. His eyebrows were furrowed, and his upper lip was folded in as he sucked on his mustache. This case chafed on him, too.

I cut a small section of frontal cortex, placed it in a Petri dish, and handed it to Dustin to label and store. The rest of the brain joined the normal pituitary in the formalin bucket.

"Think we should do the spinal cord?" I called out.

I really didn't want to, but I had a feeling this case was going to bite me in the ass.

After logging the brain, Dustin made his way back to the small animal table, hands stuffed in the pockets of his coveralls.

"What are the chances of it bein' a spinal lesion with that history?" he asked.

"Slim to none," I answered. "But I'm thinking we should anyway. This case has me all kinds of worried."

"Yeah. Guess you're right." He nodded, lips in a firm line. "I got it, Doc. Why don't you start writin' your notes, and I'll call you over when I have it out?"

"Thanks," I said distractedly, mind still stuck on the lack of significant lesions in a potential murder case.

I appreciated Dustin taking one for the team. It would be tedious work, stripping away the soft tissues before he could even get in at the vertebral bodies with the bone saw. I sat at the counter, writing anything and everything down I could think of, including what I'd checked and found normal. The bone saw buzzed as Dustin cut through the spinal column.

Before I knew it, Dustin called me over to have a look at the spinal cord. Even though I hadn't expected anything, I still felt my heart sink further when it looked completely normal.

A heavy sigh escaped.

I picked up the spinal cord gently and coiled it into the formalin bucket with the brain.

Dustin and I worked in silence, the air heavy with the fact that we hadn't found fuck-all to explain the death of an on-duty police dog. Even with all of the white fur tucked away in the cremation bag and the fresh scent of disinfectant filling the air, I couldn't shake the heavy sense of foreboding.

CHAPTER

SIX

In the locker room, I slipped out of my splattered coveralls and washed the residual blood off, feeling numb. With my civies back on, I sat on the bench next to the lockers and slowly tied my shoes. The feeling of dread was inescapable. As soon as I'd laced my last shoe, it would be off to my office to write the preliminary report on the police dog.

The task sat before me like Sisyphus's rock waiting to be rolled back up the hill. I couldn't help but take my sweet time, desperately wanting to delay the inevitable schlep back to my office.

The stuff I'd found in the dog didn't feel like *real* lesions, and it would be a waste of ink to even write them up. The whole report would be shorter than my grocery list, and that simple fact made me feel like tossing my cookies right there on the locker room floor.

To make matters terribly worse, I hadn't figured out why the dog had died. I had a sliver of hope that I might find something when I looked at the tissues under the microscope. But if histology didn't turn anything up, I had no clue where to go next.

How the hell do I even write something like this up?

I leaned my elbows on my thighs and rubbed the wrinkles between my eyebrows. This case was ten times more serious than anything I'd ever done. I couldn't postulate or add helpful comments like I normally did. I'd have to say I didn't find shit and that histology was pending in a way that wouldn't have the lawyers eating me alive if I ever had to take the stand.

Deep breaths. Little steps. Eyes on the prize, Aunty's voice whispered reassuringly.

"Quit being a baby," I muttered, the soft words echoing in the empty space.

I slunk back to my office, head down, hoping to avoid anybody. The lab's gossip tree would soon be on fire with news of this case, and I didn't want to get caught in the hallway by someone who wanted all the deets. I needed to get the report out, and then I could figure out how I was going to navigate the politics of the lab.

I made it to my office without incident, closed the door, and flopped into my chair. My computer woke with a mouse wiggle. I logged in and opened the report window for the case. The flurry of action on the necropsy floor had led to this horrible moment: me frozen at my desk with my hands hanging about an inch over the keyboard. Paralyzed.

I chewed my cheek.

A necropsy report was just a list of findings fleshed out into a narrative. I'd written a million of them, and I couldn't reconcile my reluctance to start typing. I'd done this hundreds of times.

Just the facts.

I gave myself a firm kick in the proverbial ass and started typing. The general description of the carcass was easy enough. Age, breed, sex, no tattoos, microchip number, and that trippy white coat and blue eyes—the latter being so unusual they were worth mentioning.

Writing those first few sentences was enough to get me back in the flow, and I slipped into a detailed description of each body system. It was typically taboo to write normal findings in a necropsy report, but I figured I'd include important details like the body temperature, lack of evidence of external wounds, and lack of internal bleeding. If this ever went to court, it would likely be a year or more out before it went to trial, and I wanted to make sure I'd recorded what *wasn't* there for posterity. I didn't want anyone questioning my memory.

I typed up the two paltry things I'd found: the hole the poor guy had bitten in his tongue right around death and the redness of the stomach lining. I didn't want anyone to get hung up on those, but I couldn't leave them out either. I tried to bury them in the text, but with not much else to say, the words seemed to blare from the report.

The clacking of my keyboard stopped again. The cursor blinked at the empty comment section, and I could practically hear its evil laugh.

I wanted to type "I have no fucking clue what killed this dog, and I'm going home to eat a pint of ice cream."

Instead, I wrote some fluff about how the cause of death was "elusive at this time" and that "histology was pending." It felt like the drivel it was.

Typing the report made the whole thing all the more real. I needed more information on this case to know what to do next. Looking at the tissues under the microscope might help, but the histology wouldn't come back for a couple of days at the earliest. There was no reason to order PCR or microbiology on anything at this stage; I didn't even have a bit of history or a gross lesion to give me an idea of what tissue to send or what test to order. The dog's death could be toxicology-related, but that was a black hole of testing. Until I had some idea of what to look for, it wasn't worth throwing darts at a board with my eyes covered.

I need to talk to Sandy.

The thought dialed back the burgeoning dread. As the lab's toxicologist, Dr. Sandy Bishop had been working in the field for ages and was smart as hell. She'd helped me on several cases, and I knew I'd probably be leaning on her for this one, too.

I read through the report one more time, checking for typos, and then signed it off. I thought I would feel better with that task done, but all I felt was the slow burn of acid sneaking up my esophagus.

I had about an hour before lunch. I figured I'd knock out the horse report, which would be satisfyingly simple, and then hunt Sandy down to pick her brain. After that, I'd wallow a bit in self-pity and snarf down whatever treats Carol had brought to share today.

Within fifteen minutes, the horse report was finalized and sent into the ether. It was an easy gross diagnosis, and no additional testing was required. I could wrap everything up in a tidy bow the same day the horse had landed on a table. With a sigh, I realized how much I'd needed that, and was glad I'd gotten the dog out of the way first. The colic horse was a good note to end on before lunch.

Just as I finished up, my cell phone binged with a text. I flopped back in my chair and sifted through my purse.

It was from Aunty.

> Can you please call me when you have a moment?

The text was oddly formal for Aunty and lacked the usual cheer. A thread of worry traced up my spine. Part of me wondered if the residual stress from the police dog was making me sensitive to any deviation from the norm.

I took a few deep breaths and tried to clear the image of the white dog from my mind. The effort was minimally successful. Resigned, I tapped on Aunty's contact icon and then hit the call button.

"Hello, sweety," she answered on the first ring. "Thank you for calling me so quickly."

I felt a sliver of apprehension. "Everything alright?"

"I'm not sure," she replied with worry lacing her voice.

What does that mean?

My mind raced.

I was already amped from the situation with the police dog, and my adrenals dumped another hefty load of hormones, sending my thoughts zipping in wild directions.

"Chula's not acting right," Aunty continued. "I wondered if I should bring her to the vet."

My heart rate slowed with the familiarity of the question. I could handle this.

Veterinarians received questions outside of work all the damn time. They couldn't walk into a room without someone asking for free advice about their pet. Some dipshit would wave a blurry cell-phone picture in their face and expect to walk away with a prescription and treatment recommendations. In most cases, those schmucks received a well-deserved "Make an appointment, and I'd be happy to examine Fluffy for you."

My standard answer was "I treat dead things," to which most people responded with a horrified look and backed away.

Aunty was different.

She had no problem taking Chula to the vet if something was wrong. Since Aunty had found Chula wandering the highway about ten years ago, they'd formed an unbreakable bond, and Aunty doted on her. She was also a bit of a worrywart, and if Chula even sneezed funny, she'd bring her to the vet. After a handful of "there's nothing to worry about" diagnoses, I'd asked Aunty to give me a jingle and use me as a barometer before she brought Chula in.

"What's going on?" I asked, leaning back in my chair, not feeling the slightest bit worried.

"She didn't eat breakfast this morning," Aunty started. I could practically see her wringing her hands.

My eyebrows furrowed reflexively, slipping back into the fretful creases. Chula went bonkers over food. She worshiped anything that graced her bowl like I worshiped ice cream. It was very much unlike her to skip a meal.

"And I accidentally dropped a bit of bacon on the floor this morning, and she didn't race me to it," Aunty continued.

Real worry settled in. Chula was a full-time kitchen vacuum.

"How was her appetite last night?" I asked.

"She ate all her dinner," she answered.

"Any vomiting or diarrhea?"

"Not that I've seen," Aunty replied. "She went to the bathroom first thing and has been lying on her bed since she came back in. Should I bring her to Dr. Jones?"

"Is she drinking?" I pressed, not ready to answer Aunty's question just yet.

"Yes," Aunty responded.

"And otherwise acting normal?"

"A little tired. But, yes, I think so."

One missed meal and being a little lethargic wasn't a big deal in the whole scheme of things. Chula used the bathroom and drank water. It was possible Chula's stomach was a bit irritated after eating some undercooked meat or snarfing down some random dead thing in the yard. She had a tendency to do weird shit like that.

"Do I need to bring her in?" Aunty repeated.

"I don't think so," I said after some consideration. "I'd just keep an eye on her. Are you working today?"

"Yes. My shift started at eleven, but I let the library know I'd be a little late. I was worried about Chula," she replied.

"I think she'll be fine while you're at work," I said. "See if she eats her kibble tonight. If not, offer her some boiled chicken and rice. If anything changes, like she starts vomiting or has diarrhea, give me a call. We'll see how she's doing tomorrow morning. If you're still worried, you can always bring her in then."

"Okay," she said, a thread of relief in her voice. "I'll let you get back to work. Love you, sweety."

"Love you too, Aunty," I answered. "I'll call you tonight."

We said our goodbyes and ended the call.

The details of my office pulled into focus, and the reality of the situation at work settled back in. I needed to get back to the police dog case.

Before I turned my attention to it fully, I set a reminder to call Aunty when I knew her shift would be over. With images of the white dog occupying my mind, I worried that I might forget to check back in with her. With the reminder set, I fully shifted back into work-mode and dropped my phone into my purse.

It was time to talk to Sandy.

CHAPTER

SEVEN

Sandy's office sat on the other side of the building, tucked next to the toxicology lab. I found her at her desk, reading glasses perched on her nose, typing on her computer.

I knocked on the doorjamb. "Dr. Bishop? Have a minute?"

She looked up and smiled. "Sure. Come on in." She pulled her glasses off and waved me to the chair across from her desk.

Her office was cluttered and chaotic in an oddly organized way. Stacks of papers, scientific journals, and books were piled every which way on just about every open surface. Thankfully, a seat was open, and I flopped into it.

Sandy leaned back in her chair with a slow creak and studied me with her deep brown eyes.

Normally, I might say something about the weather, ask how she was doing, something to be polite. Today, I was wired up about the police dog and jumped right in.

"I need to pick your brain about a case. It just came in," I started. "Have a minute?"

She rolled with it and fiddled with the lanyard for her reading glasses. "Sure, what've you got?"

The words quickly tumbled out. "The case is a nine-year-old, male-castrated Belgian Malinois. The dog worked with the OKC police department. This morning, the handler found him dead in the police car at Will Rogers Airport."

There was a sharp intake of breath. "Oh, boy," Sandy said softly.

My gut clenched.

I knew this case was a big deal, but the worry on Sandy's face was like the nail in the coffin. Sandy had been a veterinary toxicologist for ages and had seen just about everything. Not much shook her anymore. Those two words of cautionary sympathy after only hearing a bit about the case were enough to push me to the brink of a full-on panic attack.

Yeah, I'm fucked, I thought, and my chest grew tight.

"What were the clinical signs?" Sandy asked.

I forced myself to take a deep breath, trying to get my thoughts in order. "There weren't any, as far as I know. But I've only spoken to the detective."

"What did you find on necropsy?" she probed.

A heavy sigh escaped. "Not much. The dog had bitten his tongue, and the surface of the stomach was a little red. That's about it."

She pursed her lips, thinking, and said, "Anything in the stomach?"

"Just chunks of sausage," I replied. "I didn't see any plant bits, berries, rat bait pellets, or anything like that. I saved the contents in case we need to go back to it. But there was nothing visually suspicious in there."

Her eyebrows furrowed. "Think the redness in the stomach is actually hemorrhage?"

I shrugged. "Hard to tell. It was pretty subtle, and I won't know if it was hemorrhage, congestion, or some odd post-mortem artifact until I get the slides back. Plus, there was no blood inside the stomach, and that was the only organ affected. Even the intestines looked normal."

"Well, at least there's no evidence of trauma," she mused. "Things would've become ugly quickly if there had been."

I nodded grimly.

Her chair creaked as she shifted, eyes crinkled in thought. "It's possible it's infectious and you'll catch something on histology."

Her tone echoed my own feelings of doubt.

I switched gears. "The handler said something about the AC not being on when he dropped the dog off. But the body temp was low—so low that I'd be shocked if it was heat stroke even if we got the body an hour or two after death."

"Plus, it's overcast today," Sandy chimed in.

"Yeah, tornado weather," I agreed.

Sandy fiddled with her reading glasses. "Even with the windows closed up tight and parked in the full sun, I'd be surprised if it got hot enough in there to kill a dog on a day like today."

I nodded, chewing my cheek. Everything she said matched what I'd thought. It gave me an odd sense of reassurance.

"With minimal gross lesions and zero clinical signs, it sure feels like we're gonna be gettin' samples in the tox lab soon enough," she said with a sigh.

"I collected just about every tox sample you could possibly want. But...." I left the sentence hanging.

She knew where I was going with that. I could have all the samples in the world, but it wouldn't mean shit if I didn't have an idea of what test I wanted to run.

"I think some of the more common poisons can be comfortably ruled out," she said. "Without any clinical signs, I'd doubt it was ethylene glycol toxicosis. Without any significant gross lesions, it's probably safe to rule out rodenticide toxicosis. Strychnine is less likely, too; those cases almost always have the characteristic green-blue tinge to the stomach contents. Paraquat would cause more erosions and blistering, assuming someone could still find a bottle sitting around from the seventies. The fact that you didn't find any plants, toxic foods, or pills like acetaminophen or ibuprofen in the stomach rules out a lot of other things, too."

My sewing machine leg bounced as she hacked and slashed at the differential list.

She pursed her lips and tapped the end of her eyeglasses on her lips. "That being said, if it is a toxicosis, whether accidental or intentional, the list is still too long right now: illegal drugs, human medications that have delayed effects, heavy metals like arsenic, slug bait...I could keep going."

She shrugged and looked at me sympathetically.

I rubbed the wrinkles between my eyebrows. "I'm thinking I need to wait for histology on this one. It could be anything at this point. Everything has to be done by the book."

She nodded. "I agree. Slow and steady. Make sure all your i's are dotted and t's are crossed." After a beat, she asked, "Did you get any of the dog food?"

"No," I said. "Why? What're you thinking?"

I quickly scoured my brain, turning up just about nothing that could be in commercial dog food that would cause an animal to suddenly drop dead.

She shrugged. "I can't think of anything that really sticks at the moment. But it's worth having them save some of the food before they toss it. Once it's gone, it's gone."

My mind drifted to the Shadowhawk case and how the feed company had swept up all of the contaminated feed, hoping to skirt any responsibility.

"I'll ask them for some of the dog food," I replied. "Anything else you can think of?" I held out hope that Sandy would miracle me an answer.

Sandy tilted her head and pursed her lips again. Her eyes grew distant as she searched through the annals of her brain.

"I wish we had more information," she mused. "Does the dog have any preexisting medical conditions? What was his behavior like this morning? Those types of things. Even something as simple as him taking a bit longer to go to the bathroom might be significant."

"Agreed," I replied. "I could only interview the cops submitting the case, and they didn't know much. It'd be nice to talk to the handler."

She lifted an eyebrow. "Is that possible?"

"Not sure. One of the cops—Officer Watts, if you can believe it—dropped the dog off."

Her eyes widened in surprise. "Officer Watts?" she blurted, slightly incredulous and unable to get past that name. Officer Watts had interviewed everyone in the lab when the tiger parts had gone missing, including Sandy. His name had been burned into our memories.

"Why is an officer from Stillwater PD working up a case from the city?" she asked.

"He said he was the local liaison or something like that," I answered. "The contact on the form is the OKC police department, though."

"Hmm," she replied.

"Officer Watts said the handler was a suspect," I continued.

Sandy lifted an eyebrow in doubt.

"Yeah, agreed," I said. "Another guy came with him. A detective. His name was Powel, Pollard, or something like that. Anyway, I didn't get the vibe that the detective suspected the handler. Also, Dustin said the handler seemed crushed when he dropped the dog off. It just doesn't feel right."

"Do you think they'll let you talk to the handler?" she asked again.

"I can try," I replied, feeling hesitant. "It would be a lot easier than playing operator through the detectives. Getting any medical information from them is tough. I'd prefer to go straight to the source. But if the handler is truly a suspect, they probably won't let me."

Sandy tapped the edge of her reading glasses against her chin thoughtfully.

"Am I missing something? A test I should order now? Any ideas?" It was difficult to keep the desperation out of my voice.

She shook her head, frowning. "Sorry, I don't have any other ideas for you. Let me know what you find on histology, and we can work from there."

"Okay," I said with a slight nod, trying to hide my disappointment. I'd hoped Sandy would've waved her magic wand and a diagnosis would've appeared in my lap; she'd done exactly that on a handful of other tough cases. But I was out in the wind on this one.

"Thanks for letting me bend your ear," I added and stood up.

"Anytime," she said.

As I left, she swung her glasses back over her nose and began typing away at her computer. But the creases between her eyebrows remained.

I headed back to my office, feeling defeated before I'd even had a chance to really sink my teeth into the case. All signs indicated that I'd have to wait for histology, and patience was not my forte.

CHAPTER
EIGHT

By the time I'd made it back to my office, it was already noon. I debated calling the detective to give him an update and hopefully tease out any more useful details. But I was borderline hangry and decided to put it off until after I had a chance to stress-eat something sweet.

With my lunch in hand, I headed to the breakroom. Laughter spilled through the doorway as I walked in.

The whole crew was already there. Dustin was tucked in next to Anna, a thick sandwich in his hands. Opposite them sat Carol from the front office and Dr. Zoe Smith, a fellow pathologist. An open container of snickerdoodles sat in the center of the table like mana from heaven.

I dragged a chair over to join them. Before my ass hit the seat, I had selected a snickerdoodle and snarfed it down. The cinnamon and sugar danced across my tongue, soothing my soul.

"Thank you for always bringing treats, Carol. I really needed this today," I said with a contented sigh.

Carol had a grandmotherly air and smiled like one, too. "You're welcome, Dr. Harjo."

"Busy week on the floor?" Zoe asked me, innocently enough.

A knot in my stomach formed. Clearly, the gossip tree hadn't reached Zoe yet. If she'd known what had passed through the doors, she would've completely danced around the topic and let me silently bury my woes in cookies.

To my relief, Anna answered for me. "We got a police dog in today. So sad."

Zoe's eyebrows shot up. "A police dog?"

I nodded glumly and grabbed another cookie.

"A sniffin' dog," Dustin chimed in. "Handler found him dead in the police car."

"Oh," Zoe replied gravely.

Zoe had been a pathologist for about as long as I had and understood the gravity of the situation. After a beat, she hesitantly asked, "Did you find anything on necropsy?"

I shook my head. "Would've been nice if it was cancer or something. But I didn't find much of anything. I'm going to have to wait until histology comes back."

Even though this was a serious case, everyone in the lab had access to the report in the system and could easily look it up. There was nothing wrong with sharing the information over lunch in the breakroom.

"At least it wasn't trauma," Zoe offered hopefully.

Unable to help myself, I took a third snickerdoodle. Maybe if I acted like the Cookie Monster, I wouldn't be required to talk.

Dustin rested his arm down on the table, sandwich still in hand, and frowned. "The handler was real shook up. It's tough seein' someone like that."

We'd all seen our fair share of distraught owners. In some cases, the bulk of our job was serving as a grief counselor. Dustin carried that burden this time.

"Losing an animal like that..." Anna started, then shook her head. "My brother had a service dog for his PTSD. Rosco went with him everywhere. When he passed, my brother just about lost it." After a beat, she added, "I know this isn't a service dog, but still. There's a special bond there."

Carol nodded sagely, eyes sad.

The stress of the case ate away at me, and I was subsequently eating away at the spread of snickerdoodles. I needed to get my shit together. Focus. Work all the angles.

Officer Watts had said they were bringing the handler in for questioning. But Dustin's impression of the handler didn't jive with the narrative that Watts had spun. I needed to follow that thread a bit further.

I turned to Dustin. "Tell me more about the handler. What exactly did he say?"

All eyes around the table shifted to him.

He put his sandwich down and stroked his beard, looking a bit uncomfortable. Ever since things went down with the tiger, he tended to shy away from being the center of attention, especially with anything having to do with the police.

"Anna called me to let me know they were waitin' outside. The police vehicle was already pulled up to the dock when I went out—an SUV, K9 unit typa thing. Two guys came out. The younger one held the body. The older one stayed back, watchin' things, until I signed the chain-of-custody form; I didn't catch his name."

"Detective Pollard," I interrupted quietly, the correct name popping into my head from the ether. I fiddled with a fourth cookie, mind racing.

"The younger guy—the handler—he was cryin'," Dustin continued. "Didn't want to let the dog go. Talkin' all incoherent like."

"What did he say?" I pressed. "I didn't get much of anything from the cops."

Everyone around the table listened intently.

"He kept sayin' 'sorry' and sayin' the dog's name over and over." He frowned. "Not often you see a man like that so broken."

"You said something about the AC," I nudged. "What did he say exactly?"

"I don't remember it perfect," he said with a shrug. "Somethin' about not leavin' the AC on. The way he talked was all jumbled."

"Do you think it was heat stroke?" Zoe asked.

Dustin and I both shook our heads, but I answered, "The body temp was low. Plus, I don't think it was hot enough this morning for the inside of the car to reach a temp high enough to cause heat stroke."

"Maybe he just thinks it's that," Anna suggested. "He probably blames himself, especially if the dog died all of a sudden."

"Yeah, I wondered that myself. Like he's grasping at straws, trying to make sense of it," I replied.

"Poor man," Carol said softly.

There were a few thoughtful nods around the table.

Dustin leaned forward and caught my eye. "For what it's worth, I don't think he did anything, Doc."

The words rang true, and I trusted Dustin's gut. He'd seen his fair share of nefarious shit and always had a good read on people. I didn't think the handler hurt the dog either. I just needed to prove it.

"Thanks, Dustin," I said somberly. "I think you may be right."

A short, brooding silence spread through the group as everyone picked at their meals.

Sensing the need to shift the conversation, Anna chirped, "How 'bout that weather? It's looking pretty nasty out there. Think it'll drop a tornado?"

And with that, everyone started chewing the fat and speculating on whether or not a tornado would spill out of the ominous clouds hanging in the sky. And if it did, where it would land. All bets were on Edmond; that place was a bit of a magnet for them. Tornadoes were just a thing that happened in Oklahoma, and people who grew up around them wouldn't bat an eye. Some people would even grab a beer and stand outside to watch.

As I nibbled on another cookie, I couldn't help but feel like this case was its own wall cloud, threatening the tentative peace within our little lab. I could practically hear the tornado siren wailing in my head. All I could do was hunker down, wait for it to hit, and hope it roared right past without taking one or two of us with it.

***

After lunch, I wandered back to my office, my mind swirling with thoughts of the case. Distracted and in my own little world, I didn't notice Gerald heading straight for me until it was too late.

"Dr. Harjo," his nasally voice echoed, jarring me out of my thoughts.

He stopped just to my left in the hallway.

It was a respectable distance, and I couldn't help but notice that he hadn't blocked my avenue of escape. With this guy, any action that held a modicum of decency was a surprise. Even though I'd probably never like him, I could at least try to be polite when I could tell he was making an effort.

I forced a smile. "Yes, Dr. Richter?"

His back straightened, and he stuffed his hands in his perfectly ironed khakis. He wore an oddly neutral expression, and his usual smug smile was replaced with a frown so slight it was almost imperceptible.

"I did not receive any samples on case 43518087," he stated matter-of-factly. "Have you not considered the possibility of *Salmonella*?"

I fought the initial defensive flush of adrenaline.

This was just Gerald channeling his inner Rain Man. If I'd learned anything these last few months, it was that most of these awkward, semi-accusatory comments weren't actually insults. This was Gerald trying to be helpful.

I took a deep breath.

My mind had only picked up the word "*Salmonella*" as my brain tried to catch up, so I clung to that, thinking of the stinky goat.

"Yes, I was pretty sure it was *Salmonella* on necropsy. I sent samples for micro, PCR, and parasitology. Did you not get them?"

His eyebrows wrinkled in confusion. "Case 43518087?"

"The goat, right?" I replied. "I submitted those yesterday."

He pursed his lips, and oodles of judgment wafted off of him. "Not case 43518013. We received the samples from the goat. I'm referring to case 43518087."

He crossed his arms and puffed out his chest. I could tell he was getting frustrated and trying to bite back all the mean shit spilling through his head. I appreciated the effort, even though his body language still spoke volumes.

"Gerald," I started, and then stopped when I noticed the exacerbation in my voice. I took a small breath and tried again. "I'm not good with numbers like you are. Is that the horse from this morning? It looked like a GI torsion. I'm pretty sure there wasn't anything infectious going on in that case."

I could tell he itched to roll his eyes but fought hard not to.

"The dog," he said curtly. "The legal case."

I raised my eyebrows. "*Salmonella*. In the police dog." I tried not to snort, but it still came out slightly incredulous.

His face clouded over. "Yes, *Salmonella*," he said gruffly. "There is an active outbreak in Best Bud's Bacon Bites. The bacterial load is extremely high, and many animals show minimal to no clinical signs prior to death. It is possible that the dog was lethargic or febrile, and the owner didn't notice it."

"I don't think it's *Salmonella*," I said with certainty. "There was no evidence of enteritis on necropsy."

"Are you sure you didn't miss a lesion?" he snapped back.

The words were snarky even though his tone wasn't, and my hackles rose as I fought back the irritation.

I'd learned there were many sides to Dr. Gerald Richter. There was the mean, shitass Gerald who lobbed racial slurs and picked on women. Thankfully, that one had been shuttered since the new year. Then, there was this haughty Gerald who obsessed over work and took the title of perfectionist to a whole new level. He wasn't always correct on first guess, but he'd bird-dog shit until he found the right answer. This Gerald always felt a little off and could be annoying, but at least he wasn't trying to be mean.

"Dr. Harjo?" he said with a huff, pulling me out of my own head.

"I'm certain I didn't miss a lesion," I finally replied, voice firm as I tried to keep any snark out of my tone.

"It could still be *Salmonella*," he insisted. "This is a new strain. They don't know much about it yet. Only eighteen cases have been reported on the listserv."

I didn't know what had killed the dog, but I felt confident that it wasn't a *Salmonella* infection. Not certain enough to stake my life on it, but pretty damn close. I figured Gerald was just being Gerald; he couldn't keep his nose out of things.

"What are the gross lesions with this new strain?" I asked, more to humor him rather than genuine interest.

"The current information being shared doesn't include those details," he grumbled, sounding frustrated at whomever had dared announce an outbreak without providing every single detail.

"I still don't think it's salmonellosis. The only bacterial etiology that is still on the table right now is a streptococcal infection. And even then...." I finished the sentence with a shrug.

"Did you see any skin lesions or blood coming from the nose? You didn't put that in your report."

Of course, he's read my report already. Geez.

I felt a hint of pity. It must be truly exhausting filling the dead space in his life with everyone else's cases.

"No, I didn't see anything like that," I finally answered. "But I've had cases of streptococcal septicemia with no gross lesions." After a beat, I added, "I still don't think this one is infectious."

At least, I sure hope it isn't.

If the dog had a bacterial infection, I hadn't saved any fresh intestine to send to the microbiology lab to confirm it. The PCR lab might be able to pick up some genetic material from bacteria in the fixed tissue, but I wouldn't hang my hat on that.

Stop it. Don't let Gerald fuck with your head.

I shook off the inner monologue and looked up at Gerald.

He pursed his lips. "You should ask the owner if they purchased Best Bud's Bacon Bites with lot numbers FL1456 or FL1457," he nagged.

Sweet baby Jesus.

I threw my hands up. "Okay. Fine. If it'll make you feel better, I'll ask him."

He nodded his chin once, looking satisfied. He released his crossed arms and walked away without another word.

"Well, alrighty then," I mumbled to myself.

Frazzled, I sulked back to my office, a trail of black clouds following me. I still needed to call the detective with an update. I wasn't looking forward to that; I had fuck-all to share with him at this point.

And don't forget to ask him about the dog treats, Gerald's voice badgered.

CHAPTER
NINE

Detective Pollard's business card sat on my desk next to the submission form. I could've sworn it mocked me like Scott Farkus.

His sneering voice echoed in my head: *What, you're gonna cry now? Come on, crybaby!*

I rubbed the card between my fingers. It was relatively nice cardstock with a professional imprint. There was a slight bend on one corner, like the card had sat in his wallet for a while.

I'd made calls more difficult than this one throughout my career. Telling Rachel Hoskins that a nasty virus was circulating at Rising Run Farms had been one of them. But this call felt heavy in a way the others hadn't. Every little thing I did on the case would be scrutinized and picked apart by people who didn't live and breathe dead animals. I couldn't help but feel a preemptive desire to hide in a bunker until it was over.

I picked up the desk phone and slowly punched in the numbers. The phone rang, and a part of me wished it would go straight to voicemail.

It didn't.

On the third ring, a soon-to-be familiar voice answered, "Detective Chuck Pollard here."

"Hello, Detective Pollard," I said, reverting to using honorifics. "This is Dr. Josie Harjo from the diagnostic lab. I'm calling about Tohbi."

"That was fast," he said, sounding pleased.

"Rot waits for no one." The old adage tumbled out of my mouth before I could stop it. I tittered nervously and then kicked myself.

He huffed a laugh, rolling with it. "What'd you find?"

My stomach clenched. Even though the necropsy was finished, I didn't have anything solid to share with him.

Ruling stuff out is just as important as finding the cause of death, a previous faculty member's voice lectured in my head.

I brushed the thought away. Those were the heartless words of someone who didn't have to communicate difficult information to an owner. It was a flippant saying from someone trying to explain away their inability to take a case all the way to the finish line.

"Dr. Harjo?" Chuck said. "You there?"

Jerked from my swirling thoughts, I responded, "Yes, sorry. I finished the necropsy and wanted to give you an update."

"Appreciate it," he replied, sounding a bit eager.

"I didn't find much," I started lamely, knowing I was going to disappoint him. "There was no evidence of trauma, so that can be crossed off the list. He bit his tongue right before he passed; we see that a lot in agonal deaths, and it doesn't mean much. The mucosa of the stomach was red. It could be from an irritant or could be nothing at all. I took quite a few samples and will need to do further testing. I should have more information for you early next week."

This was met with silence.

"Sorry I don't have more for you," I fumbled.

"That's alright. Sometimes no news is good news," he replied.

That was a pretty magnanimous comment, and I appreciated the effort. My shoulders relaxed a tad.

"Any sign of heat stroke?" he asked, voice neutral.

The muscles in my shoulders bunched right back up to my ears. "I took Tohbi's body temperature when he arrived, and it was well below what I'd expect in a dog who died from heat stroke."

Did that sound defensive? I think that sounded defensive.

"With heat stroke, the core temps are usually sky high even an hour or two after death," I went on to explain. "Sometimes, the organs are even hot to the touch. If the body was kept at room temperature on the drive, it would be virtually impossible for it to have cooled down enough in that space of time. Given the low body temperature combined with the mild temp outside today, heat stroke is very unlikely."

I paused and gave him a moment to process before dropping the caveat.

"Unless the body was chilled. Then, all bets are off," I added reluctantly.

"Austin wrapped Tohbi in a blanket and placed him in the back of the vehicle before we headed to Stillwater," Chuck interjected. "We did have the air conditioning on, but it wasn't blasting. It was just enough to circulate the air and keep the vehicle comfortable."

The additional information only solidified it for me and made me more certain that it wasn't heat stroke.

"I'm not an expert in heat conduction, but I don't think running the AC on low would be enough to cool a body down in just an hour or so," I hedged, always wanting to leave myself an out.

I cleared my throat. All this talk of heat stroke made me jumpy. I didn't want to say the next bit even though I felt obligated to.

"All that said, I can't completely rule it out," I said, forcing the words out. "Other than measuring the body temp, there aren't any gross lesions associated with heat stroke. So, I wouldn't expect to see anything other than an elevated core temperature at necropsy. There's a chance I might see something under the microscope, but not all cases of heat stroke have histologic changes either. Death by hyperthermia is often a diagnosis based on the exclusion of other causes and circumstantial evidence."

I waited a beat to let all of that information settle. I wanted him to be prepared for the possibility of reasonable doubt.

Then, I added, "Don't quote me on this, but my gut says this isn't heat stroke."

"I don't think it's heat stroke, either," he shared.

My shoulders slumped back down in relief.

"Austin said he had the windows about a third of the way down, the vehicle was parked in the shade, and it was cool out at the airport this morning," Chuck said matter-of-factly. "I'm just asking because Austin keeps going on and on about the AC."

Poor guy. He's so distraught he can't stop blaming himself.

"Tohbi died under unusual circumstances," Chuck continued with a hint of sadness lacing his voice. "His death is hard to explain, so Austin's grasping at straws."

"Understandable. I'm sure they were close." I purposefully made it sound like a statement, but it was also a bit of a question. I trusted Dustin's read on the handler, but confirmation never hurt.

Chuck obliged. "Yes. Austin and Tohbi were tight. He'd take him to the lawn to play ball on his breaks. He'd order extra food for him at the drive-thru. Even though Tohbi was a working dog, Austin took him everywhere, even when he was off duty."

I was starting to get a feel for the kind of man Austin was. Owners like that always made sure their dogs were well taken care of. They took them to the vet for annual check-ups, kept their vaccines up-to-date, and never forgot to give them their monthly tick prevention. They fed them the best food and bought them toys. If Tohbi didn't sleep on the mattress with Austin, I bet he had his own cushy bed next to him on the floor.

A flicker of sympathy for Austin clutched at my heart.

I was certain Austin hadn't purposefully done anything to hurt his dog. And I just couldn't see a man like that neglecting his dog either. It wouldn't be the first time Officer Watts barked up the wrong tree.

My mind reached to fill in the blanks around Tohbi's life. What had happened that morning before he passed? How had he been acting? What was everyone else around him doing? Did anyone notice anything off? I knew they were out at the airport and there was something about a shipment, but what were they actually doing there?

"I know this is an official police investigation, but is there anything else you can share with me about that morning? Confidentially? It might help me determine the cause of death," I half-begged.

After a slight hesitation, Chuck spoke, his voice turning serious. "I can share some information with you, but it has to remain strictly confidential. I don't want facts leaking out that could jeopardize the investigation. If someone killed Tohbi, everything needs to be rock-solid for the DA."

"Yes, sir. I understand," I replied.

"We've already got reporters breathing down our necks. Someone from the airport must've called them, because the department hasn't issued a statement yet, and all of this happened off-radio. This'll be on the news tonight. There's no doubt in my mind."

Reporters? My stomach clenched.

He cleared his throat, pulling me out of my swirling thoughts of despair.

As if reading from a script at a podium, he ran through the details of the case. "Austin and Tohbi reported for duty at the Will Rogers Airport at six in the morning to inspect a freight shipment on an international flight. They passed through security at six twenty-two. Austin parked the police vehicle next to the freight inspection building. At approximately six forty-five, he and Tohbi left the vehicle to meet the onsite inspection team."

I was drowning in the minutia, and I couldn't help but interrupt. "What about Tohbi? Was he acting normal that morning? Did he eat breakfast? Go to the bathroom? Any signs of lethargy? Anything seem off?" I rattled the questions off, hoping to get something—anything, really—that could help point me in the right direction.

"Not sure," Chuck replied. "They went straight to work when they arrived at the airport. Made a big bust, too."

My head perked up like a sleepy cat catching the flutter of a bird within swiping distance.

"Made a big bust?" I repeated.

"Yes, ma'am," Chuck answered, proud. "Tohbi was the best narcotics detection dog in Oklahoma. He's busted over five tons of narcotics over his career. He's got quite the reputation."

He had *quite the reputation*, I corrected, goosebumps tracing across my arms.

"What did he find this morning?" I asked.

He could've been exposed to something while working. I'd heard of fentanyl killing police dogs during drug busts. Beyond that, I needed to crack the books. But I figured just about anything could kill a dog if the dose was high enough.

"Liquid meth," Chuck answered. "Seven hundred pounds of it. I'd appreciate it if you kept that to yourself until it comes out during the press conference tonight."

"Yes, sir," I said, my mind racing. "Anything different about how Tohbi acted before or after he alerted?"

"Not that Austin mentioned," he answered.

"Hmm," I murmured.

Tohbi must've been feeling okay when he started work. I felt pretty confident that, if anything had been off with Tohbi, Austin would've picked it up and mentioned it to Chuck. He seemed like that kind of guy. But if that was the case, how did Tohbi go from feeling fine and making a drug bust to being found dead in the cop car?

My eyebrows furrowed, trying to puzzle everything out. "So, Tohbi alerted, they seized the drugs, and then what happened?"

"Probably some 'ata-boys' before putting him back in the vehicle," Chuck replied. "Austin left him there while he finished things up with the team. Came back and found him dead a little past eight."

"Anything in the car? Vomit? Diarrhea? Blood?" I asked, grasping at straws.

"I searched the vehicle myself when I arrived on scene," Chuck answered. "The seat underneath the body was wet. Austin said he thought it was urine. But nothing else beyond that."

That fits with the empty bladder.

"Think that means something?" he asked. "People tend to lose control of the bladder and bowels when they pass, so I didn't think much of it. Is it not the same in dogs?"

"Yes, it's the same in most species," I answered. Finding urine on the seat wasn't much of a surprise to me either, and I brushed it away.

My mind shifted back to the drug bust. "Any chance he could have gotten into some of the meth?" I asked. I'd never seen a meth overdose in a dog before and had no clue what to look for.

"Doubt it," Chuck answered. "It was well concealed in the shipment." His answer felt purposefully vague.

"I'll run a drug screen on him just in case," I said. "We don't run that test in our lab. So we will have to send it out, and it'll be a while until we get the results back."

My mind raced. How would the chain of custody work on something like that? Would Tohbi's samples go to a human crime lab since this was technically a suspicious death of a police officer? Or would it go to a veterinary lab since the samples were from a dog? I'd need to talk to Sandy to puzzle that out.

Something scratched at the back of my mind. I took a moment to follow the thread.

"Ata-boys." Yes, that's it.

"I know this is totally random, but do you know if Austin fed Tohbi any treats after he alerted?" I asked.

"Not sure," he said. "Why?"

"Just asking," I replied.

I wasn't sure if it was the seed Gerald had planted about Best Bud's whatevers or something else that tugged at me. I followed the wisp of a thought to the end and found nothing, so I let it go.

Then, I remembered Sandy's request for a sample of the dog food.

"Is there someone who can drop off some of the dog food and any treats Austin had been feeding him?" I asked. "And if there's any of the sausage left that he ate before he died—cooked, uncooked, whatever—bring that by, too?"

"I'll look into getting that for you," Chuck replied matter-of-factly. "Any particular reason why?"

"Um..." I stammered, feeling slightly uneasy again. "In non-human cases of unexpected death where we don't find anything on necropsy, we like to keep all of our options open. I want to make sure we have all the samples we may need. I've seen a couple outbreaks in commercial dog food, like aflatoxin or listeriosis."

Or salmonellosis, Gerald added in my head.

"I'll reach out to Austin and try to get someone to bring it down to you today," he replied.

I could feel the call nearing its end, and I still didn't have much to go on. "Would it be possible to talk to Austin directly at some point? Ask some questions about Tohbi's medical history?"

I held my breath, prepared for a big fat "nope."

Instead, Chuck surprised me by saying, "I can arrange that. I'll have him give you a jingle."

"Thanks," I replied with genuine relief.

Chuck had given me a lot of information, but not much of it had been useful. My mind scrambled for any loose ends.

"Oh, one last thing," I added. "There's just a generic email on the submission form for the report. Would you like me to email the prelim to you directly?"

"Yes, ma'am," he said. "That'd be great. Thank you."

I shifted in my seat, feeling like he didn't have much to be thankful for at the moment.

"You're welcome." The polite gene replied reflexively on my behalf. "Sorry I don't have more for you. I'll keep you posted as results come in."

"Before I let you go...." He paused. "I didn't want to say anything in front of that sourpuss Watts, but any chance you're a relation of Lily Harjo?"

My breath whooshed out of me like I'd been punched in the gut, and I had to press reset to get my brain functioning again.

"Yes...Lily Harjo was my mom." My voice was almost a whisper.

"Well, I'll be damned," he said. After a beat, he added, "Sorry for your loss. Lily was a few years ahead of me in school. Wonderful lady." His voice was respectful and sad.

I cleared my throat uncomfortably, fighting tears. I tried not to think about my mom; it hurt too much. And I certainly didn't want to turn into a mess on the phone with a cop at work.

"I tagged along with a group of them: Lily, Leon, Will, and Molly. Sometimes Haley'd come, too, if she could sneak away. Boy, that was a long time ago. We got into plenty of trouble back then." His voice was almost wistful now.

"Small world," I murmured and forced a courteous laugh, still not fully having my mental shit together.

"You stay in touch with any of them?" he asked.

My heart skipped a beat. "Um. Yes," I answered, cautiously. My work life had always been kept distinctly separate from my life back in Ada, and I didn't like this blurring of lines. "I stay in contact with Molly."

Aunty Molly. With whom I have brunch every Sunday. Who's been like family since my mom died.

"Moll—ee Mead," he said, drawing out the words. "She was a wild one. What's she up to now?"

"She's a librarian on the rez," I answered, still feeling a little shell-shocked.

"No shit?" he blurted. "Pardon my language," he added quickly. "Lost touch with all of them when I moved to OKC. I still imagine her at seventeen, running wild. Might be about time for a visit."

I didn't know how to respond to that.

As if sensing my discomfort, he added, "Say hello to Molly for me. Would ya?"

"Yes, sir," was all I could force out.

After a pause that was just a little too long, he said, "Well, I'll let you go. I'm sure you're busy."

We said polite goodbyes, and I dropped the handset in the cradle like it was a snake. I pressed the heels of my hands against my eyes, refusing to cry at work.

The call had shaken me. I couldn't help but feel like the death of Tohbi had stirred up all sorts of shit, and not all of it was tied to that damn white dog.

CHAPTER

TEN

The ringing of my desk phone shook me out of my pensive sulk.

"This is Dr. Harjo. How can I help you?" I answered.

"Hello, Dr. Harjo. This is Anna. There's a steer for you. I asked the guy if he wanted to stay and talk to you, but he said he's just the one who transports the animals and doesn't know anything."

"That's okay, thanks," I said, feeling a hint of relief. I wasn't up to talking to anyone else at the moment, even if it might make the case easier.

We said our goodbyes, and I rose to track Dustin down.

Muffled music greeted me at the necropsy door, the melody turning to crystal clear vocals as soon as I pushed it open. The fresh, sterile smell of metal and disinfectant greeted me. I leaned through the door, still dressed in my civies, and assessed the situation.

The whirring of the hoist approached from the loading dock as Dustin came into view. A black steer hung from the hoist. A chain was wrapped around its left rear leg, and its nose was a good two to three feet off the floor. It looked small enough that the two of us could crank it out in less than an hour, assuming it wasn't anything neurologic.

Dustin noticed me and stopped the hoist in front of the large animal cooler. "Want to knock this out now, or should I toss it in the cooler for tomorrow?" he called out across the space.

My eyes danced to the clock. It was only a few minutes past two. After the police dog this morning, I really wasn't up for cutting anything else open, and I toyed with the idea of pushing it off until tomorrow.

Rot waits for no one, the self-flagellating part of me thought, tossing my own words back in my face. It was a bitter, mocking thought brought on by my own moodiness. I tried to brush it away.

"Might as well do it now," I moped. "I'll get changed."

Dustin gave me a nod and guided the steer to the hydraulic large animal table.

I made a U-turn and headed to the locker room. Within a few minutes, I was back out on the necropsy floor and dressed in a fresh set of coveralls and boots. I pulled my hair into a ponytail and scrunched it into a messy bun with the last loop of a rubber band.

Anna had already dropped off the submission form, and I pulled it out from the hanging folder. My eyes jumped to the history section and read the two most unhelpful words ever written: Dead steer.

A snort escaped.

I had half a mind to simply write "yep" as the entirety of my pathology report and call it done. But the whole garbage-in, garbage-out mentality didn't work out on the necropsy floor. We were expected to work miracles with whatever fell through the doors, regardless of the shit history.

Feeling grumpy and distracted, I grabbed my knife and dove in. Thankfully, the carcass was fresh, and we had an answer as soon as we popped the chest open. A rip-roaring pneumonia had turned the lungs into a dense mass of red tissue covered by thick mats of fibrin. I collected samples for microbiology and PCR to look for bacteria and viruses.

"You don't want to collect any tissue for histology, right?" Dustin asked, reading my mind. He'd worked with me long enough to know when I'd be content with a gross diagnosis.

Stepping back from the abdominal organs, I wiped my arm across my sweaty forehead. "Yeah, no need for histo. Won't change any-thing." The words came out with a hint of resentment.

A worried look flashed across Dustin's face before he could hide it.

"Even though it's been busy, five gross-only cases in the last two days ain't bad," he offered in an attempt to cheer me up.

I grunted a non-reply, and a frown tugged at my lips. I appreciated Dustin's effort, but it wasn't helping. Regardless of how easy some of the cases had been, I had a hard time feeling grateful with a potential legal case hanging over my head.

A potential homicide *case*, an evil voice corrected.

A case that had no diagnosis and no leads.

"Let's wrap this up," I grumbled.

Dustin rolled with it. He knew the heavy shit I was dealing with—some of it, at least—and didn't take my cantankerous attitude personally. He gave me space to process without demanding fake happiness or reassurance. I could've kissed him for it.

The music filled any need for conversation. We worked in tandem, taking the steer apart in efficient, practiced knife swipes. The clean-up went quickly. Before the clock had a chance to click to half past three, the gutted carcass hung in the cooler, and I was back at my desk in my civies.

I typed the report for the steer in less than thirty minutes, tying everything neatly with a bow and dusting my hands of it. I scanned through my case list, checking for any loose ends that I could close out before the end of the day.

My eyes stopped on the legal case. "Shit," I mumbled to myself.

Acid burbled up my esophagus. I'd been so distracted with the steer that I'd forgotten to order the drug screen before going out on the necropsy floor.

Fuck.

I jumped out of my chair. There was very little time left in the day to get this ball rolling, and I wasn't quite sure what sample to submit. I didn't have much experience with drug overdoses in dogs. Pets would occasionally eat someone's pot stash or have a lick of ecstasy, but it was rarely lethal. I'd never had to test an animal for something like meth before.

I assumed the sample of choice would be the same as in people: urine. But there hadn't been any urine to collect. I figured blood might be the next best choice, but I wanted Sandy's blessing before I pushed the paperwork through and sent the sample out the door.

Hoping to catch her before she left for the day, I sped from my office to track her down, lab coat in hand. My shoulders sagged with relief when I found her speaking with one of the technicians in the toxicology lab. I slipped my lab coat on and stepped through the door.

"Afternoon, Dr. Harjo," Sandy said kindly. "How can I help you?"

I smiled weakly. "Quick question. I want to do a drug screen on that dog that came in this morning, but I wasn't able to get any urine. What's the next best sample for a drug screen? Blood?"

"Hmm," Sandy said and pursed her lips, considering. "I assume you only have post-mortem blood?"

I nodded.

"Clotted blood may impact the test results, but we can try. The specificity is pretty good, especially since they run confirmatory testing. You can trust a positive result. But a negative...." She shrugged slightly, and her lips twisted into an apologetic frown. "The sensitivity of the test is okay, but the more degraded the sample, the less you can trust a negative result."

"Bummer," I murmured, feeling a tad disappointed.

She fiddled with her reading glasses. "It's still worth a try."

"Okay," I replied slowly, optimism still far out of reach. "Where do we even send a sample like this? A&M? Or do we send it to a human drug-testing lab because of the nature of the case?"

Sandy considered for a moment. "Let's send them to A&M. They have a rock-solid chain of custody procedure, and I've sent legal cases to them before. I think it'll be fine. Plus, they work with animal samples day in and day out. I think that's more important than anything else if this ends up going to court."

My chest grew tight at the reminder.

"Because it's a send-out, it's gonna take some time," she cautioned.

"Yeah, I figured. And I missed the afternoon pick up." I couldn't help but pout.

Seeing my concern, she said, "If you make sure it goes out first thing tomorrow, I'll call in a personal favor and ask A&M to prioritize it when it arrives."

My heart swelled with relief. "Thanks, Dr. Bishop."

"Anytime," she responded.

I hustled out to the necropsy floor to collect the blood, logging it out of the fridge, and brought the tube up to Anna, who doubled as our send-out technician.

I placed the sample on the counter with a heavy sigh, and then I kicked myself for being such an Eeyore. My exhaustion had gotten the better of me, and it wasn't fair to Anna to be huffy about it.

"Hey, Anna," I said, forcing a smile.

"Afternoon, Dr. Harjo. What've you got?" she replied with her usual cheer.

"Blood for drug testing. I think that's a send-out to Texas A&M."

"Yes, ma'am, it is," she responded and pulled out her resource binder to get started.

"Perfect. Can you send it out as soon as possible for a drug screen? Put STAT on the form, please."

"Um...we missed the afternoon shipment," she said in an apologetic tone. "The earliest this can go out is in the morning. But...tomorrow is Friday. I'm not sure A&M receives shipments on Saturdays. I can call and ask, but I might not be able to send it out until Monday morning."

Fuck!

I'd completely forgotten today was Thursday. Blood was heat-sensitive. It would need to be shipped overnight on ice and transferred right into a fridge on arrival at the other lab. That meant the receiving lab would have to be open when it arrived. If the lab were closed on Saturdays, Anna would have to wait until Monday to ship it for a Tuesday delivery. Because I'd been stuck in my own head, distracted, I might not hear anything until Wednesday at the earliest.

I can't wait that long for the results on this case. It'll kill me.

"Do you mind checking to see if someone is able to receive a Saturday delivery?" I half-pleaded. "We should also give them a heads-up about the sensitivity of the case. Chain of custody and all of that."

"Yes, ma'am," she replied. "I'll give 'em a jingle right now."

My shoulders sagged with relief. "Thank you, Anna."

"Anytime, Dr. Harjo," she said with a friendly smile.

With that done, I headed back to my office and slumped in my chair. The legal case weighed heavily, and my anxiety looped in circles. This mess with the police dog had sucked the life out of me, and I'd only received the case this morning. I couldn't help but think the ride would get bumpier before it improved.

I also had a nagging feeling that I'd forgotten something, but with the drug testing arranged, I couldn't put my finger on it. I held onto a wisp of hope that once I got out of the lab, the pressure would ease off a bit.

As soon as the clock hit five, I grabbed my purse and sped out of my office, eager to get some space between me at the legal case.

That's when it finally hit me.

I forgot to tell Fran.

I made the turn to my boss's office, my stomach tight with worry, and found the door shuttered for the day. Even though I disliked speaking with Fran, the Tohbi case was serious. I should've read her in as soon as the body passed through the doors. For all I knew, the press could be camped outside tomorrow morning, waiting for a comment. But I'd been so busy and distracted that I had completely forgotten about her.

I debated my options. Fran was a terrible boss, but she was more neglectful and selfish than truly malevolent. I fished my phone and shot her a quick text about the case. It was the best I could do at this point.

I waited a beat for a response, but my phone locked with no reply. I dropped my phone back into my purse and rubbed my hands across my face.

It is what it is. Nothing else you can do.

Fuck it.

It was time to get in my jammies, snuggle with Yersi on the couch, and devour a pint of ice cream. I quickly left the lab in my rearview mirror, eager to get away from that white dog and all of the drama swirling around it.

CHAPTER

ELEVEN

I left the lab and found the parking lot soaked from a recent wave of heavy rain. Dark puddles filled the pockets in the asphalt. The damp, heavy air had a staticky buzz and a prickly feeling that always preceded a particularly violent storm. Even though the precipitation had petered off to a faint drizzle, pregnant clouds hung ominously in the sky, threatening another round. Hail was coming. I wouldn't be surprised if a tornado or two also spun down from the angry sky.

I scampered to my car and made the short drive home. When the car thumped into the driveway, the weight of the day still hung heavily on my shoulders. Then, I saw Yersi waiting for me in the window, black fur like a shadow against the off-white blinds, and I suddenly felt like everything would be okay, even if just for a little while.

When my key turned in the door, the muffled meowing commenced. As soon as I stepped in, he swirled around my legs and rubbed on my pants.

I liked to think that he loved me so much that he couldn't express it strongly enough. Or maybe he knew how horrible my day had been, and he was offering condolences. But the realist in me knew that his stomach ran the show. If I didn't feed him within the next five minutes, there'd be hell to pay, which may or may not include a turd just outside the cat box.

I looked down at him, and my heart swelled. He was a demanding ruler, but one that I couldn't help but worship. I was firmly entrenched in the Cult of Yersi.

His purr echoed through his next meow. A slow blink followed.

"Hey, bud," I murmured affectionately. "I know, I know. Just a second."

I put my purse down on the entryway table and made a beeline for the kitchen. Yersi trotted ahead of me, tail straight.

My one-bedroom house was like a tiny actress from the 1930s. What she lacked in size, she made up for in charisma and grace. The wood floors creaked comfortingly as I passed through the cozy living room and straight into the dinette.

The kitchen was simple, and I had the fridge open lickety-split. I plopped some wet food in his dish, and Yersi buried his face with a *merf*, all thoughts of snuggles brushed to the side.

With the Great Slayer of Canned Food mollified, I headed through the back door to my yard. The garden spread before me, lush with late spring flowers. Despite the late hour and crackling feel to the air, the bees still bobbed around the lavender. The smell of jasmine was strong, and I inhaled deeply. The chickens clucked in greeting. I changed their water and sprinkled some fresh food out before heading back inside to procure my own sustenance.

The stress melted away in layers. Each simple task and deep breath of jasmine pushed the worry a little further away.

I had half a mind to bury my face in a pint of ice cream under the pergola outside, the threatening weather be damned. My garden was my happy place, and I needed a hot second to fully relax. But the clouds loomed, and storms like these tended to let loose on a dime. I figured being pelted with hail would only push me further into my depression. I resigned myself to a meal indoors.

Dinner was a bit of a let-down; anything short of mint chocolate chip ice cream would be after a day like today. I couldn't shake the images of the white dog lying on the table with its lifeless, icy-blue eyes. The case spun in my mind, the tension continuing to build just like the damn storm outside. I poked at my reheated leftovers: carnitas, rice, and beans.

When my phone binged with a text from the other room, my chest tightened. It could be anyone. Like Fran chewing my ass for not reading her in. Or the cops. Or a reporter.

Stop it, Josie. How would the cops or a reporter even get your private cell number?

In my worst moments of anxiety, I tended to go off the deep end with my paranoia. The only way to get out of the loop was to face the issue head-on. I wove to the front of the house and dug my phone out of my purse.

With a sigh of relief, I read the notification. It was a text from Armand.

Miss you.

My heart warmed, and a soft smile tugged at the edge of my lips. I headed back to the table, texting as I went.

Miss you too. Want to come over tomorrow? Bring Ileana this time?

He responded with a thumbs-up.

I knew Yersi wouldn't be pleased. He disliked the bouncy ball of joy that was Armand's dog. Even with Ileana in the picture, Yersi still ruled the house; no one dared question his leadership. But he had a sulky presence that ensured that everyone knew how put out he was when she visited.

6? Want me to pick up takeout?

That would be great.

Indian? Greek?

Whatever. As long as I don't have to cook.

Even though I enjoyed cooking, tomorrow was Friday, and I knew that the last day of the week would be just as exhausting, if not worse, than today. I wasn't in the mood to waltz gracefully around the kitchen and have the quality of our meal be dependent on a fully functioning brain.

The *bing* of Armand's thumbs-up shook me out of my thoughts.

We said our text-goodbyes, and I stared down at the cooling plate of leftover Mexican food, feeling glum. I picked at the rice with my fork, trying to tease out why I was feeling so off. My mind had shifted from one anxiety loop to another. Even though I loved seeing Armand and was looking forward to tomorrow, I couldn't help but feel down.

It's because you don't know how much longer he'll be around, a devil whispered in my ear.

That evil, little voice was spot-on.

I didn't want to think about the fact that Armand's visa would expire in early June. We'd looked for ways to extend it. Laila had even tried to get him a temporary position in the plant biology department. But with all of the budget cuts, it wasn't an option.

Armand and I had been apart before, managing to keep the relationship going with video calls. It had been an agonizingly long three months, but there had always been the promise of his return. There was a date on the calendar that we could both look forward to. This time, once he left, I had no idea when I'd see him again.

Tears pushed against my tired eyes, and I felt sick to my stomach. I scraped the rest of my dinner in the compost bin and dropped the dishes in the dishwasher. The depressing thoughts were just as bad as the looming clouds outside, hanging there threateningly, ready to let loose at any moment.

Trying to push all of the feelings in a tidy box, I flopped on the couch, determined to chase it all away with a few hours of Netflix. Yersi hopped on my lap. The comforting *ta-dum* sounded as the logo filled the screen.

Less than five minutes into some random fluff show, my phone binged again. This time, it was a text from Laila.

Up for lunch tomorrow?

Despite feeling like a grump-a-saurus, lunch with Laila sounded amazing. With all of the shit going down, I'd started to channel my inner Gru and could use some cheering up.

Yes! Bag lunch or restaurant?

The weather looks too ugly to eat outside. Red Rock at noon?

I sent her a thumbs-up. I wasn't sure what tomorrow would bring, but having solid plans to step away from work midday made it a bit easier to face whatever would land in my lap.

About halfway through the episode, my phone started ringing. My first instinct was to power the damn thing off so I could enjoy some peace and quiet.

I didn't because my phone was *actually* ringing.

The simple fact that someone had called me rather than sending a text triggered a flicker of worry. Hardly anyone cold-called anymore, and I frowned. Maybe it was a spam call. I grabbed my phone off the coffee table and was surprised to find Aunty's name filling the screen. I rushed to accept the call before it was shuffled to voicemail.

"Hey, Aunty. Everything alright?" The fretful edge to my voice surprised me.

I took a deep breath as I waited for Aunty to reply.

"I'm not sure," she said slowly, the worry in her voice discordant with the usual soothing, calm cadence. "Do you have a minute to talk?"

Everything felt off kilter: Aunty's tone, her cold-calling me, her asking if I had time to talk when I was usually the one calling her for support. All of it. My mind raced with endless possibilities. And then it hit.

Chula.

My chest tightened. In all of the chaos with the police case, I'd forgotten our earlier conversation. I couldn't help but feel like a selfish asshole for dropping the ball and not checking in earlier. I remembered setting an alarm, and a distant part of me wondered if I'd set it for the wrong time.

"Sure," I finally forced the word out through my buzzing thoughts. I tried to keep the anxiety from my voice, even though I knew Aunty would pick it up anyway. "Is it Chula? Is she okay?"

"Something's not right, Josie," Aunty replied.

My eyebrows furrowed, and I rested my hand on the sleeping Yersi for comfort. "Did she eat?"

"Yes, a little of the chicken. But she's barely left her bed since I've been home." Her voice wavered.

"Did she use the bathroom?" I asked, nerves winding tighter and tighter by the moment.

"Yes," she replied. "She went outside and did her thing like she always does."

A shred of relief allowed my shoulders to sag infinitesimally. "That's good," I replied, meaning it. "Still no diarrhea or vomiting, right?"

"Nothing like that," she answered.

I chewed my cheek, running through differentials. Even without any vomiting or diarrhea, a stomach bug was still a fairly strong possibility.

"Did she happen to get into the trash at all?" I asked.

Chula served as the resident vacuum at Aunty's house, sweeping up anything before it barely touched the floor. She was also a notorious trash bandit. Aunty had to keep the garbage can locked up under the sink or else she'd find paper towels soaked with bacon drippings torn to shreds across her floor.

"Ever since I put the baby lock on the cabinet, she hasn't gotten into the garbage," Aunty said.

I mentally crossed pancreatitis off the list.

"She's just acting tired and isn't very interested in food," Aunty added. "She's not her usual self. Should I bring her to see Dr. Jones?"

I pursed my lips, considering.

Aunty had a habit of feeding Chula bits and bobs. Maybe Chula had eaten something that had gone a little off or hadn't been cooked all the way. It was possible she'd eaten a dead mouse or something, too. She had a habit of sniffing out the rankest stuff when she roamed the creek edges with Aunty.

I couldn't imagine it being anything too terrible. I didn't know Chula's exact age, but I was pretty sure she was eleven or twelve years old. For a medium-sized mutt who was part coyote, according to Aunty, at least, I expected them to have at least a few more years together.

She's fine. Just a stomach bug or something.

"If she's eating, drinking, and using the bathroom, it could simply be a mild gastritis from dietary indiscretion. Chula might be right as rain in the morning," I offered.

I paused, tasting the words. For some reason, they didn't ring as true as I'd expected them to.

"But, if she stops eating, gets any worse, or isn't back to her normal self in twenty-four hours or so, definitely bring her in," I added. I knew Aunty would worry until Chula was back to her usual self, but I didn't want her to eat herself up overnight.

"Thank you, sweety," Aunty said, a hint of relief in her voice. "I'm sure you're right."

"I'm sure she'll be okay, Aunty." Part of me hoped saying the words out loud would help make them true. But as soon as they were out, I realized that I didn't sound very convincing.

"Hmm," she replied.

Her *hmm* was impossible to read, and my eyebrows furrowed.

"Want me to try to come down there tomorrow?" I offered, knowing it would be practically impossible given all of the shit going down at work, but I'd do it for Aunty.

"Oh, no," she replied. "It'll be fine. We'll be okay. Don't you worry."

Now, she was trying to reassure me.

I kicked myself.

"We'll see you on Sunday," Aunty continued. "Tessa's coming, right?"

I could tell she wanted to change the subject, so I reluctantly followed her lead. "Yep. I asked Armand to join us, too."

"It will be nice to see them both," she said, and I could hear the smile in her voice. "He's coming to her graduation, too, right?"

"Um-hm. Tessa was able to get enough tickets, and I know he wouldn't want to miss it," I replied.

Tessa didn't have any blood kin, so it would be just me, Aunty, and Armand cheering her across the stage. All of us promised to be there a week from Saturday, no matter hell or highwater. Aunty would be toting her airhorn, and I'd be slinging the cowbell.

"Sure you don't want us to pick you up?" I offered for the millionth time. It was a long way up to Stillwater from Ada, and Aunty didn't like driving long distances by herself.

She snorted at the offer. "I'll be fine."

"Okay," I said, and my lips cracked into a smile.

"I'm proud of her," Aunty said.

"Me too, Aunty. It's been a long road. I'm glad she's made it this far and is ready to make that next leap."

I let the happy feeling settle in my chest.

Then, a random thought bubbled up in my head. "Ever heard of a guy named Chuck Pollard?"

Aunty whistled low. "Oh lordy. I haven't heard that name in ages."

A long pause followed, and I knew that space was filled with several years of stories. According to the rumor mill, Aunty had raised a bit of hell in her teens. There were some juicy tales she hadn't shared, and I could see her hoarding them in her treasure trove.

"How'd you happen to cross paths with Chuck?" she finally asked.

Where do I even start with that....

"Um. He works for the Oklahoma City police. A detective," I answered.

"No shit?" she blurted in a very un-Aunty-like way. "Well, I'll be."

I smiled, envisioning her eyes unfocused as she went back forty years.

"He brought a case into the lab. Recognized my last name. Said he knew Mom. Asked if I knew you and some other folks. Leon? A few others I can't remember."

"Probably mentioned Will. Maybe Haley, too," she mused.

"Maybe?" I replied. It sounded about right, but I couldn't remember through the fog of the case. "Anyway, he asked me to say hi to you."

"Chuck Pollard," she repeated and huffed a laugh. "If you see him again, tell him hello back. He should come back to Ada one of these days. It'd be nice to catch up."

"I'll pass that along next time I talk to him," I answered.

Next time I talk to him. I didn't use "if." Fuck.

In my heart, I knew Chuck and I would have a few more conversations about Tohbi. It'd be practically impossible not to. If I were lucky, they'd be nice and casual. I'd get him an answer, and he'd be happy. And I wouldn't have to cross paths with him in court as a witness for the prosecution.

"Well, sweety," Aunty said with a sigh. "Thanks for helping with Chula. I know it's getting late, and I have to work tomorrow. I'll let you go."

"Okay. Give Chula a scratch for me?" I asked. "And if she doesn't eat breakfast tomorrow, bring her in."

"I will," she promised.

We said our goodbyes, and I ended the call, still feeling off kilter.

As soon as I rested my phone on the coffee table, a loud *boom* of thunder rattled the windows. This was followed almost immediately by a bright flash of light.

Yersi startled awake, claws camping into my legs. I rested a hand on him, trying to calm both our racing hearts. A few seconds later, the heavy patter of hail sounded against the roof.

I unpaused the show and turned the volume up, trying to ignore the chaos brewing outside. But as hard as I tried, I couldn't escape the apprehension from building in my bones.

CHAPTER
TWELVE

My eyes snapped open to a dark room, heart racing.

I rolled over to check the time on my phone.

It was early. Way too early.

Last night's sleep was about as shitty as they came. The weather radio had gone off almost every hour, blaring out tornado warnings. I'd wake up, lying half-lidded in bed as the counties were listed, and then crash back to sleep as soon as I learned Payne County was in the clear.

The white dog prowling through my dreams hadn't helped. The details of the dream had already begun to slip away, but I could still see the flash of his hair ahead of me on a dirt path. A creek bubbled off to one side, and the cicadas sang. The white dog stopped to turn, ears perked and eyes worried.

Goosebumps spread across my arms at the memory.

Sometimes, work came home with me in the form of a bit of missed blood on my skin or the stench of a dead animal. But that was it. I never held on to the mental images of the animals that had passed under my knife. And I'd certainly never dreamed about any of them before. I couldn't shake this case, and it chewed its way through my psyche.

I rolled over onto my stomach, folded my arms under my pillow, and thought maybe I could get a few more minutes of sleep.

A light *thud* dashed my hopes.

Within seconds, Yersi assumed his position just outside the doorway and yowled mournfully. His cry for breakfast could not be ignored. Rubbing my eyes, I swept the last of the cobwebs away and grudgingly swung out of bed.

About twenty minutes later, the morning sacrifice had been laid before the Great Ruler, and I was hunched at the kitchen counter, nursing a cup of black tea. A mushroom omelet sat in front of me, untouched. I'd made it thinking I needed a solid breakfast to start the day, but I couldn't help but lament the fact that I hadn't made waffles loaded with maple syrup. I glared at the omelet, knowing I'd need the calories but not wanting to spend them this way. Reluctantly picking up my fork, I forced the food down.

The meal didn't sit well, and I fought back burbles of acid as I dressed. Going for comfort, I chose jeans and a casual shirt that was barely passable for work. I could've brought it up a notch with a pair of flats, but my feet weren't feeling it. I laced up my sneakers with barely enough fucks to give.

As soon as the sun tipped over the horizon, I headed into the back-yard to check on the chickens. Low clouds hung heavy in the sky, and everything was damp. Thankfully, the air lacked the fierce crackle of energy from yesterday. With luck, the clouds would clear and reveal the bright cerulean sky that always followed a particularly nasty weather system.

The girls clucked conversationally as I changed their water and refreshed their food. They were eager to come out and scratch in the yard, but I didn't have enough time to watch them this morning.

"Tomorrow, ladies. I promise," I said affectionately.

It's Friday. Finally.

I just needed to make it through today. Then, I could relax. I stubbornly avoided thinking about the fact that I was on call this weekend, and that I'd be on the hook for any dead body that rolled through the door. At least I didn't have to be in the building all day.

When I pulled into the lab's parking lot, the discomfiting feeling still hung around my shoulders. When I switched the car off, my ears rang with the silence.

As much as I wanted to stop thinking about last night, images from the dream haunted me. It had been so vivid: that white dog—Tohbi—padding along in front of me, stopping to look back. The path was familiar: well-worn, with green brush pushing up along the sides.

The flowers of milkweed, yarrow, and wild garlic spotted the shrubs bordering the creek. The smell of lavender hung heavy.

It's the creek by Aunty's, I realized.

The omelet threatened to come back up again. I grasped quickly for my water bottle, taking a swig before I spilled my cookies all over the car seat.

Leaning my head back, I rubbed the base of my palms over my eyes. No matter how hard I tried, I couldn't wipe the images away.

As my hands dropped in my lap, a thought niggled at the back of my mind.

Chula.

I'd forgotten to check in with Aunty this morning. A panicky feeling raced through me. I pulled my phone out of my purse and texted her.

> How is Chula today?

To my relief, she responded almost immediately, and the ellipses bobbed as I waited for her reply.

> About the same. She ate some more chicken. Went to the bathroom.

The answer wasn't quite what I'd hoped for, but at least Chula had eaten breakfast and was still doing her business outside. I was hard-pressed to advise a trip to the vet. I didn't want to be one of those pathologists who thought their dog was dying from cancer if they missed a bit of kibble in the bowl or stumbled to catch a frisbee.

I texted Aunty back.

> Call me if anything changes.

A thumbs-up tag popped up.

I made a mental note to check back in after work and dropped my phone back in my purse. I leaned back in my seat and closed my eyes again, still troubled.

When I opened them, a gray truck pulled in next to me.

As if shit couldn't get any worse.

My heart sank. Even though Gerald had slowly morphed from troll to something resembling a human being, it had been a long journey, and he still had a long way to go to be a half-decent person. Even though I didn't want to cross paths with him this morning, being an asshole about it never helped matters.

I forced the frown away, grabbed my things, and climbed out of the car. The *bang* of Gerald's door followed quickly on the heels of mine.

"Good morning, Dr. Richter," I said through a tight smile.

His eyes narrowed infinitesimally, and for a flicker of a second, I thought he might say something mean.

Instead, he replied, "Good morning, Dr. Harjo," and left it at that.

The relief I should have felt after dodging a bullet was replaced by a weird, expectant tension. Like my body had been prepared for an attack and didn't know what to do when one hadn't landed.

We walked silently into the lab, not really together but close enough that it was a little awkward. He held the door for me, and I mumbled my thanks.

As soon as the front door swung closed, Fran pounced.

"Josie," she said sternly. "May I see you in my office?"

Fuuuuuuck.

I glanced up at Gerald, expecting to see glee in his eyes. Instead, he flashed me a look of sympathy before turning toward his office. My knees practically buckled at the shock of it.

"Josie?" Fran nagged, and my attention shifted back to her.

By her tone, I knew she planned on ripping me a new one, and I could only assume it was about the Tohbi case. Clearly, yesterday's text hadn't been enough to dig me out of whatever hole I was in.

Might as well get this over with.

My shoulders slumped, and I trudged after her. It felt like I was being dragged into the principal's office by my ear. I smoothed my expression, trying to hold back the feelings of irritation.

Fran took a seat in her bougie, ergonomic chair and gestured to the shitty government one across from her desk. "Please sit," she commanded.

The symbolism wasn't lost on me, and my lips pressed into a firm line.

Her obsessively plucked eyebrows were pulled tight in a scowl. "What is this about the police being in the lab yesterday? Why were they here?"

"They dropped off a police dog for necropsy," I said, trying to keep this short and sweet so I could get the fuck out of there.

She glared at me from across her desk.

"I texted you," I offered, weakly.

"Why is it that whenever the police are in the lab, it has something to do with you?" She leaned back and crossed her arms. "It always creates quite the mess for me to clean up."

Thankfully, my snort didn't escape.

Fran never cleaned anything up. All she did was stalk the halls like an incompetent despot while the rest of us ran around and made sure things ran right.

Figuring her question was rhetorical, I kept my mouth shut, anger simmering.

"You should have informed me immediately," she continued. "This has the potential to attract media attention."

I tried not to roll my eyes. "Yes, I'm aware of that."

"Why did you wait until the end of the day? And why, only then, did you decide that texting me was the best course of action?" She said "texting" like it was a dirty word and fluttered her fingers at the cell phone resting on her desk.

"Yesterday was extremely busy," I replied coolly. "I tried to find you when I was finally off the necropsy floor and done calling the detective, but you had already left for the day."

There. Eat that, you bitch.

Her lips pursed, and her eyes narrowed. "What did you find on necropsy? Do you have a cause of death?"

The blow hit, and her eyes flashed with delight when she caught my flinch.

I tried to brush it off and shrugged. "I don't have much more to tell you at this point. As I said in my text, the necropsy was unremarkable. Ancillary testing is pending."

She frowned.

Feeling brave, I stood and pushed my chair in, heart thudding from a dump of adrenaline. "Now, unless you have any more questions, I'm going to check in with Dustin and see what's on the docket for today."

She'd lost control of the situation, and she knew it. "Well. Fine then. But you need to keep me informed. If any results come in, I am the first to know about them. Understand?"

"Yes, ma'am," I said, having zero intention of complying.

"And you are absolutely not to talk to the press without my explicit permission," she added with a frown.

Like I would unless forced to!

"Yes, ma'am," I repeated, trying to keep the irritation out of my voice.

She dismissed me with a nod, and I escaped before my annoyance turned into verbal snark.

After dumping my things in my office, I went in search of Dustin.

There was something reassuring about finding him relaxed at his desk, cradling a cup of steaming coffee. Seeing him there, like it was just another day, brought a feeling of normalcy. For just a millisecond, I could pretend that Fran hadn't just chided me like a middle-schooler and the legal case wasn't hanging over me.

I rapped my knuckles on the doorjamb. "Morning, Dustin."

He put his cup down and smiled. "Mornin', Doc." He considered me and then asked, "You doin' okay?"

I nodded, fighting back the "no" that was sitting on the tip of my tongue.

"Just tired," I said instead.

"Weather was wild last night," he mused, studying me.

"Yup," was all I could muster. He knew it was more than the weather, but was also savvy enough to let it pass. He could tell I didn't want to talk about the real problem.

"Anything come in?" I asked.

"Yeah," he replied sympathetically. He knew I hoped for a slow day, and having a body first thing wasn't a good sign.

My heart sank.

"A racehorse with a broken leg and a cat from the vet hospital," he added.

Two! Already!

"Damn," I moped. "This week has been bonkers."

"Yeah, it has. Want to get started now or hold off a bit?"

I folded my lips in, thinking. "I need more caffeine before I do anything else. I also want to check in on the case from yesterday."

His eyes softened with understanding. "Got it. Okay."

I didn't need to say *which* case I wanted to check on. It sat in the corner like a giant turd, and everyone could smell it.

"How about we meet on the necropsy floor in about an hour?" I suggested.

He gave me a friendly salute. "Sounds good."

I left Dustin's office, grabbed my mug, and headed to the breakroom to get at least one more cup of the tea down my gullet before I waded into any carcasses.

I rounded the corner and found Gerald hovering by the coffeemaker. The brown liquid bubbled and fizzed into the pot.

My stomach flopped.

So far, he'd been half decent this morning, but I couldn't help but tense whenever I was around him. When a dog bites often enough, a person can't help but be a bit jittery around the beast.

I reached for the hot water dispenser, avoiding eye contact, and filled my cup.

He cleared his throat.

"I see that the blood is being sent to A&M for drug testing on case 43518087," he said conversationally.

"Yes," I answered, keeping my eyes on my hands as I measured tea into the steeper.

"Why?" he asked.

My hackles rose. I took a deep breath, hoping it wasn't too obvious, and dropped the steeper into my cup. Turning toward him, I finally met his gaze. "I sent the blood to A&M because the dog had busted seven hundred pounds of meth right before he died. I guess you didn't see the news last night," I snapped.

Silence swept through the room like wildfire, and I could practically hear a pin drop. Gerald's eyebrows furrowed, and he wore a confused expression. It was a new look for him. I felt a surge of malevolent satisfaction, followed by the slow burn of guilt for thinking mean thoughts.

He recovered quickly. "Did you ask if the dog had been fed Best Bud's Bacon Bites?"

Seriously?

"No, I haven't had the opportunity," I replied curtly. "I'm hoping to connect with the owner today."

It isn't infectious, asshole. Get off my back, I thankfully didn't blurt out.

I understood Gerald well enough to get the vibe that he wanted to help solve the case. He was a busybody, and I knew he couldn't help himself. He always butted into cases in an obtrusive and slightly offensive way. It raised my hackles every time he was on my ass about a case, regardless of his intentions.

I grabbed my mug. "I better get to it," I said, and left before he had a chance to grill me further. I already felt like shit today and didn't need him poking around in my business.

Back at my desk, the blinking of the voicemail light on my desktop phone greeted me with malicious glee. Clenching my cup, I leaned back in my chair and closed my eyes.

Deep breaths. Little steps. Eyes on the prize.

I took a sip of the tea, careful not to burn my tongue, and rested the mug on my desk. It was time to suck it up and get shit done. Picking up the phone, I punched in the numbers to listen to the voicemail.

"Hello, Dr. Harjo," a deep, masculine voice said. "This is Austin Carlyle, Tohbi's partner. Detective Pollard asked me to give you a call. It's eight o'clock on Friday, and I'll be here for most of the day." This was quickly followed by his phone number and a polite thanks.

After scrambling for a pen and paper, I replayed the message and jotted his number down. I pressed the hook switch with my finger and released it before dialing his number.

To my surprise, he answered on the first ring.

"Carlyle." His voice was laced with a city accent.

"Austin Carlyle?" I asked, wanting to confirm.

"Yes, ma'am," he replied.

I grabbed the pen and started spinning it between my fingers. "This is Dr. Josie Harjo from the diagnostic lab."

"Thanks for returning my call. Detective Pollard said you wanted to speak with me about Tohbi," he said, his voice cracking at the end.

"Yes," I replied. After a beat, I added, "I'm sorry for your loss. Detective Pollard said Tohbi was an accomplished police dog. I'm sure he was a good buddy, too."

It was hard to know how to react to someone's loss. Sometimes, they'd just brush it away and scoff at any offer of condolences. Other times, they'd break into tears. I'd seen the toughest cowboys lose their marbles in that little soul-sucking interview room when they brought their beloved animal in. Reading someone over the phone was difficult, and I wasn't sure what to say.

Austin cleared his throat uncomfortably. "Yes, Tohbi was a fine officer," he finally responded, his voice choppy with restrained tears.

My heart ached for him.

I gave him a few seconds before I pressed on. "I'm working hard to figure out what happened," I said softly. "I'd like to ask you a few questions. Is now a good time?"

He cleared his throat again. "Yes, ma'am."

"How was Tohbi acting yesterday morning? Did he look sick at all?" I asked gently.

"He seemed fine," Austin answered. "Ate his breakfast like normal. Went outside for a while like he always does. Then, we went to work."

My pen twirled faster. "Any vomiting? Diarrhea? Coughing?"

"No, ma'am. He seemed right as rain," he responded.

"I know you were working at the airport and that Tohbi alerted on a big shipment of meth," I started to get that messy bit out of the way. "Anything unusual about how he found the drugs? How he alerted?"

"No, ma'am," he said, his tone business-like. "He worked for about thirty minutes and sat down, just like he's trained to. Folks moved in to inspect the shipment. Popped it right open and found the buckets. Clear as day."

"Hmm," I said and chewed on my cheek. "Any chance he could have gotten into any of the drugs?"

"No, ma'am," he said, certainty ringing in his voice. "Once he alerts, we stand back and let the others take over. We stay close, in case they need us again, but not close enough that he would've been exposed. Plus, the meth was in sealed barrels. They had to open one and use a field test kit to confirm it."

Well, there goes that differential, I thought mournfully.

"Once we got the all-clear, Tohbi seemed happy, like he always does when he's done a good job," he continued.

I couldn't help but notice the slip back into the present tense.

"I gave Tohbi his toy, put him back in the vehicle, and came back to assist," he continued. "He barked a bit. But he does that when anyone walks by the car, and I didn't think much of it. Now, I'm wondering if he was crying for help."

The rational part of me doubted that, but saying so wouldn't accomplish fuck-all. This man was grieving and needed to sort through the mess of his thoughts on his own time. I let the silence sit between us.

After a beat, he continued, voice laced with shame, "I didn't think it was all that hot out. I parked the vehicle in the shade, and the windows were rolled down partway. I didn't think to put the AC on."

"Was the car warm when you found him?" I asked as delicately as I could. This was rough terrain, and I needed to tread carefully.

"No, ma'am," he said, voice wavering. "He was just lying there, sprawled out. Hair wet with pee. Saliva all over the seat. His tongue halfway hanging out...." His voice trailed off.

That was a weird detail, and I tucked it away to process later.

I decided to go out on a limb. "For what it's worth, I don't think he died from heat stroke, Mr. Carlyle," I said softly.

He let out a hushed sniff.

"I don't know why Tohbi died, but I'm going to do my best to figure it out," I said, hoping to offer a hint of reassurance.

A thought niggled its way in. Something about German Shepherds and arrhythmias. Tohbi was a Belgian Malinois, but that was close enough.

"Was Tohbi ever lethargic?" I asked, trying to keep my voice steady and calm. "Ever tire easily when playing ball?"

"No, ma'am," he said.

Fuck.

I was so sick of hearing "no, ma'am" that I wanted to ask a random question unrelated to the case just to hear the guy say yes to something.

Time to switch gears.

"Is Tohbi up-to-date on his vaccinations?" I asked.

"Yes, ma'am."

"Is he on any medications?"

"I put that stuff on his back once a month for ticks and all. That's it," he replied.

"What brand of food did you feed Tohbi?" I asked cautiously.

He rattled off a common, high-end brand of dry dog food, complete with the flavor: hearty beef and potatoes.

"Can you save some of it for me? Just fill up a gallon baggie and snap a picture of the lot number if you wouldn't mind."

"Why?" he asked, sounding confused.

I shrugged even though he couldn't see me. "Just being cautious is all. I don't think his death has anything to do with the kibble, but I want to have some handy in case we need to go back to it."

"Sure," he said hesitantly. "And just keep it somewhere?"

"Yes, please," I replied.

"Okay, ma'am."

As my pen twirled, I pictured Gerald standing at the coffee machine, going on and on about Best Bud's Bacon whatevers.

My stomach clenched.

"What kind of treats did you give him?" I had to force the words out, dreading how he might answer.

He listed off a few names that I wasn't familiar with, but no Best Bud's. I felt a thread of relief.

"Anything else you can think of? Any other little detail from yesterday?" I nudged.

"No, ma'am," he repeated.

I bit back a sigh, racking my brain for anything else to ask, and came up short. Feeling like I'd teased out as much information as I could, I thanked him. I gave him another round of condolences before we said our goodbyes.

It wasn't until I'd hung up the phone that I realized I'd forgotten to ask him about the half-digested sausage I'd found in Tohbi's stomach.

CHAPTER
THIRTEEN

With two bodies waiting for me on the necropsy floor, I needed to climb out of my head and get to work.

I slipped into coveralls and stepped out onto the floor a tad before nine. The horse was already positioned on the table, the fracture obvious across the room, and the cat lay on the table closest to the door. Between the tangy smell of disinfectant and the soft hum of music, it was like slipping on an old shoe. My mind switched into pathologist-mode, and I felt the comforting pull of making mental differential lists.

Dustin stood by the butcher's block and put a fresh edge on his knife. The *shick, shick, shick* soothed me.

"It's like deja vu, but thankfully minus the sewer goat. My olfactory bulbs will live to see another day," I quipped, joining him.

He smiled, and his chest bounced with a silent snicker. He pointed with his knife, first to the horse. "Except a different leg is broke on that one." The knife switched position. "And that cat is a tabby. And I'd bet one of Carol's sweets it ain't heartworm neither."

"You're probably right," I replied.

Dogs with heartworm were a dime a dozen. A cat with heartworm was a fucking unicorn.

"Probably lymphoma," he added. "Damn near every cat comin' through here's got that."

I huffed a laugh. "I can only hope."

We always joked that the top three differentials for any cat were lymphoma, lymphoma, and lymphoma. Today, I'd take a fractured racehorse limb and a lymphoma cat; it'd be another set of easy cases. They would also be enough to keep me busy, but not drowning.

Or left scrambling for a diagnosis in a potential murder case.

I quickly brushed the thought away.

"What's the deal with the cat anyway?" I grabbed the two submittal forms from the wall hanger and scanned them.

"Ain't a great history on the cat," he said, and he wasn't wrong; it was all of three sentence fragments that were moderately helpful.

"Diarrhea. Severely dehydrated. Owners elected euthanasia," I read from the form and shrugged. "Better than the one from yesterday. 'Dead steer' is always so incredibly helpful."

"True. At least with 'diarrhea' we know where to start lookin'," he replied with an optimistic perk of his eyebrow.

I snorted. "I wonder if they gave the cat Best Bud's Bacon Bites."

"Huh?" Dustin stopped running his knife across the honing steel and looked up at me, confused.

An awkward half-laugh escaped. "Just goofing around. I thought it would be funny, and it wasn't. There's a recall on these dog treats, and it popped into my head. My brain's all over the place today. Didn't sleep well. Sorry."

An image flashed in my mind: a white dog glancing over its shoulder on Aunty's path.

"It's alright, Doc," he said, ignoring my weirdness like it was a fart in the room. We were cool, and he could roll right along with the best of them. "It's been a busy week," he added as he hung the knife sharpener back on the peg.

I slipped a set of gloves on and chewed my cheek, still feeling the buzz in my head.

"How 'bout I take Mr. Ed, and you take Mr. Meowmers there?" he asked.

I could've kissed him for trying to keep things light. "Sounds good. Let me know if you need any help popping that one open."

"I got it, Doc," he said, and flashed me a soft smile. "Don't you worry none. Me and ole Betsy know how to get 'er done."

My eyebrows shot up, and I barked a laugh. "Betsy? The hoist has a name, now?"

"Always has. She's just shy about sharin' it, is all." He tossed me a playful wink and swept away to the other side of the room to get started on the horse.

A grin stretched across my face as I watched him go, and I shook my head. Dustin had a way of always making me smile when I needed to, and I appreciated him for it.

Feeling a bit lighter, I pulled my focus to the cat. I filled a small formalin container with the sharp-smelling, clear fluid, feeling the slight burn in my nose. The cart at the end of the small animal table held all the tools I would need. I selected a set of metal scissors, forceps, a scalpel handle, a disposable blade, and small rongeurs. I peeled the metal packaging back from the blunt end of the blade and snapped it on the handle before tugging it off the rest of the way. The tools lay in a neat line next to the formalin container. There was something about the tidiness of it all that eased the tension in my shoulders.

Grabbing the hose, I gently wet down the table around the cat. The whir of the hoist picked up, momentarily overtaking the sounds of Hank Williams.

Betsy's voice is like one of those smoky, dive-bar singers, I thought with a chuckle.

It was muscle memory from there. I'd performed a million and one necropsies and could practically do them in my sleep, which was just about where I was today. A numb and detached feeling settled over me, and I couldn't help but feel like my brain had already clocked out. About half an hour later, I blinked out of the fog and found myself bagging the cat parts for private cremation.

"What did ya find?" Dustin asked from right next to me, startling me a bit.

"Oh, um," I stammered. Once I got my mental shit together, I added, "Intestinal lymphoma."

"Ha! There ya go," he said, still trying to cheer me up. "Glad it was easy and not Best Friend's Bacon stuff."

"Best Bud's Bacon Bites," I mumbled.

"Why don't you go have a look at that horse leg? I can clean this up for you," he offered.

"Thanks," I said and started chewing on the raw tissue inside my cheek as I moved over to the horse.

I made some notes about the fracture, confident that Dustin had taken the pictures required for insurance. As I finished up, he joined me at the large animal table, having already cleaned up after the cat at a speed reserved for necropsy technicians.

"All done with the horse?" he asked, not unkindly.

"Yes, sir," I said, putting the paperwork to the side and getting ready to help out.

"I got this," he said with a smile. "It'll give me somethin' to fill the time 'til lunch. Plus, Betsy likes me better."

"Thanks, Dustin," I said, catching his eye and hoping to communicate how much I appreciated him in that single look.

He smiled back. "Anytime, Doc."

I stepped through the footbath, watching the sudsy water slosh across my rubber boots. The smell of the disinfectant filled the air. Since there was hardly any blood on me, I passed right through without needing to scrub my boots and headed to the locker room to change. Before I knew it, I was back at my desk, mind free to roam. It was dangerous territory, and a part of me wished I'd stayed to help clean. I didn't like where my mind kept circling back to.

My fingers danced across the keyboard. The two cases were run-of-the-mill, so it was easy to push the reports out before lunch. After finalizing the last report, I still had about thirty minutes before I needed to meet Laila. Even though it was only a five-minute drive, I felt antsy and itched to escape. Unable to sit in my chair a second longer, I grabbed my keys and headed out.

By the time I arrived at Red Rock, the parking lot had already started to fill up. I squeezed my Prius between two large trucks. Cracking the door, I wiggled out sideways, doing my best not to ding any paint. Foolishly, I sucked my stomach in, forgetting that it was my ass that had the widest wingspan. I still managed to squish through without doing any damage to the other vehicles and headed inside.

The restaurant was comfortably warm and filled with the smell of hearty, freshly baked bread. There was a hum of pleasant, low chatter. The moderately-sized line moved quickly. I took my position at the end and pulled my phone out to check the time. Thankfully, I wasn't grossly early; I'd left just enough time to place my order and grab a seat before Laila arrived.

Sure enough, when I flopped into a table near the front window, Laila passed through the front doors. The place was fairly busy by then, so I stood and threw a quick wave to catch her eye. She nodded that she'd seen me and pointed to the growing queue. I waved her on.

While I waited, I fidgeted with the wrapper of the straw for my iced tea. I rolled it one way, unrolled it, and then rolled it the other. Back and forth. Back and forth. The paper whisked through my fingers.

By the time Laila joined me, my food had arrived. The chicken, walnut, and apple salad sandwich sat on the plate next to a small bowl of brightly-colored fruit salad, both of them untouched. The poor straw wrapper was now worn thin, and small bits of cheap paper fell off with each spin.

Laila placed her order number and drink on the table, took one look at the mess of paper, and the skin between her eyebrows wrinkled with concern. Before sitting down, she pulled me close for a half hug. I leaned my head against her, and she patted my back before she released me.

"Hey, Laila," I said, unable to keep the exhaustion out of my voice.

She took the seat across from me and laced her fingers in her lap. "I'd ask you if you're okay, but you're obviously not."

Her eyebrows furrowed, and wrinkles pinched around her dark eyes. Despite that, everything else about her looked perfect. Her beautiful black hair hung straight to her shoulders and had a healthy, glossy sheen. She wore a silky purple dress shirt with little orange flowers and dark blue fitted jeans. I was glad to see her looking so well, especially after everything that had happened with her parents over the winter break.

"Work?" she nudged.

"Yeah, it's been a thing," I huffed, eyes back down, watching my fingers twirl.

Roll, unroll, roll.

"You should eat," she nudged.

Roll, unroll, roll.

"Psht. Seriously, Stacy?" she asked in a perky, high school cheerleader voice.

My eyes jumped up, and I felt a flitter of shock.

Laila grinned. Then, she dropped the smile to give me a fake judgy look. She continued in that same playful voice, "The chicken salad always makes the bread *wet*. Like *ew*. That is *so* nasty. *Blech*. You need to eat it, like, now, or it's going to get *so* gross."

It was a damn good imitation of Cher Horowitz, and I couldn't help but crack a smile.

One eyebrow lifted, and she sneered down at the sandwich. "Seriously, Stacy. Like, if you don't, I will. And then I won't fit in my prom dress. And Brad will leave me for Amber," she said of her imaginary high school drama.

Unable to help myself, I let out an exaggerated sigh and rolled my eyes dramatically. "*Fiiine*, Becky. But only because I *hate* Amber, and Brad is *hot*."

"Yes, he is," she said with a self-satisfied hair-flip.

We giggled like schoolgirls, and I was finally able to let go of the straw wrapper.

"I love you, Laila," I said with a smile.

The wrinkles around her eyes softened. She looked a bit smug when I took a bite of my sandwich.

"Back at you, Josie," she said.

She sipped her drink and glanced around the restaurant. "Busy today," she remarked.

"The last stragglers are getting their fix before the semester ends," I commented.

She nodded. "The department is busy finalizing grades and prepping for graduation. The Ag College graduation is on Sunday. I'll be leading the Plant Bio section. It'll be my first time. Wish me luck."

I flashed her a supportive smile. "You'll do amazing," I said, meaning every word of it. Oklahoma State University was lucky to have her as Chair of her department.

"I hope so." She smiled shyly. "How about you? The vet school graduation is on Saturday, right?"

"Yep," I said. "But I just have to sit with the rest of the faculty and clap. I don't have any speeches or have to call out names."

I took a bite of my sandwich, enjoying the crisp bite of the apple.

"Is Tessa all set to walk?" she asked.

Since my mouth was full, I just nodded with a proud smile.

"That's awesome," she said. "You did good by her."

I'd leaned on Laila quite a bit when we'd been in the thick of things with Tessa. She'd even helped Tessa find emergency housing and just enough money to scratch by until she could finish her senior year. It'd been Ted Colbert who'd helped with the legal side of things. Aunty had also been there, providing emotional support. It had taken a village, but Tessa had made it. I couldn't wait to see her walk across the stage and planned on bringing lots of Kleenex.

"What's it like being Chair with the end of the school year closing in?" I asked.

"Meh," she answered. "Other than the graduation stuff, not much different. Same problems. Just less classes and less students to worry about."

"And hopefully less Ian Murray?" I added.

Every department had a work troll, and for the plant biology department, it was Ian Murray. He spread his own special brand of toxicity.

She snorted. "Yeah, and less Ian Murray. Thankfully, he's absconding off to fuck knows where for the summer. I'll finally be able to breathe for a hot second."

My heart went out to her. Gerald definitely took the title of work troll in the diagnostic lab, but he seemed to be coming around in his own weird way. I didn't have much hope for Ian; that guy was slimy as fuck.

"How about you?" she asked.

I held my hands up and shrugged. "If animals are dying, I'm working. But the students are off the floor for the summer. It makes everything else I have to deal with a bit easier."

Like trying to solve a murder, the evil part of me whispered, trying to drag me back down into despair.

My lips tugged down into a frown, and I started to fold back into myself.

Laila's expression softened with concern.

"It's a shame Armand has to go back," she said, misreading my dismay.

My chest grew tight. Of all the troubles I'd been avoiding thinking about, Armand's impending departure was right up there.

I avoided Laila's gaze and took a sip of my drink, forcing the iced tea down.

"We tried to find something else—some way to extend it or bounce him to another visa," she said apologetically. "It's difficult with the current administration and new limits on funding."

"Yeah," I murmured, my shoulders sagging.

"My friend in the soil and water resources department said they're cutting three positions. *Three*." She shook her head. "I'm just grateful we don't have to cut any in plant bio."

"They're holding a couple backfills in the vet school, too," I said. "Asking people to not retire if they can help it so they don't lose positions."

My thoughts drifted to Sandy, who brushed against retirement age. Selfishly, I wanted her to stay because I couldn't imagine the lab without her. But the friend in me wanted her to follow her heart. She'd talked wistfully about retiring but worried about the toxicology department falling apart if she left. Though I'd never admit it, I had a feeling her reservations were founded. I wouldn't be surprised if Fran closed the department down when Sandy retired.

Laila sensed the shift in the conversation, and there was a brief lull. The chatter of the other diners and the clang of utensils on plates filled the silence.

I'd managed to eat about three-quarters of my sandwich, and I was feeling pretty proud of myself. It had tasted good—everything from Red Rock was delicious—and the bread hadn't been soggy. But I still felt sick to my stomach.

I looked up and noticed Laila studying me, slowly chewing on her own bite of sandwich.

She swallowed and asked, "So, what's really going on?"

"Just work stuff," I replied, trying to dodge the question.

She wasn't having any of that. "Gerald?"

"No. Yeah. Sort of. I don't know. I guess, no," I stammered.

"Fran, then?"

I sighed. "Fran is a shitass, but that's nothing new."

She took a sip of her drink, waiting for me to dish it out. When I didn't oblige, she asked, "Is it that case on the news?"

My eyes shot up.

"OADDL is the only lab that does necropsies in a three-hundred-mile radius, and you were on duty this week. I figured the police dog had probably landed in your lap." She lifted one eyebrow.

"Yes, it came to the lab," I answered. I searched for the straw wrapper and couldn't find it. My sewing machine leg started up instead.

"The story was on my feed this morning," she replied. "Not much info. Just said they found a police dog dead and sent it in for a necropsy. I know you can't share any details, and I'm not asking for them. I'm just wondering if that's what's on your mind."

There was a flash of the white dog, trotting ahead of me on a dirt path, bushy tail low and nose to the ground.

I blinked the image away before he could stop and turn his head. Before he could look at me.

"Josie?" Laila asked, real concern on her face now.

"Yes. Sorry." I forced a weak smile. "It's my case."

"Why do you always get all of the legal cases?" she asked, frowning. "That sucks."

It was so close to what Fran had said, my brain tripped over the words. At least, when Laila said them, I felt her empathy and concern.

She was genuinely worried and knew these cases weighed heavily on me.

"It is what it is," I said.

I brushed all of the messy thoughts away, locking them into a black box in the corner of my mind to unpack later. If I didn't, I was going to cry like a little bitch in the middle of a packed Red Rock.

"I'm here if you need anything. Want to come over to my place tonight? We can play Lords of Waterdeep and eat ice cream for dinner," she offered.

I shook my head. "Thanks, though. Armand is coming over tonight."

"Good," she said, worry still creasing her eyebrows.

And though she didn't say it, I could still hear the "as long as you're not alone" tagged at the end.

The conversation shifted to fluff. I wanted to feel better. I really did. But my shoulders were still tense, and I couldn't escape the constant urge to fidget.

After our plates were cleared, she glanced at her phone. "I've got to get back. I have a meeting at one thirty."

She looked back up at me, eyes soft. "Call or text anytime. Night or day. Green?"

Catching the movie quote that we always ping-ponged back and forth, I responded with the obligatory, "Super green."

A smile tugged at the edge of my lips.

CHAPTER
FOURTEEN

When I pulled into the lab's parking lot, my stomach clenched and the acid burbled up into my throat. All of the good vibes I'd soaked up from Laila were instantly dashed away when I saw the news van parked out front, plain as day.

"Channel 4 News" was splashed across the side in bold, white caps against a deep blue background. Of course, no one watched the news on cable anymore, but plenty of folks still streamed it, especially for the weather and the traffic. The "Channel 4" just seemed to stick.

They could only be here for one reason.

Fuck.

I hated the spotlight. The thought of being interviewed in front of a camera was up there with sticking bamboo slivers under my nails, especially when I had nothing to share.

I chewed my cheek and studied the van through my rearview mirror. It was a big, fat rattlesnake, resting on the heat of the pavement in the sun. If I could sneak by without waking it up—without hearing the *shicka, shicka* of the tail—I might make it to the other side in one piece.

I thought about just squatting in my car until the van took off, but I knew I was already on Fran's shit list. If I didn't buck up and get my ass in there, I'd only dig a deeper grave. With a sigh, I turned my engine off and gathered my things.

By the time I'd exited the car and clicked the key fob to lock the doors, a trio of people hustled out the front door, lugging video equipment. I froze like an opossum and, no joke, actually toyed with the idea of playing dead. I wondered what I looked like, standing in the parking lot like a deer in the headlights.

One of the techs slid the van's panel open and helped the guy with the camera load the gear in the back. The third person hung back, checking his phone. He was all jazzed up in a fancy suit with a sweep of hair that had been styled into an impossible poof that surely required an entire bottle of hairspray. I wasn't much into the news, but I vaguely recognized his face.

What's his name? Don? Devon? Dylan? My mind raced, stuck on trying to place the guy.

He glanced up and noticed me standing in the middle of the parking lot, clutching my purse like a damsel in distress.

Damien. I'm sure he's the harbinger of doom. My *doom.*

Semi-hysterical laughter threatened to bubble out. I fought it back with every fiber of my being and took a step forward. I tried to look past them and make a beeline for the door.

The spiffed-up guy seemed to dismiss me and turned his attention back to the van. He climbed into the front passenger seat just as the techs clanged the van's panel closed. In less than a minute, the engine fired up, and they drove out of the lot, not even sparing me another glance.

Relief flooded through me, and my shoulders relaxed. I wasn't sure how I escaped that noose, but thanked my lucky stars.

I made it all the way across the parking lot and up the steps before it hit me. Though I'd dodged the bullet and avoided the camera, Fran was going to be pissed that I hadn't been there. No one had told me reporters were coming, and I wondered if they'd dropped by without giving anyone any notice. It wouldn't matter; Fran made a habit of pointing fingers even when someone wasn't guilty. There was nothing I could do about it, and I might as well face the music.

Taking a deep breath, I whisked open the door to the lab. The cool air washed over me, spreading goosebumps across my arms. Before I made it through the foyer, James pounced.

"Oh! There ya are, Dr. Harjo," he said, his good-ole-boy Oklahoman accent threaded with a mixture of worry and relief. "I've been running all over lookin' for you."

James was fresh out of high school and worked up front with none other than the lab's cookie-dealer, Carol. Like Sandy, she was nearing retirement, and James would be the one stepping up on the work-side of things. Lord help us when that happened. Not because of James, though. Rather, our little lunch group would die of hypoglycemic shock without Carol. No one could ever fill the empty space she'd be leaving behind.

"Hello, James. What's up?" I said, trying to sound casual.

James looped his thumbs around the large belt buckle that graced the front of his tight, starched jeans. He wore a light green, checkered, snap shirt. There was a permanent indent where his cowboy hat rested on his head when he wasn't indoors.

"The news people were just here!" he said, eyes going wide. "Fran wanted you to talk to 'em. Had me looking all over the building for you. I said, 'If she ain't lunching with Dustin and Anna and all, she's probably out.' But Fran didn't believe me." He gave a single, curt nod to punctuate his statement.

"Sorry about that," I said before I could stop myself. I had the annoying habit of apologizing for shit that wasn't my fault. Even though I was trying to stop, the words always seemed to slip out. "I ate lunch off campus today. I didn't know they were coming."

"I don't think anybody knew," he said. "Fran was looking mighty worked up about it."

"Hopefully, she was able to answer their questions?" I asked, hooking my thumb over my purse strap.

Please, please, please say they won't be back.

"Yup," he said, nodding.

Well, there's that.

"They got what they needed and just left. Did you see Darryl Castor?" he continued, eyes wide.

Darryl. I knew that guy's name started with a D. But there was no joy in remembering that pointless piece of fluff.

"Yeah. I saw him just now when I was coming in," I replied.

"Whoo-wee," he said and huffed a nervous laugh. "Carol practically fainted."

I *hmmed*, not feeling super impressed. I was still getting over my relief at having avoided a press interview.

"They talked to Fran a bit, and then Fran asked Gerald to stand in since you was out," he added.

My chest went tight. "Gerald?" I asked weakly.

"Yes, ma'am," James said with a nod, not realizing the grenade he'd rolled toward me.

Fucking Gerald.

I sighed and rubbed my fingers over the creases between my eyebrows. My mind raced with a million and one scenarios of how *that* might've gone down. The sandwich knocked at my esophageal sphincter, asking to make its way back up.

"Welp," James said, misreading the look of abject horror on my face. "Fran was upset that you were gone. You might want to stay hunkered down for a bit."

"Thank you, James," was all I could manage.

He gave me a nod, and we parted ways, him heading to the front office and me slinking through the hallways back to mine. I didn't want to see Fran or Gerald at the moment.

It was Friday, and there were only a few more hours left in the workday. I planned on checking in with Dustin and then making myself scarce, just as James had advised. If I were lucky, I could skate out of here without getting my ass chewed. Things might calm down over the weekend.

To my relief, no more bodies came in that afternoon. I hid in the histology lab, trimming the fixed tissues from the police dog. If they went on the processor tonight, I might have slides on my desk come Monday. Unfortunately, I was only able to trim the thoracic and abdominal organs. The brain and spinal cord were still too raw to cut, and would have to percolate in the formalin over the weekend before they'd be fixed enough to section into cassettes. It would mean further delay, but I didn't have much of a choice. If I pushed it, I'd just trash the tissue and have to start all over again.

By some miracle, I was able to sneak out of work just before five and avoid any awkward conversations. With each step away from the lab, my shoulders relaxed a tad. On the drive home, angry clouds hung in the distant south, threatening the crisp blue sky over Stillwater.

I pulled into the driveway, relieved to be home.

Yersi swirled around my ankles, greeting me with a purr-filled *meow*. I tossed my purse by the door and headed into the kitchen to feed him. With that task done, I headed outside with the back door clanging behind me.

The cicadas sang, and the smell of jasmine washed over me. I took a moment to soak in the last rays of sunshine, closing my eyes. A faint, warm breeze danced across my skin. I took a deep, cleansing breath. The soft clucking of the chickens gently pulled me from the moment.

The chickens danced at the edge of the Eglu, eager for me to open the gate and let them roam the yard. Again, I promised them some roaming time tomorrow, when I could sit outside to watch over them. They didn't seem too pleased with that, but were happy enough when I tossed a couple of handfuls of chicken feed into the large enclosure.

By the time I'd taken care of the girls, I had about fifteen minutes before Armand arrived. I thought about madly dashing around, maybe even trying to squeeze in a shower, and decided to park my ass on the couch instead. We'd been together long enough that I was allowed the occasional off day.

Yersi hopped up next to me, delicately wiping his face with his paw. "Hey, bud," I said.

He paused his bath to give me a slow blink. A smile tugged at my lips, and I traced my fingers across his back. He responded with an appreciative *merf* and continued his bath, licking his shoulders and down his chest.

The phone drew my eye. With a start, I realized that I hadn't checked in with Aunty. Today had been hectic. I sent her a quick text.

> How's Chula?

My phone locked before she responded. I wasn't expecting an instant reply. I knew she was working today, and she might have picked up the later shift. Her hours at the library could be a little wonky sometimes.

With his bath finished, Yersi crawled into my lap. I stroked his smooth hair, and a low rumble started up in his chest. I felt my shoulders relax.

My phone binged. I reached over, trying to check it without disturbing His Royal Highness. Aunty had responded.

> She ate all of her chicken. I had to coax her outside, but she's snuffling around the kitchen for snacks again.

I hearted her text.

> Glad she's feeling better.

> Me, too.

The screen went dark.

I spent the last few precious, quiet moments with Yersi, trying to clear my mind. I loved Armand and liked being around him, but part of me wished I could have some quiet time to myself tonight. The Tohbi case weighed heavily on me, and I didn't want to drag Armand down with my moodiness.

My thoughts were soon interrupted by a loud shuffling coming from the other side of the front door. Yersi's nails clamped into my thighs. He flashed me a disdainful look and fled to the bedroom. The doorbell rang a millisecond later.

I opened the door to find Ileana practically bouncing on her feet. Her rear shifted side-to-side with the enthusiastic wagging of her tail.

It was impossible to ignore the power of a happy dog. "Ileana. Look at you," I cooed.

All sixty pounds of her almost fell over in excitement.

I bent down to scratch her ears as I looked up at Armand. My heart fluttered as it always did.

"Hello, *iubita mea*," he said softly. One hand was holding the leash, and the other a large bag of takeout.

I didn't care if his hands were full. I leaned into him, squeezing my arms around his waist. He tried to wrap his arms around me in return. It wasn't easy with an ecstatic dog tugging on one hand and takeout weighing down the other.

I inhaled deeply, enjoying the pleasant smell of his aftershave, and stepped back.

"Come in," I said, feeling so much better that he was here. I'd thought I'd wanted a night to myself, but I realized having him there made everything so much better.

As I closed the door, he released Ileana with a click of the leash. She bounded off in glee, nose snuffling on the floor, no doubt seeking The Great Slayer of Canned Food to implement her toolkit of kitty-torture techniques.

"Chinese," Armand said, lifting the bag. "I hope that's okay."

"Sounds amazing. Thank you for picking it up."

My appetite was still hiding somewhere behind the police tape, but I figured a tiny white lie was allowed when trying to be polite.

I followed him into the kitchen and pulled out a couple of plates as he unpacked five white boxes. The smell of soy sauce and sesame oil filled the room. Normally, I'd be wiping the saliva off my chin. Today, it made me a tad nauseous.

Just as we were getting ready to sit down, my phone started ringing from the living room. My eyebrows wrinkled in a mixture of irritation and confusion.

"I need to check that," I said. "I'm on call this weekend." I wasn't sure why I thought that. Our on-call student, Josh, always texted when something came in. But the words simply spilled out.

"You go. I'll wait for you," Armand replied, moving to set the table.

"Feel free start," I said, nodding to the plates. "It's probably a spam call. I'll be back in a sec."

I headed to the living room and picked my cell phone up from the coffee table.

Zoe's name filled the screen. Surprised, and even more confused at having a fellow pathologist cold-calling me after-hours, I picked up.

"Hey, Zoe," I answered. "What's up?"

"Oh my God, Josie," she said, words spilling out of her mouth in a rush. "Did you see the news?"

A vise gripped my chest, and I couldn't breathe.

"No," was all I managed to push out.

"Here. I'll text you a clip," she said. "You're not going to believe this shit." My phone binged with the text before she finished her sentence.

I wasn't sure I wanted to watch it, and my phone suddenly felt like a snake ready to strike. I glanced back into the kitchen, seeing Armand settle down at the table. Ileana took up her usual position at his feet.

"Um," I mumbled.

"The clip is only a minute," she said, still buzzing. "I'll hold."

I couldn't tell if the energy in her voice was excitement or anger. It was an odd mix.

Better to face it and move on, I thought glumly.

"Putting you on speaker," I said, opening the text chain and tapping the clip to play.

Darryl Castor stood in front of the lab, hair perfectly styled and a dramatic, somber expression furrowing his eyebrows and tilting his lips down in a frown.

"Today, I'm at the Oklahoma state diagnostic lab with an update on the Ofi' Tohbi Ishto' case," he said, mangling the pronunciation.

I realized with a start, that "Tohbi" was short for a Chickasaw name. Goosebumps broke out across my arms.

"Tohbi was a canine officer at the Oklahoma City Police Department and was found murdered yesterday morning."

"Murdered." Really? Fuck. What a way to get everyone riled up.

Zoe's voice spoke over Darryl's, "Wait for it."

The scene changed to show the window that looked out onto the necropsy floor. Darryl and Gerald stood on either side, framing the space. Centered between them was a view out to the cold, steel necropsy tables.

Darryl turned toward the camera. "I'm here with Dr. Gerald Richter, leading veterinarian at the diagnostic lab—"

Zoe snorted loudly.

"—more information about the case. Dr. Richter, what can you share with us?"

The frame shifted, and the camera focused on Gerald.

Gerald cleared his throat, looked directly into the lens, and dove right in, practically preening. "The deceased arrived yesterday morning. Because of the gravity of the situation, a necropsy was performed immediately."

My stomach clenched, and I felt like I was on the rise of a roller coaster.

"Can you explain what a necropsy is for our viewers at home?" Darryl interrupted from off-camera.

"A necropsy is the procedure of dissecting an animal to determine the cause of death. It is similar to an autopsy in people," he explained, and I had to give him credit for doing a good job of it.

"And what was found during the necropsy?" Darryl probed.

"As this is an active investigation, I defer to the police department as to what information should be disclosed to the public."

"Huh," I said under my breath, surprised at Gerald's professional response.

"Is it true that there were no significant findings on the initial examination?" Darryl pushed.

An irritated expression flickered across Gerald's face so quickly that, if you didn't know him, you probably would've missed it. I couldn't blame him; I was pissed, too.

"Are you at all concerned that you won't be able to solve this case?" Darryl asked.

My eyebrows jumped up in surprise at the guy's nerve.

Gerald stiffened, and his Manson lamps slowly shifted away from camera toward where Darryl stood out of frame.

"Waaaiiit for it," Zoe chimed in, her voice now almost a whisper.

"We have a superlative team at the Oklahoma Animal Disease Diagnostic Lab," Gerald said coolly. "I have faith that Dr. Harjo will have this case solved within the week. She is exemplary at her job, having tackled several difficult cases over the course of her stellar career."

I flopped on the couch in shock.

Gerald's eyes narrowed, and he took a deep breath like he was getting ready to say more. I knew that look. It meant he was really going to lay into the guy. But before he could, the scene cut, and a view of Fran at her desk filled the screen.

"You can turn it off now. The rest is bullshit," Zoe said.

I paused the clip, feeling completely numb. I took the phone off speaker and held it to my ear.

"What the hell was that?" I said in a slow half-whisper.

"Right?!" Zoe exclaimed. "Who *was* that pod-person? Did we have an alien invasion, and I missed the memo?"

"Wow," was all I could get out.

Gerald had defended me. Like, hardcore stood up for me. And I was pretty sure whatever he'd said after the scene cut had been brutal. When Gerald went on the attack, someone always left bleeding. And I was utterly dumbfounded that it wasn't me.

"Anyway," Zoe said, voice calmer now. "I wanted to make sure you saw that."

"Yeah, uh," I stammered. "Thanks."

"Have a good weekend!" Zoe said cheerfully.

We said our goodbyes.

I sat holding the phone, feeling like the rug had been yanked out from underneath me. I was glad I hadn't been interviewed. That reporter smelled blood in the water, and I wasn't sure how I would've responded.

I also wasn't sure how to process Gerald sticking up for me. Sure, I'd spoken up on his behalf with the whole tiger thing. But even after that mess, I wouldn't say he'd been kind to me. We'd just entered a stage where we had the occasional awkward conversation.

I jumped when Armand put a hand on my shoulder. "Everything okay?"

I shook my head, trying to push the messy thoughts away. I forced a fake smile. "Yeah. Everything is fine," I lied. "Let's go eat."

CHAPTER

FIFTEEN

I managed to eat a little bit of dinner; the call of the cashew chicken was too strong to resist. But all of the oil didn't sit right in my stomach. Hoping jasmine tea would help, I brewed a small pot. I cupped the warm mug and inhaled deeply before joining Armand in the living room.

"What would you like to watch?" he asked, flipping through the streaming options. He was already nestled into the corner of the couch. His left arm rested across the armrest, remote dangling from his hand. Ileana was curled up at his feet.

"Hm," I said, unsure. "You choose."

Cradling my mug carefully, I moved to sit next to him. He lifted his right arm, draping it gently around my shoulders. I snuggled into the crook, grateful to feel him so close.

"*Fargo?*" he asked.

We were on season three of the series, and it was such a good show that I didn't mind rewatching it with him. The characters were often nasty, but the dry, sarcastic storytelling gave the show a wonderfully unique flavor. All that said, I had to be in a certain mood to watch it, and I wasn't feeling up to it. I hated to poo-poo the first option Armand had tossed out after I had so recently relinquished all decision-making rights. But that show was heavy in a way that I just couldn't sit through today.

Trying to make things light, I teased, "Well, when I said 'you choose,' I meant nothing with police, crimes, detectives, murders, or anything sort of illegal-ish. But, again, you choose."

He smiled at me with a playful sparkle in his eye. "*Bridgerton*, then?" He highlighted the show's thumbnail, finger poised, threatening to press play.

I fake gagged, and a mangled *guork* sound burbled out. "Okay, you choose. But nothing with police, crimes, detectives, murders, anything illegal-ish, or *romance*."

He smiled back smugly, knowing he'd got me.

Clicking through the thumbnails, he browsed some more until he landed on a sci-fi drama that didn't appear to have any police, crimes, detectives, murders, or romance. With an approving nod from me, he pressed play, and I sipped my tea.

Yersi appeared from his hiding place, which sat just outside of time and space. He hopped to the back of the couch with an irritated *merf* sound. Ileana picked her head up, the tags on her collar jingling. Her tail thumped loudly on the ground. Yersi glared at her and folded himself into a tense meatloaf position on the back of the couch, just out of reach.

My shoulders relaxed.

As stressful as the Tohbi case was, I loved being able to come home and curl up next to Armand, sipping on delicate tea and enjoying a show together.

Before I could stop myself, I said, "I'm going to miss this."

His body tensed, and he curled his arm more tightly around me. "What do you mean?" It came out soft and inquisitive, but I knew him well enough to hear the tension behind it.

I leaned my head against his chest. "I just..." I started, but my throat caught before I could finish.

He paused the show and twisted his body a bit so that he could see me better.

I pulled away and risked a glance up at him before dropping my eyes back to my mug. "I don't know what's going to happen in June when your visa expires."

He ran his fingers through my hair and watched me sadly. "I don't know, either."

I uncurled from him and shifted back, folding my left leg up on the couch between us so I could face him. My free hand reached out, fingers winding through his.

"I don't want to lose this," I said softly.

"Me neither, *iubita mea*."

"Surely there has to be a grant or a position somewhere or something. They can't make you go back, can they?" A pleading tone edged into my voice.

His lips tilted up in a slight, almost resigned smile, and his eyebrows deepened with worry. He squeezed my hand gently.

"I'll keep looking," he promised.

It wouldn't be enough. Even on the off chance that he found something, he'd have to go back home for who knows how long before the new visa kicked in. It all seemed so hopeless, and tears pressed against my eyes.

"What if you don't find anything?" The words came out hesitantly, as if I were too scared to say them out loud. Maybe I was.

He gave my hand another gentle squeeze. "Then, I have to go home. But I promise I'll try to find a way back. No matter what it takes."

I knew he was trying to reassure me, but he couldn't hide the doubt in his voice. The chances of him getting a third round of grants and a visa without a position at the college were slim to none. The current political climate only made things worse. He did amazing work that would benefit Oklahoma agriculture, but without any funding, it didn't matter.

He released my hand, and his eyes shifted to Ileana. In that subtle gesture, I knew it was too hard for him to look at me.

That wonderful, annoyingly gorgeous curl slipped down over his forehead. I coiled my fingers around it and traced down his cheek.

He sighed deeply and looked back up. "You could come to Romania."

The floor fell out beneath me.

"What?" The word tumbled out in a clipped half-whisper.

"With your qualifications, I think you could get a work permit. Would you like me to ask around at the college?"

"But I don't speak Romanian," was all I could force out as I tried not to blow oily chunks of cashew chicken everywhere.

He lifted one shoulder nonchalantly. "Some professors lecture in English. I think it'll be fine."

He clasped my hand and looked down at our intertwined fingers. "Many American professionals are leaving the US right now. Especially the scientists. And other countries are welcoming them in."

"I...." *I hadn't even thought about going to Romania.* The words stuck in my throat.

My mind raced. I couldn't imagine leaving everyone behind: Aunty, Laila, Tessa, and all my friends at work. Plus, even though Fran was a horrible boss and Gerald was *Gerald*, I loved my job. Like, really, really loved my job.

Do I love all of that more than Armand?

The question weighed heavily, and my chest grew tight.

Armand gave up everything to come here, an evil voice whispered, mocking me for my selfishness.

It was true; Armand wasn't asking me to do anything that he hadn't done himself. But that didn't make the situation any easier. The rational part of my mind kicked in. If moving to Romania was the only way we could stay together, I seriously needed to consider it. I started thinking through all of the practical implications. But when I looked deep into my heart, I didn't want to leave. I was tied to the land, and I couldn't imagine living anywhere else. And yet, I didn't want to lose Armand, either. My heart had two pieces, and they would soon be six thousand miles apart.

My internal struggle must have been written all over my face because Armand reached over and gently squeezed my knee.

"I don't want to pressure you," he said in a hushed voice.

"What department would I even work in at the college?" I said, my mind dancing around in circles.

"The vet school," he said with certainty. "I know they would hire you, even if they don't have a position open."

"I mean...like where? In the pathology department? Do they even have a necropsy floor?"

He replied with a shrug. "I'd have to ask around."

I started chewing on my cheek, fighting the feeling of panic while, at the same time, wondering why I felt so scared.

"You and Yersi could live with me."

The air sucked right out of my chest, and I felt like I couldn't breathe.

Is this a fucking panic attack? Really?

I forced myself to take a deep, shuddery breath.

My mind continued to spiral. I'd have to find someone to take care of the chickens. And rent my house. Or sell it. I'd lose my job; I knew Fran wouldn't wait for me to come back. Simply thinking about all of that made me sick.

Armand's eyebrows creased. "I didn't mean to worry you. I apologize. You've had a difficult week. I shouldn't have brought it up."

"It's.... I just.... It's a lot to think about," I stammered.

"You don't have to answer now. The offer is there."

He took my hand and gently guided me back to the crook of his arm. I let him fold me into a comfortable spot and rested my back on his chest.

"We can talk more another day," he said gently. "Let's forget I even said anything and watch the show."

"Okay," I replied, still reeling.

He pressed play and lightly ran his fingers through my hair.

The show's music reached its crescendo, but my mind was elsewhere. There was no way in hell I could brush aside everything we talked about and be distracted by laser cannons and alien fights. Even though Armand sat right beside me, I felt a crushing sense of loss. I kept reminding myself that I should enjoy the here and now. Take advantage of this moment, folded in his arms. But an impossible choice crouched before me, and I couldn't escape.

CHAPTER
SIXTEEN

That night, I dreamed of the white dog.

He trotted slowly down the path about ten feet ahead of me. He paused briefly to lift his nose and sniff the air. The warm humidity pressed in, and sweat started to bead on my skin. Dark clouds hung heavy in the distance. They hadn't formed a wall cloud, but seemed to be working up to it. The song of the cicadas turned shrill.

Even though I recognized the well-worn path from Aunty's, I felt a burning sense of dread. I didn't want to be there, and I certainly didn't want to follow the white dog. I knew I wouldn't like what he was going to show me.

The dog stopped. His cool, crystal-blue eyes turned to me, watching intently.

I woke with a start, heart racing and chest damp with sweat. My hands clenched the blankets, and I had to consciously force them to relax. My eyes were wide open, and I knew that I had a snowball's chance in hell of going back to sleep.

I leaned over to check the time on my phone, trying not to disturb Armand. It was early for a Saturday, but not so early that I should force myself to try to go back to sleep. I lay back on the bed, trying to calm my speeding heart.

A slight *thud* announced Yersi dropping to the floor. The jingle of Ileana's tags followed. It was an evil portent. Soon, Ileana would seek a playmate, and Yersi would respond with a "fuck no." A ruckus would ensue.

Before the two of them could wake Armand up, I slipped out of bed and took Ileana gently by the collar. "Come on, girl," I whispered.

Ileana turned into a sixty-pound bundle of happy-dog wiggles with the attention. She trotted along next to me, tail waving excitedly as she tried to lick my hand, my face, or whatever was within her bouncy reach. I led her outside as quietly as possible, careful not to bang the door, and let her do her doggie thing.

Back inside, I made my morning offering to Yersi. He chomped through his food with a grateful *merf*, stopping ever so often to scan for the great, four-legged blond beast. When Yersi finished, he slinked away, skipping his usual post-meal bath on the counter chair. He definitely did not enjoy sharing a space with Ileana.

I clicked the kettle on and listened to the building rumble of the water. My mind drifted, and wisps of last night's dream flitted through my head. I rubbed my eyes, trying to chase them away.

By the time the kettle clicked off, Ileana was waiting patiently by the back door. I let her in, giving her ears a scratch as she passed. Her short hair was damp from the mist.

She snuffled around on the floor, toenails skittering happily. She made her way to Yersi's bowl and licked it a couple of times. It clanged with gusto.

Yersi was going to be *pissed*.

In an attempt to hide the evidence, I tossed the bowl in the dishwasher.

"Ileana, sit," I said firmly.

Her bum hit the ground faster than lightning as she assumed her "pretty girl" pose, ears alert and a line of drool starting along the edge of her lips. She quivered with barely contained energy, shifting her weight back and forth on her front feet. I poured some of her sleepover-kibble into a cereal bowl. As soon as the bowl touched the ground, she buried her face in it.

With the Ceylon tea poured, I cradled the cup and watched Ileana snuffle around the kitchen. It was nice having her here, and I liked the fact that Armand would soon join us. But I still couldn't imagine giving everything else up to move halfway around the world.

I sat at the table, nursing my cup of tea as the sun rose. The early morning rays danced across the wood. Through the window to the backyard, I watched as the sun chased away the last of the morning mist, revealing a rain-soaked garden.

"Good morning," Armand said softly as he walked in.

I smiled, feeling my heart warm. "Morning."

We'd been together long enough that he helped himself to the instant coffee and joined me at the table.

"You woke up early," he said, a crinkle of worry settling between his brows. "Is everything okay?"

I looked down at my mug, fumbling for an answer. "Nightmares," I mumbled.

Images of the path and the white dog flickered in my mind. I didn't want to think about it anymore, but I couldn't force the thoughts away either.

Maybe I should talk about it.

I took a sip of my now-tepid tea and sighed. "I've been having this recurring dream about the police dog. He's on the path by the creek at Aunty's. You know the one?"

Armand nodded.

I clasped my mug with both hands. I stared at the speckles of fragmented tea leaves that now rested on the bottom.

"The dog is jogging ahead of me. I'm following him, but I don't want to. And even though the path is familiar and I can practically feel the hum of the cicadas in my bones, I don't want to see where he's taking me." I rubbed my forehead with one hand. After a beat, I asked, "Did I tell you the police dog had a white coat?"

He shook his head.

"You just don't see Belgian Malinois with white hair," I said, disconcerted. "And he had these icy-blue eyes. Being on that path with him feels like I'm following a ghost. It's creepy."

"Maybe he's leading you to the answer. The reason he died," he offered.

I chewed my cheek in doubt.

"In Romania, there is a legend that says a white wolf fought alongside the Dacians against the Romans. I know the story is about a wolf and not a dog." He shrugged. "Pure white animals play a role in folktales in many countries. It's okay to be uncomfortable with it."

I sipped my tea, thoughts of a white wolf tumbling through my head as I tried to make sense of my unease.

"There's a Japanese story," he said, sifting through his memory banks. "I don't remember the name of the story. But the dog's name is Shiro. He protects the couple, finding them gold and bringing trees back to life. A neighbor ends up killing Shiro because he was jealous."

"That's horrible," I said with a hint of bitterness.

He looked up, and worry crinkled the skin around his eyes. "Sorry."

I waved it away, not unkindly.

A stray thought niggled in my head, and I tried to grasp at it. Armand and I both geeked out on folklore, and I flipped through my mental notes, trying to find what was bugging me. An image of Darryl Castor flashed through my head. He held the artificial somber expression as he reported on the case.

Ofi' Tohbi Ishto', his voice echoed in my mind.

Goosebumps rose on my arms.

"Oh fuck," I said more to myself.

"Hmm?"

I shook my head, trying to chase away the heebie jeebies. "It's an origin story. There's a folktale Aunty used to tell me. A white dog named Ofi' Tohbi Ishto' led the Chickasaw and Choctaw tribes to their ancestral lands. He was a protector and guide. The police dog had the same name."

"That's an odd name for a dog," Armand mused.

I shrugged. The dog's name hadn't been what spooked me.

"It's not that weird. Tons of people name their dog Athena or Zeus, which isn't much different if you think about it. They called him 'Tohbi' for short," I said distractedly, still trying to put my finger on what bugged me about the whole thing.

"I wonder if they named him that because he guided them to drugs," Armand offered.

The idea didn't seem to fit right, but I replied with a noncommittal, "Maybe." My mind was elsewhere.

Why am I freaking out? Is it because a story my Aunty told me ages ago is now manifesting in my dreams like some cheesy scary movie?

I felt like a spooked little girl, and my thoughts churned into an even soupier mess.

"I bet the cause of death is in your mind somewhere," Armand said, still on a line of thought that was miles from my own. "You are dreaming of him because he can lead you to the answer. Maybe you should follow him?"

The dreams brought dread, not curiosity. I didn't think the dog was leading me to some miracle diagnosis. There was something dark at the end of that path. Something I didn't want to face.

Maybe he's leading me to Romania.

I shook off the uncomfortable thought.

Armand took a sip of his coffee. "White dogs symbolize many things: loyalty, protection, guidance. Could the dog from your dream be protecting you from something?"

"Or warning me," I murmured.

Like Pele's white dog, sent out to warn the island's people of an impending volcanic eruption.

I really didn't like where that stream of consciousness was headed.

I waved my hand to brush everything away.

"Whatever. It's just a dream," I said, forcing cheer into my voice. "I'm hungry. What do you want for breakfast?"

"I'm game for anything. Want help?" he said, rolling with it.

"I've got it," I said, forcing a smile.

Armand watched me closely as I pulled out the eggs and bacon. I wasn't sure if he'd noticed how shaken the dream had made me. I couldn't help but feel silly about the whole thing.

The routine of cooking quickly forced the dark thoughts away, and my shoulders slowly relaxed. We ate a pleasant meal together, and the conversation soon shifted to lighter things. When we finished, Armand cleared the plates and loaded the dishwasher. I knew he had moved his soccer game to today so that he could join us for brunch tomorrow, but there was a tug at my heart as I watched him get dressed.

Before I knew it, he kissed me on the cheek and headed out with Ileana in tow.

I stood at the door, robe pulled tightly around my body, and watched him pull away. I felt like a part of me was leaving with him.

CHAPTER
SEVENTEEN

The rest of Saturday meandered by. Before I knew it, Sunday morning arrived, and Armand was back in my arms.

I drove, Tessa rode shotgun, and Armand had graciously folded himself into the backseat. After two hours of driving through low pastureland, the tires crunched onto Aunty's driveway.

Aunty's house came into view. The flap-board sides of the small home were painted a cheery yellow and trimmed with white. The large wraparound porch was stuffed with soft chairs where Aunty and I had spent plenty of hours sipping tea, smelling the lavender from the farm next door, and watching the chickens scratch around the yard.

As I pulled close to the house, Chula watched us from her favorite spot on the porch. It gave her a perfect view of the yard. She regularly camped out there to stand guard over the chickens.

Today, the chickens were spread out around the yard, clucking merrily as they scratched around the wild grasses. Chula was lying down, her head resting on her front paws. Her coyote-like tail wagged weakly.

"What's wrong with Chula?" Tessa said, her concern cutting like a sharp knife.

I didn't have a chance to answer.

As soon as the car was in park, Tessa opened the door and called out, "Chula, girl, come say hi." She crouched and patted her legs.

Chula lifted her head slightly and looked at Tessa with eyes that said everything.

That moment—seeing Chula look like she wanted to come over to Tessa and simply couldn't—that's when I knew that something was seriously wrong. My heart tumbled all the way to my feet.

Armand and I climbed out of the car.

"Is Chula okay?" he asked.

He'd only been to Aunty's a couple of times. But once was enough to know that Chula was typically full of energy. Just last week, she'd bounded off the porch to greet me, all wiggles and licks. Today, both of her airplane ears drooped.

Tessa was at her side first, stroking her ears. "Chula, honey, what's wrong?" she said in a sweet, soft voice.

Tessa turned to me, eyebrows creased. Armand and I joined them at the top of the stairs, and Chula stood slowly. She looked like Bambi on weak, shaky legs.

I crouched to pet her. "Hey, Chula," I said softly.

Her tail swished slowly in response.

"How long has she been like this?" Tessa asked, not unkindly.

"Aunty called me on...Thursday, I think? She said she wasn't acting like her normal self." I turned to look at Chula, and a deep well of concern opened up. "I didn't realize it was this bad."

Tessa stood. She chewed her bottom lip.

"Let's go in," I offered. "We can get a good look at her inside."

"I wish I had my stethoscope," Tessa murmured.

I stood and opened the front screen. "Come on, Chula," I called in a sing-song voice, patting my thigh.

Chula shuffled inside, her right back foot catching slightly on the threshold as she crossed.

There was a tense moment where we all hesitated to follow her in. Tessa and Armand wore identical worried looks, and I was sure my expression wasn't much better. I'd been peripherally thinking about Chula, but the seriousness of the situation hadn't really sunk in until I'd gotten eyes on her.

We followed the sounds of clanking in the kitchen. Aunty turned from the stove and wiped her hands on her apron.

"Hello! Come in, come in," she said with her usual cheer, folding us each into a warm hug. "Have a seat," she said, gesturing to the table. The pleasant upward inflection of her voice didn't change the fact that her eyebrows were furrowed, and her smile fell as soon as she looked away.

Chula lapped up what felt like gallons of water at the bowl by the end of the counter.

"Tea?" Aunty asked.

"Yes, please," Armand answered, as he took a seat.

Tessa and I nodded, eyes locked on Chula as she made her way to the small kitchen rug and flopped down.

Normally, we'd chit-chat about the weather, the drive, or some other fluff topic before moving on to anything else. But the worry chased away any modicum of Oklahoma-polite in my bones.

"Did Chula eat this morning, Aunty?" I asked.

Her back was turned to us, and her long, gray braid traced a line between her tensed shoulders. "Yes. She still won't eat her dog food, but she did eat some boiled chicken." She forced a laugh. "I guess she's just spoiled."

"How long has she been acting like this?" Tessa asked, repeating her earlier question.

"Oh, I'd say since Wednesday night," Aunty replied. She tried to be casual and upbeat about it, but her voice shook ever so slightly.

She measured out the tea into the pot, back still turned.

"Has she been going to the bathroom normally?" Tessa asked.

"Yes," Aunty said. "She's just tired. Sleeps a lot. Doesn't want to play."

Tessa turned to look at me. "For at least four days." Her eyebrows crinkled.

I knew what she was thinking, because the same thoughts swirled in my mind. Dogs could be off for a couple of days if they got into the garbage can or ate something they shouldn't have, but they usually bounced back. The fact that Chula had been so lethargic for this long also ruled out some of the nastier, sudden things like being hit by a car or a ruptured splenic tumor. But there were still plenty of scary differentials sitting on the list.

My mind went to the dark places, to the terminal diseases that chewed away slowly. All of the air whooshed from my lungs.

When I finally got my mental shit together enough to speak with a normal voice, I said, "I think Tessa and I should examine her. After we eat, maybe?" I framed the last bit as a question, wanting Aunty's blessing.

"Sure, that would be lovely," Aunty said.

Tessa and I exchanged another concerned look. Aunty was the epitome of the wise, old grandma. Her almost-British reply felt fake and forced.

When Aunty turned around to pass out the tea, her expression floored me. She looked crushed. A soft frown tugged at her lips, the skin around her eyes was tense, and her eyes were just a little too wet not to be fighting tears. I'd only seen Aunty like this one other time in my life: when my mom had been dying.

A chill twisted around my spine.

Suddenly, Aunty straightened her back and put her fists on her hips. "Look here," she said sternly. "I only get to see y'all once a week. We're going to eat a delicious meal, enjoy each other's company, and then we're going to sit on the porch and calm our spirits."

A sad smile tipped my lips, and I noticed Tessa fighting one as well.

"Yes, Aunty," we both mumbled in unison.

Armand, who'd only met Aunty a couple of times, stayed silent, which was probably the safest bet.

With a satisfied nod, Aunty went back to the stove to turn the hashbrowns.

Armand cleared his throat and said to Tessa, "Less than a week until graduation. How does it feel?"

And with that, the conversation shifted. It felt forced, especially with all of us sneaking glances at Chula. But Aunty wanted to have a nice meal together, and I wasn't going to be the one to take that away from her.

Heaping plates of crispy hashbrowns, bacon, and scrambled eggs filled the table. Small bowls of grits were passed out for each of us, a pat of half-melted butter sitting in the center. Despite all of the stress, my stomach rumbled, and we all tucked in.

As always, the food was amazing. Aunty seemed to relax, enjoying the meal. We even managed to get a few laughs out of her, especially when Tessa and Armand continued their long-standing debate about soccer versus football.

With our bellies full, Aunty said, "Shall we go sit on the porch?"

With the weather being as nice as it was, we'd usually head out for a walk along the creek, picking up litter as we went. The shift to the porch could only be for sweet Chula, who probably couldn't make the walk and wouldn't want to be left behind.

We all rose to clear the table.

"I'll take care of the dishes," Armand said. "You three go outside, and I'll meet you."

Aunty gave him a wink.

I leaned over to peck his cheek. "Thanks," I said softly.

"Let's take the iced tea," Aunty said.

Tessa and I each grabbed some glasses, and Aunty took the pitcher to bring out to the porch. Chula rose to follow, taking careful steps. I held the screen door for her with my elbow as she followed us out.

We settled into our chairs.

The air was warm and heavy with humidity. Clumps of clouds meandered across the crystal blue sky. A slight breeze brought the smell of lavender from the fields across the way. The cicadas served as background singers to the chirping birds.

"Aunty," I started and stumbled. I licked my lips. "May Tessa and I have a look at Chula now?"

Aunty folded her lips and then said, "Sure."

Tessa and I took a knee on either side of Chula. She rolled on her side, tail thumping lightly on the porch.

"Hey, girl," I said softly.

I scratched her ears as Tessa did a head-to-toe examination. Without the usual tools of the trade, we had to skip taking her temperature and listening to her chest. But Tessa still palpated every inch of her.

"She's still peeing and pooping normally, right? No diarrhea?" I asked Aunty as I watched Tessa run through her exam.

"She pees for a long time. But other than that, yes," Aunty replied. "She just seems really tired and doesn't want to eat."

"She's on Revolution, right?" Tessa asked, looking up at me.

I nodded.

I knew what she was thinking. Being on preventative medication ruled out a couple of things, but several others were still stacked on the list. Tessa didn't have to ask if Chula was vaccinated; of course, she was.

Even though Tessa was doing her own exam, I took a peek at Chula's gums, pressing my thumb down and releasing it. Chula's gums blanched briefly and then turned bright pink within a few seconds.

Scratching her ears, I looked into her eyes. She watched me back, fully trusting us, and her tail wagged weakly.

Tessa pressed slightly on Chula's abdomen. Chula tensed, but didn't cry out.

"Sorry, girl," Tessa murmured, meeting my eyes. "Abdominal pain? Maybe splenomegaly? I don't want to hurt her. I wish I had an ultrasound machine."

I pressed my lips together, thinking.

Chula seemed protective of her abdomen, and I knew why Tessa was reluctant to push too hard. We'd all heard the story of the dog that had been palpated by so many vet students at the teaching hospital that the diseased spleen eventually ruptured. Whether it was true or not, it scared the bejesus out of us, and we were all extra gentle when palpating abdomens.

Tessa returned to her exam.

After a few more minutes, Tessa sat back on her heels and sighed. "I think we need to bring her in," she said softly, looking down at Chula. "She obviously doesn't feel well, and I think her abdomen hurts, but there's nothing obvious."

Tessa looked over to me. "With the PU/PD, do you think it could be Cushing's?"

Chula had been going at the water bowl all morning, and Aunty had said she seemed to pee forever. Given her age, Cushing's disease was right up there. Part of me hoped it was that. Even though Cushing's disease was a lifelong illness, lots of dogs got it, and it was manageable with treatment.

"Could be," I said. "She seems awfully tired and inappetent for Cushing's. If she was far enough along to be this lethargic, I'd also expect muscle wasting, a pot belly, some skin lesions, something." I ran my hand over Chula's coat, which still had the shine of health.

"Cushing's can be weird," Tessa debated. "She could still have it even though she doesn't have the other clinical signs."

I couldn't counter that; Cushing's disease caused wacky changes in hormones, and dogs presented with a wide variety of symptoms. But this didn't feel like Cushing's, especially with what seemed like abdominal pain. I don't know how I knew it wasn't Cushing's, but I did. I'd bet the farm on it.

"We need to start with some blood work and go from there," I said. I looked up at Aunty. "She'll need to go in as soon as possible."

"I'll call tomorrow and try to get her in to see Dr. Jones," Aunty said. Her tone was matter-of-fact, but a deep well of sadness sat behind the words.

Tessa and I exchanged a look.

"Aunty," I said softly. "I...." My voice caught.

Tessa stepped in for me. "Can we take her up to the vet school? Josie and I can pull some strings and get her in."

"That's two hours away," Aunty said. "There's no need to drive that far when Dr. Jones is right here."

"We might be able to get a discount for you," Tessa added, hoping to sweeten the deal.

"Dr. Jones charges fair. It'll be fine," Aunty said. Her voice was calm and respectful, but there was a slight tensing of her shoulders that made her look defensive.

I moved to sit next to Aunty and held her hand. "I know Dr. Jones is amazing, and I trust him with Chula. It's just…Tessa and I want to look after her. If she's at the vet school, I can make sure she's getting everything she needs. Plus, if they need to do any testing or surgery, they have everything right there."

"Dr. Jones does surgery," Aunty replied stubbornly.

In my heart, I knew Chula would be fine visiting her local doctor. I was pretty sure Dr. Jones had all of the bells and whistles in his clinic. Maybe not an MRI machine or the ability to do radiation treatment. But Dr. Jones had just about everything else he might need to diagnose and treat whatever might be plaguing Chula.

I still felt uncomfortable having Aunty and Chula more than two hours away when I was pretty damn sure Chula was really sick.

Tessa watched me, sitting crisscross-applesauce at Chula's side. After her exam, Chula rolled to lie on her sternum, and her head rested on Tessa's lap. Tessa slowly stroked her ears.

"Dr. Jones, it is," I acquiesced.

Aunty squeezed my hand.

"But she has to go first thing tomorrow," I insisted. "If they don't have any open slots, come to Stillwater, and we'll get you in at the vet school."

Aunty nodded. "Dr. Jones will see her," she replied with certainty.

"Want me to try to get the day off work? I can go with you to the appointment," I offered.

"We'll be fine," she said. "Thank you, sweety."

She pulled her hand from mine and patted my arm. "We'll be fine," she repeated. "Truly."

Aunty's brown eyes looked deep into my heart. There was a softening around them, as if she had accepted what was coming, no matter what it was, and that we'd walk the path together.

I leaned back in my chair and studied Chula. The thread of worry coiled tightly in my chest.

Armand broke the silence, slipping through the screen door, hand on the handle so it didn't bang closed. His eyes sped across each of us, and his eyebrows crinkled.

"Thank you for doing the dishes," Aunty said and stood up, her mumu floating around her. "Have a seat. I'll pour some more iced tea. It's lovely outside today. And with another system moving in, we should enjoy being outside while we can."

He took the chair next to mine and accepted the glass with a quiet thanks.

After refilling everyone's glasses, Aunty sat back down and breathed deeply. "Doesn't the lavender smell lovely? This time of year is always so beautiful."

We sat on the porch for another hour, enjoying the early afternoon sunshine. There was quiet conversation, interrupted only by the occasional clucking from the chickens as they moved about the yard. Chula had moved to camp at Aunty's feet and snored softly. It was peaceful, and I treasured every second.

It wasn't until we were driving away and the cheery yellow of the house faded in the dust that the heaviness settled back around my shoulders.

CHAPTER

EIGHTEEN

It was hard to face the lab on Monday morning, and I sat in the parking lot, soaking up the last few moments of peace.

On the one hand, I was grateful to finally be off necropsy duty. I had a mountain of cases to wrap up, and the last thing I needed was more work heaped on top. On the other hand, being off duty meant I'd be tied to my desk. It also meant I had idle time to think about all of the crazy shit happening around me: the Tohbi case, Armand leaving, and Chula.

Oh, Chula.

My heart ached.

Maybe it will be okay, I lied to myself, hoping that it would make me feel better.

It didn't.

There wasn't much I could do other than worry. Resigned, I grabbed my keys and collected my purse to head inside. As if on cue, Gerald's truck slipped into the parking space on the passenger side of my car, looming over my Prius. I felt the usual dump of adrenaline.

The defensive rush felt unwarranted, given that Gerald had actually said some nice things about me to the reporter. And he'd done it in one of the most public ways possible. I shouldn't be feeling like a cornered schoolgirl.

A deep, shuddering breath escaped as I fought through the mess of feelings.

I slung my purse over my shoulder, stepped out of the car, and hit the key fob to lock my car. Then, I did something that I hadn't done in the seven years I'd worked in the lab: I waited to walk in with him. The small smile on my lips didn't even feel forced.

He climbed out of his truck, eyes shifting to me and away, obviously uncomfortable. He looked like a trapped animal, and I half expected him to start hissing at me. Part of me worried that he would reflexively revert to nasty-Gerald to protect himself.

I didn't know why he reacted that way. Was he scared of someone being kind to him? Maybe it was easier for him to deal with people who were mean to him? I guess if he expected people to be evil, he'd never be disappointed.

A wave of pity washed over me.

"Good morning, Dr. Richter," I said pleasantly.

His eyes darted away again, and he hit his key fob. The lights flashed on his trunk, and there was a low *thunk*. He straightened his shoulders and eyed me cautiously. "Good morning, Dr. Harjo," he replied.

I moved to cross the parking lot, and he joined me, walking in step.

"Thanks for covering the news interview for me," I started hesitantly, risking a glance.

He met my comment with an awkward, stony silence. The old Gerald would have snarked about me shirking my duties or called me something demeaning. This Gerald, whatever version of him this was, still hadn't snapped at me.

Yet, an evil part of me whispered. *He hasn't snapped at you* yet.

I chewed my cheek.

When we reached the stairs into the building, I stopped. His steps faltered, and he turned to me.

"Thanks for saying what you did," I said. "You didn't have to. I appreciate it." I met the cool blue of his eyes, trying to read his expression.

"You're welcome," he replied stiffly.

I rolled my lips in, unsure of what to say next, and broke eye contact. With a slight nod, I headed up the stairs. I held the door for him, and he entered the building without a single quip.

Less than a minute later, I tossed my purse next to my desk and flopped into my chair.

Well, that happened.

Looking back, I could see how everything spun back to the tiger. The one little choice to stick up for him had sent him down a different road. A weaving path that led to a lemon bar from Carol and an apology for Dustin. One that brought us here, where he would defend me during a news interview, and we could have a conversation as we walked into work without throwing barbs.

A sudden feeling of contentment with my job washed over me. Working at the state lab was like a comfortable pair of well-worn jeans. They might look a little rough and ready and have a small tear in the rear pocket. But they simply *fit* like nothing else. Despite all of the messiness with the tough cases and the lab politics, I loved the lab, and it would be agony to leave it.

My eyes drifted to the stack of cardboard flats holding oodles of slides on my desk. It would take me at least a day to crunch through them all. Instead of feeling overwhelmed, I felt ready.

Just as I reached for the top slat on the stack, my phone binged. I quickly fumbled through my purse. It was Aunty.

> Dr. Jones was able to fit Chula in. I'm bringing her in at 8:30.

I felt a flood of relief.

In less than twenty minutes, Chula would be in an exam room and having tests done. I tagged Aunty's message with a heart.

> How is she doing?

> The same. She is very tired. She'll eat chicken if I coax her, but nothing else. Not even her treats.

I chewed my cheek. Even though I knew she was going to the doctor, worry coiled in my guts like a snake ready to strike. I didn't like being in the dark. I had half a mind to take the day off so I could be down there with them. But in my heart, I knew that wouldn't accomplish anything and might freak Aunty out even more than she already was.

Let me know what he says?

She sent a thumbs-up.

I put my phone on my desk and picked up a pen to fidget. It was just a few minutes after eight, and I knew she wouldn't have much to share until after nine at the earliest. I was pretty sure Dr. Jones had squeezed her in around already-booked appointments. It would be a while, and if I didn't do something to distract myself, I'd gnaw a hole through my cheek.

I opened the first flat of glass slides, determined to get some work done and hopeful that it would take my mind off things. Soon, I was lost in the flow of the cases, glass slides slipping across the microscope stage as I finalized each report. I was two cases in when my cell phone rang.

I snatched it up, heart racing and barely registering Aunty's name on the screen before hitting the accept icon.

"Hey, Aunty," I answered, feeling a bit breathless.

"Hello, sweety," she said, voice sad. There were sounds of people talking in the background, and I could tell she was still at the vet's office.

My heart clenched. "What did Dr. Jones say?" I asked in a half-whisper.

Aunty sighed. "He's not sure what's going on. He said her heart and lungs sound fine, and she doesn't have a temperature. But he knows something is wrong. Josie, I had to lift her into the car. She couldn't even get in by herself...." Her voice caught, and I could tell she was doing everything in her power to keep her shit together.

I waited, not wanting to push her.

A small dog started yapping in the background, filling the silence.

"Chula's in the back now," she continued, voice even. "They're taking blood and pee to send off. He's going to send her home with some appetite stimulants. But he doesn't want to do much else until he knows what's going on."

"He's sending her home?" I asked, sounding slightly incredulous.

I wasn't sure how I felt about that. If Chula was healthy enough to go home, that was a good thing. But I also knew that she was very much *not* okay. The idea of her sitting at home, waiting for test results, chafed.

The damn dog continued to chirp in the background like an annoying bird.

"It's okay, sweety," Aunty said, her voice an impossible mixture of resignation, love, and reassurance. "Chula will be happier at home until we know more. It's where her spirit wants to be."

I knew she was trying to make me feel better, but it wasn't working. Trying to hide my angst, I replied, "Yes, she'll be more comfortable at home."

After a beat, I added, "Plus, that little dog is fucking obnoxious. I'm sure Chula wants to eat her. Why does anyone own those stupid yappy things anyway?"

As I'd hoped, Aunty forced a laugh.

I checked the clock. "It's still pretty early. You might get the results back this afternoon."

"Yes," Aunty replied. "That's what Dr. Jones said."

I didn't like the idea of Aunty carrying the weight of this all alone and offered, "Want me to come down there?"

"No," she replied. "We'll be fine. Don't you worry."

I knew her well enough to hear the lie, but I also wanted to respect her wishes.

"Call me when the results come back?" I nudged. "Please?"

"Of course, sweety," she replied. "As soon as I know, you'll know."

"Give Chula some scratches for me?"

"I'll give her lots of those," Aunty said with affection. "Now, I know you're busy. Don't you worry about us."

"Okay, Aunty," I replied, still reluctant to let her go. "Love you."

"Love you, too, sweety."

We said our goodbyes.

I slowly placed my phone back on my desk, feeling numb. I stared at it, a mixture of feelings swirling through my mind. I kept picturing Chula yesterday. I couldn't stop thinking about how weak she'd been and how she'd still tried to wag her tail. I didn't have a clue what ailed her, and I couldn't offer Aunty any hope until Dr. Jones had a diagnosis. It was weird being on the other side of the fence, worrying the inside of my cheek and waiting for an answer.

I rubbed at my eyes, hoping I could press the tears away.

Don't freak out until you actually know what's going on. You'll know more soon.

But soon couldn't come fast enough. Between now and then, I knew I'd eat myself alive fretting over it.

Desperate for a distraction, I slipped a glass slide on the microscope stage. It took me a while to focus on what was in front of me, but soon the rhythm of the work pulled me away from my messy thoughts, and I didn't come up for air until several hours later.

As soon as the clock ticked over to noon, reality swept back in. I desperately needed one of Carol's sweets to fill the weeping hole in my chest, and my ass couldn't leave my seat fast enough. I grabbed my lunch and made a beeline for the breakroom. I arrived first, with Carol and Anna hot on my heels.

"Hello, Dr. Harjo," Carol said.

She placed a square plastic container in the middle of the table and popped the lid before sitting down. Today's cookie offering consisted of raspberry jam and poppy seed thumbprint cookies. The sweet smell of the jam hit me, and my stomach grumbled.

"Oh my gosh. I love those." Anna sighed in longing at the sight of the dainty cookies topped with bright red kisses.

"Thank you, Carol," I said, as we all helped ourselves. I placed my cookie on a napkin, forcing myself to eat my salad first, which was almost impossible.

Dustin and Zoe joined us about ten minutes later. Zoe had a harried expression.

"Everything okay?" I asked, surprised to see her so ruffled.

She waved a hand dismissively. "Yeah, just busy this morning."

My eyes bounced to Dustin for confirmation, and he nodded as he took a bite of steak sandwich.

"It was hectic last week, too," I mused. "Thankfully, most of them were gross-only."

Zoe huffed. "If only. Except for the steer with blackleg, I'll be doing histology on all of them."

"What'd y'all find in that dog?" Anna asked Zoe. "The owners were mighty upset. They were waiting outside when we opened up, and the wife wouldn't stop crying."

I was secretly grateful I hadn't been the one interviewing them today. I might've lost it.

"Yeah, she was distraught," Zoe said sadly, a slight frown pulling at her mouth. "The death was unexpected."

"What's the history?" I asked, more to keep the conversation going than true interest. The jaded part of me figured they had pointed a finger at the neighbor, and it would end up being garbage-can gut or something.

"They went on a camping trip. When they came back, the dog was off for a few days—not eating, not wanting to play, that kind of thing. They made an appointment to bring her in. The vet said she looked normal, but ran some routine tests to be on the safe side. The dog died at home, waiting for the results."

Goosebumps traced up my arms.

"We didn't find much on necropsy, either," Zoe added. "I collected a bunch of stuff, but I'll just have to wait for the histology to come back."

"Maybe it's tick-borne?" I offered.

The idea fell flat, and I somehow knew in my heart it wouldn't be one of a handful of blood parasites carried by ticks in Oklahoma.

"I called the vet and asked for the results of the bloodwork," Zoe replied. "They said they'd email it over. Might be something there. But I think this one's just going to be difficult. At least the other cases were easy: steer with blackleg, a horse fetus, and a sheep with diarrhea."

I was still stuck on Zoe's case. The similarities to Chula's clinical signs nagged at me.

The bite of salad I'd eaten sat unsteadily in my stomach, and I pushed the container away from me. My eyes landed on the cookie resting on the napkin; it winked at me with its red center. A bit of acid trickled up my esophagus.

The conversation flowed around me, and I zoned out for a few minutes. It wasn't until the group went abruptly silent that I was jerked back into the moment.

Gerald stood at the end of the table, holding a mug of coffee. "Good afternoon."

Everyone sat still as statues.

Dustin leaned forward, crossing his arms on the table, and asked, "Howdy, Dr. Richter. What can we do ya for?" His tone was friendly, and there were no hidden jabs despite the turn of phrase.

"Hello, Dustin," he said, tone prim and proper. He turned to Zoe. "Dr. Smith. I'd like to discuss case 43518162."

Zoe's shoulders tensed, and her eyes grew wary. "The dog I just finished?"

I was surprised she remembered the case numbers. Of all of us, Gerald was usually the one who had the knack for memorizing that kind of stuff.

"Yes," Gerald replied. "Were there any lesions on necropsy? The gross report isn't in the system yet."

The comment teetered on the edge of being an insult. I couldn't tell if this was his normal awkward bluntness or him trying to be a shitass. Residual bad blood remained between the two of them. I wasn't sure how far our unspoken truce extended into the friend group.

"No. There weren't any lesions," Zoe responded curtly.

Everyone else around the table remained still, waiting for the next move.

"There's an outbreak of *Salmonella*," Gerald said. "You didn't send any samples to my lab to test for it."

Here he goes again, I sighed to myself. It took everything in my power not to roll my eyes.

Zoe put words to my thoughts. "There was no history of vomiting and diarrhea, and the intestines looked normal."

"The situation with Best Bud's Bacon Bites is different," he insisted, sounding a bit petulant. His eyebrows furrowed in frustration, and he frowned. "The affected animals present with lethargy and die within a few days. Reports on the listserv have confirmed sepsis in several cases."

"The vet ran bloodwork." Anna chimed in and turned to Zoe. "Wouldn't that pick up sepsis?"

"I don't have the results yet," Zoe replied without really answering her question.

Zoe looked at Gerald like he'd fallen off his rocker, and I couldn't help but think the same thing. It was simply too hard to connect the dots between oral ingestion and sepsis without GI signs in between, especially with a *Salmonella* outbreak. Even if the owner had missed any signs of vomiting or diarrhea, the infection should've been glaringly obvious on necropsy, just like the goat I'd had last week.

"I advise questioning the owner about what treats they've given the dog," Gerald directed.

Zoe's lips pressed into a line, and I cringed inwardly.

If there really was an outbreak of *Salmonella* in dogs from this brand of treats, asking the owners about it wouldn't hurt. But Gerald had a habit of saying shit in the worst possible way, even when he didn't mean to.

Gerald turned to me. "The handler of case 43518087 should be questioned as well. It is possible that they missed the initial signs. Have you asked him yet?"

I jerked my head up. Given the context, I knew he referred to the Tohbi case, even though I didn't immediately recognize the accession number.

I felt a slim bit of pride when I was able to reply in the affirmative. "Yes, I asked him what he fed him, including what kinds of treats."

Gerald's eyebrows furrowed. "Did you ask specifically about Best Bud's Bacon Bites?"

"Not specifically," I replied, hating the defensiveness that had leaked into my voice. "He listed off a bunch of brand names, and he didn't say that one."

Gerald made a noise that was halfway between a huff and a *hmm*.

"Keep me apprised of the situation," he said and turned to Zoe before adding, "in both cases."

"Yes, we will. Thank you," Zoe said, exacerbation slipping into her tone.

We both knew Gerald would bird-dog both cases in the system and know any results as soon as they were released. Even though I knew he was simply trying to help, it was annoying to have him insist on keeping him *apprised*.

Gerald lifted his mug in a weird salute and left the breakroom.

"Best Bud's Bacon Bites," I huffed to myself, slowly shaking my head, eyebrows raised in disbelief.

Then, I felt a slight tug on a thin wisp of a memory. Hadn't I seen a box of treats like that in Aunty's cupboard recently? I stood quickly, startling everyone at the table.

"You okay?" Dustin asked.

"Huh? Yeah. I'm fine," I mumbled as I frantically packed my lunch up. "Gotta run. See ya."

I stumbled out of the breakroom, feeling my friends' eyes trace my path out. I headed straight to my office, practically threw my shit on my desk, and dug out my phone to text Aunty.

What kind of treats does Chula get?

She replied immediately as if she'd been waiting by the phone.

Lots of kinds. Why?

Does Best Bud's Bacon Bites sound familiar?

> Maybe? I'd have to check when I get home. Why?

> There's an outbreak associated with them. Let me know if you find anything.

> Is the bloodwork back yet?

> No. Dr. Jones said it wouldn't be back until late this afternoon.

> OK. Thanks. Sorry to bug you.

I placed my cell phone down and chewed my cheek. If it were sepsis, wouldn't Chula have a fever? Chula looked awful yesterday, but I couldn't help but think she should've looked ten times worse if she was septic. The whole dog-treat thing didn't feel right, but I couldn't help but try to stuff the round peg into the square hole.

And then there was Tohbi.

I picked up my pen and twirled it as my mind raced.

Could some innocent treats loaded with a whopping dose of bacteria have been enough to take out the police dog? Had the handler missed some subtle clinical signs? Or was Tohbi so excited to work, as most sniffing dogs are, that the adrenaline had covered up any of the associated clinical signs? Was the excitement enough to tip him over the edge?

I dug through the sticky notes on my desk, found Austin's number, and called him from my desktop phone. Voicemail picked up on the fourth ring. After the beep, I left my message.

"Hello, Mr. Carlyle. This is Dr. Josie Harjo from the state diagnostic lab. I'm calling about Tohbi. Did you feed Tohbi a brand of treats called Best Bud's Bacon Bites? It's a long shot, but there's an outbreak right now, and I wanted to rule that out. Please call me back." I left my number and hung up, frustrated.

My mind raced with the possibilities. The worst part of the whole mess was that there was no way to get an answer for Chula or Tohbi within the next few hours. I couldn't turn my worry into action. All I could do was wait for the results. Wait for Chula's bloodwork. Wait for the drug test results and histology on Tohbi. Wait, wait, wait.

The pressure of it all was going to kill me.

CHAPTER

NINETEEN

As the clock tipped past three in the afternoon, Sally swept in with a flat of slides.

"Here's your STAT case, Dr. Harjo," she said, all business.

My heart lurched. I'd been expecting the slides back from the Tohbi case today, but I was still a bit surprised—and if I was honest with myself, a bit nervous—to see Sally bring them in.

"Thank you, Sally," I replied, taking the cardboard flat from her.

She left with a silent nod and headed back to the histology lab.

The cardboard flat sat in my hands like a Hello Kitty surprise bag. I itched to open it. But just like those stupid expensive bags, the chances were fairly high that I'd be disappointed with my pull.

I flipped back both flaps to reveal all of the slides from the case, each graced with slivers of pink-purple tissue. The slides skated across the stage of my microscope. With each slide, my heart dropped further into my shoes. When all of the slides had made a tour across my scope, I sat back in my chair with a frustrated huff.

Nothing.

There had been absolutely nothing. Despite the stomach being red at necropsy, the histology sections were completely blah histologically. At a stretch, the vessels might be a bit congested, but even if they were, congested vessels didn't mean much in the context of the case.

Fuck.

Gerald nagged in my head, and I felt a flutter of panic that he might be right about Best Bud's Bacon Bites.

With a sigh, I picked each slide up again, scanning every tissue with more scrutiny than on my first go. Maybe I'd missed a tiny thrombus, some bacteria, a cluster of inflammatory cells, *anything* that might suggest sepsis. But the slides were just as boring the second time around.

"Well, so much for that," I grumbled to myself.

I didn't have many places to go from there. The brain and spinal cord would be back in a day or two, but I didn't want to put all of my eggs in that basket. The only other pending test was the drug screen on the blood. I spun back to the computer to check the toxicology results. My fingers sped across the keyboard with hopeful determination. When I finally got the toxicology window open for the case, a big, fat "pending" filled the screen.

I felt a flicker of disappointment.

The case notes indicated that the samples had been shipped on Friday, which was fabulous; Anna must have confirmed that the lab would be open on Saturday to receive the package. But even if a diagnostic lab was open to receive samples, it didn't mean that every department would be running tests on a weekend. Hopefully, Sandy had enough clout to get them to rush the sample today, and the results would be ready before five.

Even with the pending toxicology, I still needed to get the histology results out. I navigated to the pathology window and typed up the histologic findings. Like the gross findings, the histology result section of the report was repetitive and unhelpful. Line after line of "within normal limits" filled the screen. In the comments, I wrote some drivel about how the "cause of death remains elusive" and mentioned that histology on the brain and spinal cord was still pending. I added a note at the end about the pending toxicology test.

With dread, my mind jumped to what might be said on this evening's news report. I couldn't help but imagine the worst. Darryl Castor would be dressed in a suit, hair styled like a Ken doll, and have a serious face. I could hear his voice: "Despite the optimism of her coworkers, including world-renowned Dr. Gerald Richter, Dr. Josie Harjo was unable to find anything in the poor, deceased police dog. Will Tohbi find justice despite the bumbling work of an inept pathologist? Tune in next time."

Sinking in my chair, I buried my face in my hands.

Cut it out with the self-pity, Aunty's voice chided.

I rubbed my forehead, trying to shake myself out of it. Self-flagellation wouldn't get me anywhere. I closed my eyes and leaned back.

Deep breaths. Little steps. Eyes on the prize, Aunty's voice continued.

My eyes flipped open, and a feeling of resolve washed over me. I quickly released the histology results before I could further mind-fuck myself.

As I sat there glaring at the screen, the report made its way through the ether and into Chuck's email. I owed the guy a call, even if all I could tell him was I hadn't found anything yet. I picked up the phone and dialed Chuck's number, half-hoping I'd get his voicemail.

No such luck.

"Detective Pollard, here," he answered gruffly.

"Detective Pollard. This is Dr. Josie Harjo from the diagnostic lab," I said.

"Dr. Harjo! Good to hear from you," he replied, his voice turning friendly. "What've you got for me?"

I picked up a pen and started spinning it in my fingers. "Not much, I'm afraid. I got the slides back on the internal organs today, and they were normal. Histology on the brain and spinal cord are pending. Drug testing is also pending."

"Well, darn," he sighed, sounding deeply disappointed. "When can we expect those results?"

"I'm hoping the drug testing comes back later today. We had to send it to another lab. Our toxicologist, Dr. Sandy Bishop, called in a favor to get the case pushed to the front, but there are a lot of other factors in play, so no promises. Worst-case scenario, we'll get them tomorrow."

That isn't the full truth, though? Is it?

The real worst-case scenario would be a declaration that the sample was non-diagnostic because the blood had been collected postmortem. Then, we'd be back to square one. But I figured I'd cross that bridge when I got there.

The pen twirled through my fingers. "I'm also waiting on the sections of the brain and spinal cord. They take longer to fix in the formaldehyde solution than the other tissues. I trimmed those in today for processing, which takes another twenty-four hours or so. I should have those sections back by tomorrow afternoon."

"What are the chances we find anything?" he asked.

"In the brain?"

"Yeah," he replied.

He forced me to say what I knew deep down in my heart. "Given that Austin didn't notice any clinical signs prior to death, I'm not holding my breath," I replied, resigned. After a beat, I added, "Sorry."

"It's alright," Chuck said, and he sounded like he really meant it. Like he knew I was doing my best.

"We've ruled a lot of stuff out," I offered. "There's no indication of trauma, cancer, or inflammation. That rules out a lot of differentials." My pen started twirling faster. "But there are still several other possible causes on the table. The kind of things that are more difficult to definitively diagnose."

"Like what?" Chuck asked.

Like heat stroke, an evil voice whispered in my head. *Or a really nasty, acute sepsis from a dog treat that has a stupid name.*

There was no way in hell I was going to say that shit out loud, especially to a detective. I pressed my lips together and buried the thoughts deep into my psyche.

"It could be an acute toxicosis," I offered instead. "Sometimes animals get into things, like human medications or supplements. Or they chew on a toxic plant."

I quickly brushed away the fact that I hadn't found pills, plant pieces, or anything else sketchy in the stomach. Those differentials went in the box with heat stroke and *Salmonella*-induced sepsis.

An image of half-digested sausage flashed in my mind.

I still need to ask Austin about that, I reminded myself.

"We just have to take it one step at a time and keep ruling stuff out," I finished lamely.

"I understand," Chuck said, obviously disappointed. "Thanks for keeping me posted."

"I'll call you as soon as I know more," I said.

"I appreciate that," he replied.

Just as I was about to say goodbye, I remembered Aunty's message.

"Oh! And before you go. Molly says hi back. She hopes you're doing well." I knew it was a quick change of subject, but the words tumbled out before I could stop them.

"Huh!" he said, more to himself. "Any chance I can get her contact info? It'd be nice to catch up."

"Sure," I replied. I rambled off Aunty's phone number from memory, knowing she'd be fine with it.

Chuck thanked me again, and we said our goodbyes.

A mixture of feelings swam through my mind when I hung up the phone. On the one hand, Chuck had taken my not-an-answer remarkably well. On the other hand, the guilt at not solving the case continued to eat away at me. Either way, I was glad to have that call over with.

The rest of the day petered by in a series of glass slides marching across my microscope. At thirty minutes to five, I came up for air and checked for the toxicology results one last time.

"Pending" glared at me from the screen.

If any word could mock a pathologist, it was "pending" after an ancillary test result. The only other words that could initiate feelings of doom were "within normal limits," but these were usually self-inflicted.

I needed to find Sandy. It was possible that A&M had sent over the results, but they hadn't been entered into our system yet. I wasn't sure how busy Sandy's lab was. Deep down, I knew Sandy would be watching for that one, likely as anxious as I was. But I couldn't sit around and do nothing for the last bit of the day.

I left my desk and found her plunking away at her keyboard. My knuckles tapped the doorjamb before entering.

"Hello, Dr. Bishop."

She looked up over her reading glasses and smiled. "Hello, Dr. Harjo." She stopped typing and leaned back. "Let me guess: here to check on the drug test results?"

"Yep," I said, stepping into her office but not having a seat. "Any news?"

"No, ma'am," she said with sympathy. "I've been keeping an eye on the tox lab email, waiting for it to pop up, and it hasn't yet. Want me to give A&M a call?"

I shook my head. "It's okay."

Even though this was an important case and people were eager for answers, I didn't want to bump a herd-health case out of line because of it. Further, when a lab is already really busy, people calling for results only slowed things down. I needed to trust.

Sandy nodded as if she had read my mind. "I'll keep an eye out until I leave. I'll enter them as soon as they come in and give you a holler."

"Thanks, Dr. Bishop."

I slumped back to my office, feeling horribly disappointed. I'd be leaving work empty-handed. Again.

TWENTY

As I packed up to leave, my cell phone began to ring. Aunty's name filled the screen.

My chest clenched uncomfortably.

"Hey, Aunty," I answered and moved to close my office door.

The latch clicked before Aunty responded.

"Hello, Josie," she said, her voice soft and tired.

"Any news?" I asked, sitting down on the edge of the office chair. I leaned forward, resting my elbow on the desk, and rubbed the wrinkles between my eyebrows with my free hand.

"Dr. Jones called with the bloodwork," she said, the normal smooth cadence of her voice troubled and harried. "He said Chula doesn't have enough cells in her blood, and that's probably why she's tired. He doesn't know why. He said something about having a doctor look at it to help us figure it out? I don't know. And he wants to see her tomorrow for an ultrasound."

I was having a hard time making sense of everything. Dr. Jones had clearly translated the information into non-scientific terms for Aunty. I struggled trying to get everything back into medical terminology. It was like playing operator in different dialects of the same language.

"Did he send you a copy of the results?" I asked.

"No, but I can ask for them," she replied. "They're all so wonderful there. I'm sure they'll send them right over."

"Can you please? And then email or text them to Tessa and me," I advised. After a beat, I asked, "Is he referring Chula somewhere else? You said something about another doctor?"

"Oh, no," she answered, not unkindly. "It has something to do with the blood. He wants another doctor to look at the blood."

The lightbulb clicked on. "Oh. He's probably waiting for a pathologist to look at the slide."

My mind raced, trying to think of all of the possible reasons to request a clinical pathologist to review the case.

"Did he run any tests to check for blood parasites? Tick-borne diseases?" I asked.

"Yes. When I was still in the waiting room," she replied. "He checked her blood and said it was negative."

I could only assume he ran a four-way tick-borne disease test, which would catch heartworm, Lyme, *Anaplasma*, and *Ehrlichia*. It was pretty standard in Oklahoma because of all of the ticks; no one could step outside without the little buggers crawling all over them.

I shuddered at the thought. I hated ticks almost as much as I hated maggots. The worst was when a dead carcass came in loaded with them. The ticks would abandon ship in waves and crawl up my arms as I tried to cut the body open. It was horrible. We even kept bug spray on the necropsy floor for that exact thing. I could handle just about anything on the pathology floor, but ticks and maggots were my kryptonite.

"Dr. Jones ruled out some of the more common bloodborne parasites," I explained. "I think he wants a pathologist to look at the slide to cover all his bases."

"A pathologist? Could he send it to you?"

Oh, hell no!

That was my knee-jerk reaction to anything related to clinical pathology. I couldn't help it and was glad I hadn't let it slip out. Instead, I said, "Different kind of pathologist. One who looks at fluids. I examine bodies and whole tissues."

And I suck at hematology, I sulked.

I could've looked at Chula's blood smear. But honestly, I didn't trust myself. It'd be like me running a toxicology test or setting up a PCR. I knew just enough to be dangerous.

"Oh," Aunty said, a tad disappointed.

"I'm sure the clinical pathologist will do an amazing job. It'll be okay." After a beat, I asked, "How's Chula doing?"

"About the same. I'm at work right now. But after her appointment, I got her settled on her favorite bed before coming in.... I had to help her out of the car." Her voice caught.

I could feel her pain through the phone and wished I could reach through to give her a hug.

"What time is her ultrasound tomorrow?" I asked hesitantly.

"Same time," she answered. "Eight thirty."

"Want me to come with you?" I offered.

"It's okay, sweety. I know you're busy with work. We'll be fine."

If anyone but Aunty had said those words, I'd know they were full of shit and wanted me to come. But Aunty's voice was sincere. She was a tough cookie and fiercely independent. If I pushed it, I'd be a shitass. So, I let it slide.

Instead, I said, "I'm here if you need me," and left the offer hanging there.

"Thank you," she said softly.

"Give Chula a pat for me?"

"Absolutely," she replied.

After we said our goodbyes, I sat back in my chair, gnawing my cheek raw. Unanswered questions hung heavy on my shoulders. I needed to get my eyes on the bloodwork before the worry ate me alive. I guessed it would be at least fifteen or twenty minutes before Aunty forwarded them to me.

Just enough time to get home.

I had no idea what the blood results would show. It might be enough to send me over the edge, and I didn't want that to happen at work. With a decision made, I jumped up and hurriedly finished packing. I headed out the door quick as a flash, eager to be home before she sent them to me.

There really hadn't been a need to rush.

By the time my phone binged with a notification, I was at the kitchen counter, anxiously picking at leftovers. I quickly unlocked my phone, relieved to see a text from Aunty. I opened the text chain and found the PDF of Chula's blood test results.

With just one look, my heart sank into my shoes.

Several of the values were off, but only slightly and not in a way that was very specific. Her red blood cells were low, so she did have a mild anemia, but it was regenerative, and her body was trying to make more cells. She also had low platelets and low protein.

I checked the white blood cells, unable to help myself. They were normal, with no evidence of toxic changes.

Sepsis is unlikely, then.

The pathologist's review would confirm that, but it was likely that Best Bud's Bacon Bites had been cleared.

My eyes drifted down to the chemistry results, and I was surprised to find that Chula's liver values were high; Aunty hadn't mentioned that. It was common enough to see liver values a smidgen off, especially in older dogs. But Chula's numbers were through the charts.

I switched from the group chat to text Tessa directly, asking if she could call. My phone started ringing immediately.

I answered with a "What do you think?"

"I'm not sure," Tessa replied, hesitantly, echoing my thoughts. "There's a mild regenerative anemia, mild thrombocytopenia, and hypoproteinemia for starters. Did they do a 4 Dx?"

"Yes, the tick-borne disease testing was negative. He's asked for a path review on the blood smear," I replied. "Thoughts on the liver values?"

A few seconds of silence slipped by as she mulled it over. "They're pretty high, especially the ALP," she finally said. "But it could just be an old dog thing. How old is she again?"

"We don't know for sure, but around eleven."

"That's pretty old for a dog who's half coyote," Tessa said, her voice wavering, and then she forced an awkward laugh, trying to make things light.

A small smile tipped my lips. "Yeah, for a half-coyote," I replied softly.

"With the PU/PD, it could be secondary to Cushing's," she said.

"They're doing an ultrasound tomorrow," I said. "That'll give them a chance to look at the liver and adrenals."

"Any chance of them running an ACTH stim test or low-dose dex test when she's in?" she asked, referring to some of the tests used to diagnose Cushing's disease.

"Aunty didn't mention it," I replied. "But I'll nudge them that way if the ultrasound is boring."

The conversation lulled as we both puzzled over the case. In my heart, I knew there wasn't much more we could do today. An ultrasound might turn something up, but I wasn't placing my bet on that horse.

"At least we know it's not Best Bud's Bacon Bites," I mumbled, feeling huffy.

"What?" Tessa asked with a half-laugh.

I waved my hand dismissively and sighed. "Oh, nothing. There's just an outbreak of *Salmonella* in some dog treats."

"Chula doesn't have GI signs," Tessa interrupted.

"Yeah, I know," I said, not unkindly. "I haven't looked into it much myself. But Dr. Richter says the affected dogs present with lethargy and sudden death from sepsis."

"Hmm," Tessa said, sounding doubtful.

"He just mentioned it as a differential for two other cases: one of mine and a case Dr. Smith got in today." I shrugged. "But Chula's white blood cells are normal. I'd be shocked if she has sepsis."

"Agreed," Tessa said.

"Well, I guess we wait for the ultrasound then," I said.

"I guess so," Tessa replied softly. After a beat, she added, "I'm really worried about Chula, Josie."

"Me, too," I finally admitted. Saying it out loud made it real, and the words tasted like ash.

"Keep me posted?" she pleaded.

"Definitely," I said. "I'll let you know as soon as I hear any-thing."

"Thanks," she murmured.

We said our goodbyes, and I ended the call. I placed the phone on the counter next to my plate. I stared down at the cold piles of three-day-old Chinese food, my appetite suddenly gone.

CHAPTER

TWENTY-ONE

The white dog trotted ahead on the dirt path, tail held low. The cicadas hummed, and the smell of lavender was thick on the breeze. The air felt heavy, and dark clouds formed a looming gray-green wall in the distance. Every muscle in my body tensed. My feet kept pulling me forward even though every fiber of my being told me to get the fuck out of there.

Suddenly, the cicadas stopped their screaming, and an eerie silence fell over everything. The white dog stopped and lifted its nose to sniff the air. It turned to me, eyes sharp, and let out a single alert bark.

My eyes slammed open. My body was frozen and drenched in sweat, despite the chill in the room. As control over my limbs returned, I slowly unclenched my fingers, panting.

The room was pitch black. I reached over to check my phone, the electric light creating deep shadows in the corner of the room.

It was just after one in the morning.

Yersi shifted his weight next to me and blinked. With an irritated tail flick, he rested his head back down and closed his eyes.

This recurring nightmare was killing me.

I lay back down, staring into the darkness, trying to force myself to sleep. I changed positions a million times, trying to get comfortable. My eyes were heavy, but sleep remained elusive. After about thirty minutes of this, Yersi left the room, disgusted.

I rolled onto my back and rearranged my pillow yet again. A deep pressure hung heavily around my eyes. I was so incredibly tired, but I couldn't calm my brain down enough to relax back into sleep.

After what felt like forever, I must've dozed off because the wailing of my alarm woke me a few hours later. As soon as I silenced my phone, Yersi started up his moaning.

Foggy, I rolled out of my bed, half-awake. I went through the motions of my morning routine in a daze, tipping back cup after cup of black tea, hoping to get enough caffeine in my system to make it through the day.

Next thing I knew, I was in the lab, sitting at my desk with my palms pressed against my tired eyes. Flashes of the white dog flitted through my mind, and I could still hear the echoes of the single sharp bark. A knock at the doorjamb pulled me from the haze. Looking up, I found Sandy standing at the threshold.

"Good morning, Dr. Harjo," she said cautiously. "Are you alright?"

"Yeah," I replied, trying to wipe the cobwebs away.

"Have a second?" she asked politely, still standing just outside my office.

"Yeah. Of course. Sure." I waved her in. "Sorry. I didn't sleep well. I'm kind of out of it."

Sandy drifted into my office and took a seat. Leaning back, she crossed an ankle over her knee and laced her fingers across her stomach. She watched me intently.

"We got the results back from the police dog," she started.

Every muscle in my body tensed.

"You're not going to believe it," she continued. "They detected a pretty high concentration of cocaine in the blood. Nineteen point three micrograms per milliliter."

My eyebrows jumped up in shock.

"Wait. What? Cocaine?" I blurted, my mind scrambling to catch up.

She nodded.

"But they found meth in the shipment," I insisted.

Sandy shrugged. "Well, the dog's blood tested positive for cocaine."

"But..." I started, still trying to brush the fog of exhaustion away so I could make sense of everything. "Cocaine," I repeated, dumbfounded.

I rubbed my palms against my eyes. "I assume the concentration of cocaine was high enough for an overdose." I opened my eyes to watch her expression. "Is that what you're thinking?"

"Mm-hmm," she said, eyes sharp. "High enough to result in acute cardiovascular and respiratory arrest. I suspect he went pretty fast."

The neurons finally started firing in my brain. Austin had mentioned saliva on the seat. He'd said Tohbi's hair had been wet with urine as well.

And he'd bitten through his tongue. Don't forget that.

"He must've had a seizure," I mumbled, more to myself.

Austin said he was acting normal when he worked the shipment. Don't overdoses happen fairly quickly?

"How long does it take for cocaine to show up in the blood?" I asked, trying to build a timeline.

"Depends on route of exposure, but fifteen minutes or so," Sandy said without hesitation. I figured she must've looked that up when she saw the results; cases like this didn't come through our doors often enough to have that tidbit sitting on the tip of her tongue.

"Let's say he somehow got enough cocaine in him to overdose, have a seizure, and die," I pressed. "How soon after exposure might we see neurologic signs and death?"

"With a dose high enough to reach that concentration, I would expect fairly quickly. Ten to fifteen minutes, maybe?" She lifted one shoulder in a shrug. "I'd have to pull some articles to confirm that. Knowing the route of exposure would help. But I can't see it being more than thirty minutes."

"The timing doesn't make any sense," I replied, shaking my head with frustration. "How did he get into cocaine while locked in the car? When would he have even had an opportunity to?"

"That's an excellent question," Sandy said matter-of-factly.

"He was working a *meth* bust," I asserted, unable to get past that niggly bit.

She held up her hands as if to say *It is what it is*.

"You're a hundred percent sure the dog died from a cocaine overdose?" I asked again.

"Yes, ma'am," she replied confidently. "Now, if you'd found something on necropsy to suggest differently, I might hem and haw a bit. Say it was a contributing factor or something. But this is pretty clear-cut."

"Crap," I muttered, finally realizing how messy this whole thing was going to get.

A police dog died from a cocaine overdose on a meth bust.

I shook my head slowly, still feeling the shock.

"Any idea how the dog might've gotten into cocaine?" she asked gently.

"No clue," I said bitterly. I chewed my cheek, trying not to freak out. There was no way I could solve this on my own. After a beat, I added, "I guess I'd better call the detective."

And hopefully, he can help me put all of this together.

"I'll wait an hour to release the results. Give you a chance to give him a verbal heads-up first," she offered.

"Thanks," I replied, mind racing.

Sandy gave me a sympathetic look. "I'll leave you to it, then. Let me know if I can help at all."

"Thanks, Sandy," I said absently. I was already five steps ahead, trying to figure out how to tell Chuck that a police dog had died from a drug overdose.

Sandy left with a quiet goodbye and closed the office door behind her. She knew I needed some privacy for what I had to do next.

I stared at my desktop phone for a good twenty minutes before I felt brave enough to pick it up. My fingers reluctantly typed the numbers into the keypad, and the ringing jangled in my head.

"Detective Pollard, here," he answered.

My palms started to sweat at the sound of his voice. "Hello, Detective Pollard. This is Dr. Harjo from the diagnostic lab. I have an update on Tohbi. Have a minute?"

"Good morning, Dr. Harjo. Sure, what've you got?" he replied, somehow managing to sound relaxed and business-like at the same time.

"Um." The words froze in my throat.

I finally knew what had killed Tohbi, but so many pieces were still missing from the puzzle. Plus, I couldn't help but feel like I was about to kick a hornet's nest. No one could blame me for hesitating.

I swallowed. "The drug test results are back. Dr. Bishop should be releasing them shortly. There was enough cocaine in his blood to cause an overdose."

"Cocaine?" His tone was slightly incredulous. "Are you sure?"

"Yes, sir. Cocaine," I replied.

"Huh," Chuck said, sounding as flabbergasted as I'd been when talking to Sandy.

"Just to confirm, Tohbi found methamphetamine in the shipment that morning. Correct?" I asked.

"Yes, ma'am."

My pits joined the palm-sweat party. Sure, I'd seen my fair share of serious cases: animals worth over a million dollars, animal cruelty cases, and nasty outbreaks that dropped animals like flies. But the severity of this situation had reached a whole new level.

A canine police officer had died from a drug overdose while on duty. And I didn't know if it had been a horrible accident or a murder. The whole thing had me in knots.

"Any chance there was cocaine in the shipment?" I asked.

"There's always a chance," he said gruffly. "I'll ask the team to have another look. But I think it's unlikely."

A slim chance was better than none. The timing of exposure still didn't make sense.

I took a deep breath. "The reason I'm asking is...cocaine overdoses happen fairly quickly. That puts the likely time of exposure within fifteen to twenty minutes of death. Maybe half an hour if we push it."

A horrible, tense silence stretched between us as Chuck processed what I'd said.

"So Tohbi was exposed while working the shipment or while he was in the police car," he said more to himself.

"Exactly," I replied.

"I can't imagine a dog accidentally snorting enough cocaine while working a shipment to OD," he said, his voice grim.

My stomach clenched, and something tugged at my mind. "Maybe he didn't snort it," I said quietly, thoughts racing.

"What?" Chuck asked sharply.

I shook my head, trying to jiggle the thoughts back into place. "Maybe he didn't inhale it."

"You think someone injected him with it?" he asked, slightly incredulous. "That'd be pretty damn hard with DEA agents and police swarming the hangar."

"Maybe, it wasn't injected...." My voice trailed off. I was missing something. It sat just on the edge of my mind, and I was so exhausted, I couldn't reach it.

I closed my eyes and rubbed the crease between my eyebrows. The image of the white dog on the path instantly popped into my head, and a sharp bark made my eyes snap open.

"What if someone fed it to him?" My words came out as more of a statement than a question.

"Say what?" he asked, voice stern.

"We get cases sometimes—rarely, really—of someone who kills their neighbor's dog. Like with poison. Rat bait or whatever." My words jumped all over the place, trying to keep up with my swirling thoughts. I took a deep breath and started again. "What if someone laced dog treats or something with cocaine and stashed it in the shipment? Or somehow fed it to him?"

What if they put cocaine in something like sausage?

"Holy shit," I blurted, voice hushed.

"What?" Chuck said.

"The sausage," I said, feeling that rush of certainty that always came over me when I'd finally hit the mark. "There was sausage in Tohbi's stomach. I wonder if it was laced with cocaine. I asked Austin what treats he gave Tohbi—there's an outbreak in a brand of dog treats, but that doesn't really matter." I shook my head, trying to focus. "Anyway, Austin told me what he fed Tohbi that day and what treats he gave him when they were working. He never once mentioned sausage."

"Do you still have any of that sausage?" he asked.

A smile tipped my lips. "As a matter of fact, I do. I'll get that sent off today for drug testing. We might've already missed the morning pick-up, so the results might not come back for a couple of days, but I'll call you as soon as they come in."

"I'll give Austin a call," Chuck said. "Just to confirm what he fed Tohbi that morning. See if there's anything else he noticed. We need to walk back through things and figure out who might've had access to Tohbi the hour before Austin found him."

"This might sound like a stupid question, but is there camera footage from that morning?" I asked.

"Yes, ma'am," he answered. "We went through the footage first thing."

Of course, they did, I thought glumly.

"There are some blind spots around the hangar. There's footage of the police vehicle, but the detail isn't good enough to see inside. Still, it doesn't hurt to give the security footage another once-over. We might catch something we missed the first time 'round, especially now that we know what we're looking for." After a beat, he added, "Thank you, Dr. Harjo. I appreciate all your hard work."

"You're welcome," I replied, heart still thudding in my chest.

"Well, I'll let you go," he said, not unkindly. "I'm sure you're busy, and I've got some phone calls to make.

We said our goodbyes, and I hung up the phone.

I wiped my palms on my pants and took three deep breaths. Everything was starting to come together. Just a few more pieces, and this case could be in my rearview mirror.

CHAPTER

TWENTY-TWO

As soon as I hung up the phone with Detective Pollard, I made a beeline for the necropsy floor.

The crooning of Hank Williams and the whir of the hoist filled the air. There was a flurry of activity. Zoe and Dustin were fully geared up and knee-deep in a large bull. Dustin looked up from across the room when I walked in.

I raised my hand and called out, "Just grabbing a sample. Be out of here in a jiffy."

He gave me a nod and went back to it.

My shoe covers scuffed across the floor. I dug through the freezer and found the stomach contents. I was so damn grateful I'd saved it.

My pen sped across the sheet clipped to the fridge as I logged the sample out. With the container in hand, I headed straight for the receiving department, only stopping to toss my shoe covers in the bin before stepping out.

"Hey, Anna," I said in greeting and plopped the plastic container on the counter.

"Hello, Dr. Harjo. How can I help you?"

"I have some stomach contents to send out," I said as she passed me a request form.

"A&M, again? Is it from the police dog?" she asked.

"Yes, ma'am."

"You just missed the morning pick-up. Sorry. But I'll make sure it gets out this afternoon," she said, taking the paper as I passed it through to her.

"Thanks, Anna. I appreciate it."

If the samples could make it out today, they'd arrive at A&M to-morrow. If I were lucky, I'd have the results by Thursday. I was eager to get this case buttoned up.

I swept back into my office and landed in my chair with a heavy sigh. The conclusion of the Tohbi case was within reach. Hopefully, the results from the stomach contents would tie a neat bow on the whole package. If not, I didn't really know where to go from there. And honestly, it probably didn't matter. With the cause of death confirmed, the ball was in Chuck's court to figure out how it happened.

I pulled another flat of slides from the stack and returned to the flow of case-reading. A smidgeon before lunch, the *bing* of a text drew my attention. I pulled my phone out of my purse. A text from Aunty popped up in my notifications, asking me if I could talk.

A wave of concern washed over me. I immediately pressed the call button, and Aunty answered before the first ring finished.

"Hello, sweety," Aunty said, voice hushed and laced with sadness.

"Hey, Aunty," I replied hesitantly.

"They did Chula's ultrasound," she said, leaving the sentence hanging all on its own.

My stomach clenched. My poor body could only take so many hits today, and I felt broken. I leaned forward, resting my forehead in the palm of my free hand.

"And?" I nudged, trying to be kind.

"They said her liver and spleen are big. They used a needle to take a few cells and sent them off."

I pressed my palm against my forehead as tears threatened.

Aunty had just described a fine-needle aspirate. And given all of Chula's other signs, they could only be thinking it was cancer. My hopes of something common and manageable like Cushing's disease flew out the window. I clenched my teeth, and I forced the welling sadness into a tidy box.

"So I guess we wait," I replied, trying to be strong. Despite my best efforts, the words came out in a defeated sigh.

Aunty didn't reply.

"How's Chula doing?" I asked softly.

"They said she's doing fine," Aunty replied. "They wanted to keep her for the afternoon to make sure there was no bleeding after they put the needle in her. I'm getting off work early to pick her up later."

"Give her a kiss for me?" I asked.

"I will, sweety. I will. And all of the chicken if I can get her to eat."

I forced a small laugh. "And maybe some ice cream. I think you both deserve some today."

"She does love her peaches and cream," Aunty said, a smile edging into the sadness of her voice. "I'll pick some up before I get her."

"I'm sure she'd appreciate that," I said softly. "And Aunty...buy a pint of rocky road for yourself, okay?"

That got a small laugh.

We shared somber goodbyes, and I ended the call, feeling completely and totally wrung out. I looked at the stack of glass on my desk, and buried myself in work.

Later, I skipped lunch in the breakroom, feeling too exhausted to be social. Instead, I focused on the slides from the previous week's cases between bites of salad.

At some point, my phone binged again. I fished my cell out of my purse and found a text from Armand.

> Want to have dinner tonight?

Given everything that happened today, my knee-jerk reply was a hard no. A pint of mint chocolate chip ice cream sang to me like a siren from my freezer, and I was more than happy to mope on my couch and devour the entire thing by myself. But a small part of me hoped that dinner with the person I loved might cheer me up. Even if it didn't, I knew I could still crush a pint of ice cream in his presence without judgement.

My decision made, I texted back.

> Sure

> Want to go out? Louie's?

I absolutely did not want to go out. I wanted to head home, get in my jammies, and cry. I ran my fingers through my hair, trying to figure out the best way to respond.

> Not really. Mind coming over to my place again?

The ellipses bounced for a bit, disappeared, and bounced again.

> I can come over there. Want me to get takeout or I can cook for you?

> Sure. Whatever is easiest.

I honestly didn't care what we ate. I'd only nibble at whatever he put in front of me, and only so I could lie to myself that the fuck-ton of ice cream I inhaled later was simply dessert rather than a meal.

He sent a thumbs-up. We confirmed a time, and I dropped my phone back in my purse, feeling huffy and not understanding why.

The rest of the afternoon waddled by. I hid in my office, working through my cases. I tried not to think about Tohbi or Chula or all of the other stuff swirling around in my head.

I scooted out a tad early, hoping to have some quiet time to myself before Armand came over. Even though we hadn't explicitly texted about it, a part of me hoped he wouldn't bring Ileana. I wasn't in the mood for the bouncy cheer of a dog right now, and I didn't feel like hosting an overnight guest.

As soon as I passed through my front door, I fed Yersi and changed into soft sweatpants and a T-shirt. Cradling a pint of ice cream, I leaned against the counter and allowed myself a few stolen bites. The minty taste tingled in my nose, and the sweet chocolate flakes melted on my tongue.

Yersi swirled around my legs, tail twining around my calves. He looked up at me and gave me a slow blink.

A smile tugged at my lips, and my shoulders relaxed. "Love you, too, bud."

He silently trotted into the living room, clearly expecting me to follow like any good worshiper should. I fit the lid back on the ice cream container, placed it in the freezer, and headed after him. We snuggled on the couch for a good thirty minutes, his throaty purr calming my mind.

At six, Yersi lifted his head and hopped off my lap. The doorbell rang a few seconds later.

Armand stood at the door, a grocery bag in one hand. "Hello, *iubita mea*," he said and leaned in to kiss my cheek. The smell of his aftershave washed over me, and my heart softened.

Maybe I don't want to be alone after all, I admitted to myself and stepped to the side to let him in.

"I brought food to cook for you," he said, holding up the bag and grinning like a man who'd caught a prize boar.

I closed the door behind him. "Thank you."

I followed him into the kitchen and took a seat at the counter as he started to unpack the groceries. He laid out a package of ground pork, polenta, and fresh green beans. He quickly got to work, massaging an ungodly number of spices into the meat before shaping them into large sausage patties.

"Want any help?" I asked.

"No, no," he said, the edges of his lips tipping into a smile. "Just relax."

I asked him about his day and listened as he talked about root growth patterns and a not-so-great student who worked for him in the greenhouse. My mind drifted over his softly accented words, grateful for a break from the mess that clouded my own mind.

The minutes slipped by, and before I knew it, we were seated at the table, the smell of heavily spiced sausage making my mouth water.

"Thanks for cooking," I said. "It smells delicious."

He smiled, and that irritatingly sexy curl slipped over his forehead.

About halfway through the meal, he put his fork down and leaned his elbows on the table. "I booked my flight back to Romania today," he said softly.

My stomach clenched, and acid burbled up my esophagus. My hand froze with the fork halfway to my mouth. I stared at him, unable to blink.

I couldn't help but feel like he'd dropped a stinking turd on the table between us. The last fucking thing I wanted to talk about today was him leaving.

"I don't have a choice," he said apologetically. "I don't want to leave, but my visa expires soon. I can't stay."

I slowly lowered my fork and tucked my hands into my lap.

"The offer is still there. You can come to Romania. Stay with us." His voice was filled with hope, and his eyes were practically pleading.

"I...." My voice caught in my throat.

"Maybe just come visit? Talk to people at the veterinary school? See if you like it there?" he offered.

I chewed my cheek, mind racing. I was operating on only a few hours of sleep, and what little bandwidth I had was still being consumed by restless thoughts of Tohbi and Chula. I just couldn't deal with this shit right now. It was too serious a thing to talk about without giving it my complete attention.

"Sorry. I'm really tired today," I said, trying to dodge the question. "A visit sounds nice. Maybe we can talk about it this weekend?"

He smiled at me, his eyes kind. "Sure. Maybe after Tessa's graduation?"

With a start, I realized that I'd completely forgotten about this weekend's festivities.

How the hell could I forget about something like that?

All of the vet school staff, myself included, would attend the ceremony this Saturday. We even had an area reserved in the auditorium for faculty seating. Armand had a ticket for the guest section. Aunty had one, too, assuming she was still able to come with all of the shit going on with Chula. We'd all planned on coming back to my place for dinner afterward.

"Yeah, after graduation," I answered, glad to hang all my baggage on that date. "Want to stay the night after the party?"

He nodded and reached over to give my arm a gentle squeeze. "I love you, *iubita mea*," he said, eyes soft.

"I love you, too," I replied without hesitation.

But I'm not sure it's enough to leave everything behind, a secret part of me added.

CHAPTER

TWENTY-THREE

When I closed my eyes that night, the white dog was already waiting for me.

After a darting glance over his shoulder to make sure I followed, he moved steadily down the path. Humid heat pressed in, and the cicadas sang shrilly. A sense of urgency drove me, and even though I didn't want to, my steps quickened so as not to lose sight of him.

He rounded a small bend and slipped behind thick shrubs and scraggly trees. Panic swept in as I lost sight of him, and I switched to a jog. Sweat dampened my shirt, and I started breathing heavily. As soon as I rounded the corner, I stopped dead in my tracks.

Aunty's place sat before me. The sun had started to set, and the sun's rays traced the edges of the house, leaving the porch in shadows.

My chest grew tight. Dream after dream, I'd known I was on the path near Aunty's house. But I'd thought I'd been going *away* from her place to some unknown destination. Yet, here I was, standing before her home. The white dog had been leading me here the whole time.

The white dog circled back to me and nudged my hand with his nose. His icy blue eyes pierced through me, and tears started to stream down my cheeks.

I woke with a start, heart thudding wildly in my chest.

My sheets were soaked with sweat. I rubbed my hands across my face to find them wet with tears. I blinked through the fog, trying to escape the vivid feelings of crushing sadness that had swept over me right before awakening.

There was no going back to sleep. I was too afraid of what I'd see when I closed my eyes again. I climbed out of bed and splashed cold water on my face. The fresh sting was enough to bring me back to the present.

***

After crawling into the lab, I tried to hide in my office. The stack of flats on my desk was shorter today. I figured I had just enough work sitting there to keep me busy until lunch. I put some music on and dove in, eager for a distraction.

Around mid-morning, Sally appeared with a few flats of slides. They included the last vestiges of glass from Friday's cases. The brain and spinal cord from the Tohbi case sat right on top.

After a quick thanks to Sally, I pushed aside the case I'd been working on and turned my attention to the Tohbi case. The slides skated across the microscope stage one by one.

Absolutely boring.

If I crossed my eyes a little, I could maybe pretend a few of the neurons in the hippocampus were slightly shrunken and maybe dead. But in my heart, I knew it was simply artifact; brains were fussy in that way. Since I now knew Tohbi died from a cocaine overdose, I hadn't expected to find anything earth-shattering in the sections from the CNS. But I couldn't help but feel a little let down.

I quickly updated the report and added a comment that toxicology testing on the stomach contents was still pending.

The results went out, leaving me with mixed feelings. With the exception of the checking the partially digested sausage for cocaine, the case was pretty much done from my end. But I still had a million unanswered questions, the most important of which was how a police dog had overdosed on cocaine during a meth bust. I knew it wasn't my job to answer that question, but it chaffed at the puzzle-solver in me. That last niggly bit would sit like a pebble in my shoe. I wouldn't be able to put this case to bed until I knew where the cocaine had come from.

About an hour or so after lunch, I grabbed my iPad and stylus and headed to the weekly team meeting. I'd been dodging Fran since she chewed my ass last week, and I knew I'd eventually have to deal with her. I hadn't told her about the toxicology results, and part of me was too tired to care. At least I'd have the rest of the pack there as a buffer if she came down on me too hard.

When I arrived, almost everyone else was already seated. Sandy and Zoe were on one side of the table with an empty chair on the end. Manuel and Gerald were on the other, an empty seat in between them. Fran, of course, perched at the head of the table like Yertle the Turtle.

I took the spot between Gerald and Manuel without even thinking. It wasn't until I caught Gerald in my peripheral vision that I realized that I'd actually chosen a seat next to him. It slowly dawned on me that being that close to him didn't bug me like it used to, and I wondered when that change had started to happen.

Dr. Tom Lang, the third pathologist at the lab, hurried into the room, interrupting my thoughts.

"Apologies," he said sheepishly to no one in particular and took the last empty chair.

Fran cleared her throat and leaned her elbows on the table. "I have no updates for this week. Shall we go around and hear from each department?"

It wasn't a question.

Gerald lifted his hand slightly. "I'll start," and then he continued without waiting for a reply. "I'm sure you are all aware of the outbreak of *Salmonella enteritica* in Best Bud's Bacon Bites." He paused and scanned the people around the table, seeking a reaction.

Fran picked at a hangnail. A slight crinkle sounded as Tom fidgeted with a piece of paper. Zoe leaned over and whispered to Sandy. Manual's chair creaked as he shifted uncomfortably.

Gerald's eyes bounced around the table, and his lips drew into a thin line.

Everyone was being incredibly rude, and to my surprise, I found myself irritated by my coworkers.

I caught Gerald's eye. "Yeah," I replied, trying to throw him a bone. "That's the outbreak you brought to our attention last week. Very unusual presentation for salmonellosis. Any updates?"

An expression crossed his features so quickly I almost missed it. There was a hint of relief in it. Like I'd saved him from something.

His eyes softened.

He turned back to the group and continued, "After consuming the contaminated treats, patients rapidly develop septicemia and die. It's difficult to calculate a mortality rate at this stage of the outbreak, but this strain appears to be particularly aggressive and often presents without the typical clinical signs of diarrhea."

"No GI signs?" Tom asked, just as surprised as the rest of us had been when Gerald had shared that nugget on Monday.

"Correct," Gerald replied, chest puffing up a bit. "And no intestinal lesions have been reported on necropsy, either. The pattern of infection resembles a subset of non-typhoidal *Salmonella* infections in people. In those cases, they develop septicemia without prior evidence of gastrointestinal signs. They present with lethargy, anemia, and high fevers."

Gerald paused for effect and looked around the table. "We've had four confirmed cases in the microbiology lab in the last seven days."

My eyebrows shot up.

In the world of outbreaks, it was unusual to have four fully confirmed cases come into a single lab in under a week. The affected dogs had to meet strict case-inclusion criteria, and the strain of bacteria that was isolated had to be a genetic match to the organism associated with the outbreak. There were a lot of hoops to jump through for a case to be defined as "confirmed." Further, the cases that came into our lab only represented a fraction of what was happening out in the real world. The actual number of cases in the region would be exponentially higher than the four cases that had passed through our doors.

"The first case was Dr. Smith's, 43518162," Gerald continued.

My back stiffened with surprise, and I caught Zoe's eye across the table. She gave me a slight nod.

We'd all rolled our eyes at him during lunch on Monday, but Gerald had been right all along. I couldn't help but feel a burgeoning respect for the guy.

"We isolated the organism from the feces in Dr. Smith's case," Gerald pressed on. "In the other three cases, we isolated the organisms from the blood. All three dogs subsequently died."

Tom let out a low whistle.

Gerald tipped his chin slightly. "The affected batches of Best Bud's Bacon Bites have been recalled, but the information has not been adequately disseminated to the public. Therefore, I expect that we will continue to receive samples for at least one to two weeks."

"Has the information been pushed out to vet clinics?" Sandy asked.

Gerald nodded. "It is my understanding that the information has been communicated via the listserv."

"Veterinarians are busy. I suspect many of them haven't even seen the email," Zoe said with a worried frown. "The vet was shocked when I sent him the results from my case."

"Perhaps we should contact the media," Fran said, pursing her lips. I could only imagine she was weighing the cost-benefit ratio as it related to her own position.

Gerald flashed a smile, and I couldn't help but think he looked like the Cheshire cat. "I'll speak with Channel 4 News again."

Fran made a single, slight nod. "Yes. Please do that. You did an exceptional job when you had to stand in for Josie on the legal case."

Zoe's eyes jumped to me, and I could tell she was angry on my behalf at Fran's slight jab. I shook my head slightly, hoping no one else would notice. It wasn't worth the fight. Plus, I'd been relieved to have someone talk to the press in my stead, and Gerald had even done a good job.

"Speaking of which, where do we stand on the police dog?" Fran asked sharply.

I instantly regretted not sharing the toxicology results with her yesterday. Things had been so hectic, I'd entirely forgotten, and now, I'd pay the price. My eyes bounced to Sandy and back to Fran. Sandy looked unfazed, and I knew she'd have my back if Fran decided to jump in my shit.

I tried to appear relaxed and put on a mask of cool indifference. "We've just about wrapped it up," I answered.

Gerald stiffened and turned to look at me.

Fran's eyebrows jumped up. "Oh, have you now?" Her words were like dark clouds, threatening a tornado.

I leaned forward on the table and met her glare. "Yes," I replied firmly. "The dog died from a cocaine overdose."

A surprised hush fell across the table.

"We detected high levels of cocaine in the blood—four times the lethal dose," I pressed on. "We think he died from an acute overdose and suspect he was exposed within fifteen to twenty minutes before he died. He was working on a shipment before he died, but they found meth—not cocaine—stashed in the shipping containers. I'm still trying to determine the route of exposure. We sent the stomach contents off to A&M yesterday afternoon to see if he ingested it. I'm hoping to get the results back tomorrow."

"You think someone fed him cocaine?" Tom asked neutrally.

I shrugged. "I'm not sure. There are reports of dogs being exposed to cocaine through inhalation when working, but again, the police are holding firm that it was a meth bust. I guess it could've been injected, but from what I understand, Tohbi was uncomfortable around anyone but his handler. All I can think of is someone spiked some food. We've seen that more than once."

Sandy nodded. "Not often, but every once in a while, someone does put a bit of rat bait in some burger and tosses it over the fence."

A horrified look folded Zoe's eyebrows into creases, and her lips drew down into a frown. "So it *was* a murder, then."

Bile tricked up my esophagus. "I don't want to speculate too much. The cops will figure that part out. But it's difficult to imagine a situation in which Tohbi was exposed to that much cocaine accidentally."

Silence spread across the table.

Fran's eyes looked panicky. "You'll need to testify. In court."

I tried not to sigh. "Yes, that's very likely."

As veterinary pathologists, we were rarely called into court. Most pathologists could go their whole career and never have to appear. Animal cases weren't prosecuted like human deaths. But Tohbi was a police officer who died while on duty and would be treated as a person in the eyes of the law. Unless whoever did this pleaded guilty, I didn't see any way that I could avoid court.

Moving halfway across the world might not be a bad idea after all, I snarked to myself.

"I have every faith in Josie," Sandy announced. "She's been very thorough in this case, and all of the procedures have been followed to the T, including chain-of-custody. I suggest we move on to other topics." And with that, Sandy effectively shifted the Eye of Sauron away from me, and I was able to shrink back into the wallpaper as the meeting flowed around me.

I sulked in my seat. Fran had fanned the flames, and my mind was stuck in a loop over the Tohbi case. There wasn't much else I could do. The only thing pending was the damn stomach contents, and it wasn't up to me to figure out how the cocaine entered his system. But the not-knowing slowly chewed away at me.

I tuned out the rest of the meeting and shuffled back to my office. I flopped in my chair and checked the time. There were almost three hours left in the day, and I felt like a part of my soul would die if I had to spend another minute at my desk. I felt fidgety and needed to escape. I wanted to be in my garden, smelling the jasmine and hearing the chatter of the birds. Deciding to cut out early, I packed my things and headed out, leaving a message with Carol and James to give me a call if anything important came up.

The sound of cicadas greeted me as I swung the door open and stepped out of the lab. The sky was a clear blue, but the air teetered on the edge of uncomfortably hot, and the humidity was high. As soon as my ass hit the driver's seat, I started the car and blasted the AC. Before I could shift my car into gear, my cell started ringing from my purse. I dug it out, fully intending to silence it until I saw it was Aunty.

"Hey, Aunty," I answered. "Everything okay?"

"Josie," she started.

That single word was loaded with anguish, and the world came crashing down around me.

CHAPTER
TWENTY-FOUR

The hum of the car's air conditioner filled the silence. My breath caught in my throat as I waited for Aunty to speak.

"Josie," she repeated. "Chula has cancer."

"No," I whispered, unable to accept what she was saying.

Even though I was a vet and I saw cancer day in and day out. Even though I was practical, and it was my job to cut up dead things. Even though I'd lost my fair share of family members. I simply could *not* accept that Chula had cancer. She couldn't leave us. Not now. Not in this way.

"Josie, sweety," Aunty said a third time.

My mind raced. Maybe it was something easy. Something treatable. Maybe it wasn't as bad as Aunty thought. Maybe the heart-wrenching sorrow in her voice was misplaced.

"What kind? What kind of cancer is it?" I asked hurriedly, fighting tears.

"Lymphoma," Aunty answered.

I felt a glimmer of hope. With chemotherapy, remission rates were as high as eighty percent in dogs with lymphoma. There was a chance that Chula's cancer would respond to treatment; it all hinged on what type of lymphoma she had. My mind spun.

"Did Dr. Jones tell you anything else? Like what kind of lymphoma it is?"

"The bad kind," Aunty replied.

What does that even mean? My heart tumbled back down to my shoes.

A low anger started to burn, built on logs of fear, resentment, and frustration. I needed more information. I needed all of the cards on the table so I could figure out what the fuck was going to happen. I had to know how long Chula would be with us.

"Aunty, what's the clinic number? I'd like to call Dr. Jones, if that's okay with you."

I shifted my phone to my shoulder and fished in my purse for a pen and paper. "I'm ready," I said, pen in hand.

Aunty read me the phone number.

"I'll call him right now," I said with authority.

And then it hit me. I was moving so fast, I hadn't even thought about how Aunty was handling the news. I was behaving like a soulless robot.

I took a deep breath. Closing my eyes, I leaned my head back on the seat. "How are you managing, Aunty? Do you want me to come down there?"

"You don't need to come down," Aunty said. She sounded dejected, but I knew she meant it. "I'll be fine. Chula and I are going to sit out on the porch and eat ice cream."

If I closed my eyes, I could see them enjoying the last bit of sun before it tipped to dusk and the mosquitoes came out. Chickens out in the yard. The scent of lavender in the air. Aunty spoon-feeding Chula ice cream.

A deep ache bloomed in my heart, and I wanted to be with them so badly that it hurt.

"I'm taking the rest of the week off," Aunty said. "I'll come up for Tessa's graduation Saturday. But I'll be spending the rest of the time with Chula."

"Let me call Dr. Jones. It may not be as bad as you think." The words sounded flat, and we both heard it.

"Okay, sweety," she answered, and I couldn't help but feel like she was indulging me in a lost cause.

"I love you, Aunty," I said, my heart breaking.

"Love you, too."

We said our goodbyes, and she ended the call.

The hand that held my cell dropped to my lap. Tears pressed in.

Get your fucking shit together, Josie.

I closed my eyes again, taking deep breaths and fighting the tightness in my chest. After halting the advancing tears, my eyes flicked back open.

The last thing I wanted to do was to make this call from my parked car, AC running, and in front of the lab. But I didn't want the clinic to close before I had a chance to connect with them either.

Resigned, I dialed the number Aunty had given me.

"Hello. Oak Hills Animal Hospital. This is Julie. How may I help you?" a feminine voice drawled in a thick accent.

"Hello, my name is Josie Harjo. I'm a relative of Molly Mead. I'm calling about Chula Mead. I know it's a long shot, but is Dr. Jones available?"

"Just one moment, ma'am. I'll go check," she replied with the usual pleasant cheer that most vet receptionists managed to maintain despite the endless parade of clients.

Hold music drifted through the earpiece, with occasional pauses to espouse the value of heartworm prevention and regular dental cleaning.

After what felt like forever, there was a *click,* and a gravely masculine voice answered, "Hello, this is Dr. Jones. Is this Chula's family?"

My shoulders sagged with relief at hearing his voice. I thought we'd be playing phone tag for the next day or so. "Hello, yes, this is Josie Harjo. I'm a relative of Molly Mead. I'm a pathologist at the diagnostic lab."

I was always uncomfortable throwing that latter piece of intel around. He might already know I was a veterinarian, but if not, it was always best to give him a heads-up. That way, we could talk about the nitty-gritty details of the case in medical terms.

"Sorry we have to meet like this," he said, echoing the words I often used when interviewing clients.

I bit my lip trying to fight the tears. "Thanks for taking my call," I managed. "I'm sure you're busy."

"Yes, ma'am," he said. "It's foxtail season."

"We get our fair share of those on the necropsy floor. They can get pretty nasty," I replied, the polite part of me unable to skip the idle chit chat.

"Yes, indeed. But I know you're calling about Chula, not foxtails," he said, not unkindly, mercifully cutting the how-do-you-dos short. "How may I help you?"

"Would you run me through the test results? Molly shared the high level, but...." I drifted off, figuring he could fill in the blanks.

"Well, let's see here," he said, and a keyboard clacked in the background. "Mild regenerative anemia and thrombocytopenia. Path review confirmed there were no parasites. Hypoproteinemia—both albumin and globulin. ALP and ALT were through the roof. Bilirubin was up as well." He paused and cleared his throat. "On ultrasound, there was hepatosplenomegaly. No enlarged lymph nodes."

"Adrenals were normal, I take it?" I interrupted, unwilling to let go of the sliver of hope that it was Cushing's disease.

"Yes, ma'am," he replied. "The GI tract and kidneys looked normal, too. We did an FNA on the liver and spleen and got the results back this afternoon. Small cell lymphoma in both."

Everything went numb.

"I've ordered ICC on the aspirates. But I suspect it'll be a T-cell."

Fuck.

"I'm so sorry," he repeated.

He didn't need to say anything else. I knew how all of those pieces fit together: Chula had hepatosplenic T-cell lymphoma. It was the shittiest of pulls from the lymphoma lottery and not treatable. Most dogs died within a week of diagnosis.

Tears streamed down my cheeks. Trying to hide it from my voice, I said, "Thank you, Dr. Jones. I guess it's lots of love and steak for Chula from here on out."

"I gave Molly the number of an at-home euthanasia service if things get bad," he said, voice laced with sympathy. "Chula didn't seem to be in any pain when I saw her. But if she starts looking uncomfortable, you give us a jingle, and we'll get her some pain meds to make her feel better."

"Thanks," I replied, my brain trying to catch up and wade through the agony.

Chula. The thought echoed in my mind, low and painful.

I couldn't remember saying goodbye or hanging up, but I must have, since I was holding a locked phone when I rose from the fog of despair. I hoped I'd been polite about it. I stared at the phone in my hands, air conditioning humming through the vents in my car.

A knock sounded on my window.

Startled, I looked up to see Gerald. I was so wrung out that the only response I could muster was pressing the button to roll the window down.

He eyed me shrewdly, face unreadable. "Are you okay?"

I nodded, still in shock over Chula and unable to say a word.

"Do you need a ride home?" he offered all business-like.

I shook my head.

He pressed his lips together. "Fine," he said curtly. He whipped back around and stomped into the lab.

Unable to process what the fuck just happened, I rolled my window up, buckled my seat belt, and fled home.

***

Fifteen minutes later, I stood just inside my house, keys still clutched in my hand, staring off into space. Yersi swirled around my legs, begging for dinner even though I was home early.

I threw down my keys. They skittered across the entryway table and clanged to the floor. It barely registered. I pulled my phone out of my purse and tossed my purse on the floor.

Feeling numb, I went through the motions of feeding Yersi and taking care of the chickens. With the chores done, I flopped down in a patio chair beneath the pergola. I'd left the back door cracked open so Yersi could join me once he finished his meal.

The sky was bright blue and twinkled like a sapphire. Bees bobbed around the late spring flowers. The buzzing song of the cicadas was interrupted by the occasional chirp of a squirrel as they chased each other through the trees. A hummingbird buzzed up to me, gave me an appraising look, and zoomed over to the bell-shaped, magenta flowers of the penstemon. Yersi sauntered out and slumped down on his side in the sun, tail swishing.

All the life swirling around me was almost too much. The tears started again. I let them flow, knowing that they wouldn't be the last.

Chula.

I didn't know how much time we had left with her. But I knew that the time we did have would be rough. I wouldn't be throwing a ball for her or walking with her down the path by the creek. I'd be watching her body slowly give up, and the thought of it all was fucking agony.

And there was Aunty. From our call earlier, I suspected she'd made it through the denial phase a hell of a lot faster than I had. But Chula was her buddy. They'd been together for so long, I couldn't imagine Aunty without Chula by her side.

Then, it hit me that Tessa still didn't know. My chest grew tight. I sent her a quick text, asking if she was available for a call. I figured she'd be busy with work this time of day, but I also knew she'd want to know as soon as I did.

Tessa had only been part of our found family for just under a year, but she loved Chula like she was her own. Along with the rest of us, Chula had been there to help Tessa through her rough patch. Even when Yersi had been a dick, Chula had seen through Tessa's pain and sadness to love her for the woman she was.

My phone started ringing within a minute. Tessa's name lit up the screen.

"Hey," I answered solemnly.

"Is it Chula?" Tessa asked, unable to hide the worry in her voice.

"Yeah. Hepatosplenic lymphoma," I said, cutting to the chase. Tessa would want to know all of the details later, but I wasn't going to pussyfoot around the hard news.

She sucked in a clipped breath. "Oh no."

I wanted to give her a hug. Hell, I wanted *her* to give *me* a hug. This was some tough shit to carry alone.

"ICC is pending, but…." I paused to take a deep breath, trying to loosen the tightness in my chest. "It's a small-cell, there's hepatosplenomegaly, and they didn't find any enlarged lymph nodes on ultrasound."

"Oh no," she repeated. This time, the words were drawn out and grave.

The tears started up again, and streams trickled down my cheeks. I knew I wouldn't be able to hide it.

"Chula," Tessa barely whispered, still processing it all.

"She's back at home with Aunty. It's palliative care at this point." After a beat, I added, "Dr. Jones gave Aunty the number of an at-home euthanasia service."

"I need to see her," Tessa said, her own tears edging into her voice.

As soon as she said it, I realized how right she was. I'd been so caught up in processing everything, I hadn't even started to think about next steps.

"Want to go together?" I offered. This was one of those things that was easier to tackle with a friend.

"Yes," she said. "When?"

"Umm," I stalled, trying to give my head a moment to catch up with everything.

The Tohbi case wasn't completely wrapped up, and the results of the stomach contents were expected tomorrow. I wasn't sure I could take Thursday off. Fran didn't consider ill animals a "family emergency." But I was fairly certain I could get away with taking Friday off, especially with graduation on Saturday.

Hopefully, Chula can make it to Friday.

"Do you think you can get Friday off?" I asked.

"Yes. I'm certain of it. Charlie will understand," she answered.

I knew she was right; Charlie Anderson was just one of those guys, a keeper if there ever was one. For the millionth time, I thanked the universe that Tessa had landed a job with him.

I wiped the tears away, grateful to have a plan, some way to stay distracted. "Okay. Want to come over at nine, and I'll drive us down? I'll text Aunty to make sure it's okay, but I know she'll say yes."

"Sure," Tessa said.

We said our goodbyes. I sent Aunty a text, asking if we could come on Friday. She sent back a positive reply followed by three hearts in a row.

When all was said and done, the only thing left to do was to lay my head on my arms and lean into a good, solid cry.

CHAPTER

TWENTY-FIVE

I didn't have any nightmares that night. Even though I'd slept a full eight hours, I still woke up emotionally tired. The type of tired where my body felt okay, but my mind wanted to check out for another four to five hours.

But checking out wasn't an option.

As soon as the wailing ruler of Casa Harjo had his face buried in breakfast, I texted Aunty.

How is Chula?

The ellipses bounced for a few seconds. I knew Aunty would be up, but I was still grateful she had been by her phone. While I hadn't dreamed of the white dog last night, my sleep had been broken, and all I could think about was Chula.

She's about the same. Maybe a little weaker.

Is she in any pain?

I don't think so. Just tired.

I'm going to stay home with her today.

I hearted her text.

> Is there anything I can do?

No, thank you. We're good.

> OK. Text if you need anything. See you tomorrow.

Love you.

> Love you too.

My heart ached with sorrow, and tears threatened my already puffy eyes. Flashes of Chula, one brown ear perked up straight, and the other flopping down to the side, filled my mind. I could practically hear her tail thumping on the wooden deck of Aunty's porch and feel her little, welcoming kisses on my hands.

I worried about Aunty, too. I couldn't imagine how she was feeling. It seemed like Chula had always been there. Dogs come and go, but Chula had made her mark on all of us. The thought of going to Aunty's and finding her all alone in that little farmhouse was unthinkable.

Even though I didn't feel like eating, I went through the motions of pulling some breakfast out of the fridge. All I could be bothered to put together was yogurt and toast.

Yersi must've sensed my distress. He took up his post on the chair at the counter and watched me. Yellow eyes traced my path as I moved around the kitchen. His ears were perked.

"It's okay, bud," I said softly, giving him a gentle scratch behind his ears.

He closed his eyes and purred quietly.

As I packed my lunch, my phone binged. I felt a jolt of concern and swooped it off the counter. It was from Armand.

Good morning.

I felt a thread of relief that it wasn't Aunty, and it dawned on me that I would be on pins and needles until I could get down there to be with her and Chula. This was immediately followed by a weird feeling of guilt that I hadn't updated Armand on the situation. Was I just so caught up in all of the craziness that I forgot?

Slowly, I realized that I'd been avoiding him. I dreaded the impending conversation about what came next between us. Part of me thought that, by putting the conversation off, I could just keep skipping along like our relationship wasn't about to turn into a dumpster fire.

All of the thoughts slammed through my mind, one after another, all because of a simple "good morning" text. I tried out a dozen responses before landing on a bland one.

Good morning.

Feeling better?

How do I even answer that? Tears threatened again.

I hated that about myself. Whenever anyone showed even the slightest hint of sympathy or care, it broke me. It had always been hard to keep my emotions bottled up. If I needed to power through something, I had to stay tough and shuck off any attempts to make me feel better, or else I'd turn into a sniveling mess. I knew in my heart that Armand cared about me, and I loved him back. It was just hard being vulnerable around anyone, especially when it came to losing a family member.

After a deep breath, I decided to be direct and truthful. That was who I was down at my core, and if I fell into a sobbing mess on the floor, so be it. I sent my reply.

> It's messy. Chula is really sick. I'm not sure she'll make it through the week.

My phone went dark before he responded, and I knew I'd probably shocked him. He'd seen Chula on Sunday, so it wasn't a surprise she was under the weather. But I was pretty sure he'd thought she'd be fine in a couple of days.

I held my phone, waiting.

> Is there anything I can do to help? Want me to come over?

It wasn't the response I'd expected, and slow tears started leaking down my cheeks. I didn't know what I thought he would text back—maybe questions about what had happened, declarations that it couldn't possibly be true, fist waving at the universe, or even worse, the "I'm so sorry" comments that always felt flat and hollow. His reply had been absolutely perfect, and that was what made it all the more difficult to read. How could I possibly let this wonderful, considerate man go?

Fuck.

I put my phone down and rubbed my eyes with my palms. There was too much going on, and I felt completely and totally overwhelmed.

Yersi stepped across the chairs lined up on the counter and pushed his way onto my lap with a concerned *merf*. I rested my arms on the counter and leaned back to make space for him. A low purr started up as he curled into a ball.

I scratched him under the chin, a smile tipping through my tear-streaked face. I took a deep breath and picked my phone back up.

The ellipses bounced, stopped, and then started bouncing again. I knew he was worried and trying to figure out the best way to be there for me. I didn't blame him for being unsure; even I wasn't really sure what I wanted from him.

And once again, his reply was absolutely, positively perfect. The tears started again, and I rested my head on my arms, forming a small cave over the purring Yersi.

***

Cold compresses hadn't done shit, and my eyes still looked puffy and red when I rolled into the lab. I made a beeline to my office, determined to bury myself in work and tie up the rest of my cases before the end of the day. I closed the door behind me, something I didn't usually do, hoping to dissuade anyone looking for an idle chit-chat.

About an hour into the morning, there was a knock at my door.

I leaned back from my scope, rubbing my eyes. "Come in."

Sandy peeked her head around the door. "Got a minute?"

My heart lurched in anticipation. I waved her in, chewing on my cheek.

She took the seat across the desk, and studied me. Concern flashed briefly across her face before she tucked it politely away. She rested one hand on top of the other on her loosely crossed legs and sat back.

"The results are back on the stomach contents," she announced. "Positive for cocaine, and quite a hefty amount, too."

I slumped back in my chair. "Holy shit," I blurted.

"Yeah. Holy shit," she replied and folded her lips into a tight line.

"That...that doesn't just accidentally happen. Someone did this to him," I said, the full horror of it slowly dawning on me.

Sandy raised her hands slightly, palms facing up, and tilted her chin to the side. If there ever was a "there it is" gesture, then that was it. Someone had laced the sausage with cocaine and fed it to Tohbi. Someone had meant to kill him.

"I...wow," I fumbled. "This is...huge."

"Yep," she said with a single tight nod.

"Fuck," I whispered, throwing every ounce of courtesy out the window.

Sandy replied with another flat, "Yep."

My mind had finally caught up and shifted into action mode. "I'll let Fran know first. Then, I'll call the detective." My eyes snapped up. "Have the results been entered?"

She nodded. "Yes, but I haven't released them yet. This is gonna require some delicate orchestration."

Boy, did she have that right.

"Okay, let me tell Fran. Then, I'll call Chuck. Then, you can release your results, and I'll release the final report. Does that work?"

She nodded.

My stomach clenched, and I had to ask, "Do you think we'll have to go to court on this one?"

If the case went to trial, there was a damn good chance I'd get called to the stand to talk about the necropsy results. Sandy and whoever the poor sod was who ran the tests at A&M might very well join me. Veterinary pathologists weren't trained to be witnesses. My experience with this type of shit was limited to watching the occasional true crime documentary on Netflix, and I was starting to panic. I didn't want to sit there while some asshole questioned my ability or nitpicked the test results in an attempt to free a guilty party.

Sandy let out a heavy sigh and took a moment to ponder the question.

"I'm not sure," she eventually replied, and I respected her for telling the truth. "But either way, the work is solid," she added. "It's always tough up on the stand. But the data is the data. And we did a good job on this case."

I could tell she wanted to reach across the desk and give my hand a pat. Instead, she gave me a slight, reassuring smile, for which I was grateful. A hand pat might've pushed me over the edge, turning me into a sobbing mess.

"We've got this," she said. She stood and pushed the chair in. "Anything I can do to help other than releasing the results when the time is right?"

I smiled weakly and shook my head. "No. Thanks for the offer, though." This was my shit to sort out; it was the hand I was dealt. And I was going to suck it up and work with what I'd been given.

I stood to follow Sandy out. We parted ways in the hallway. I headed toward Fran's office, dreading every step.

Fran's office door stood open, and she was tucked into her desk, focused on her computer. I wasn't sure if I was happy to find her there so I could get this god-awful conversation over with or if I was glum that I couldn't put it off for a bit longer.

I knocked on the doorjamb and said, "Good morning, Fran."

She looked up and scowled. "Yes, Dr. Harjo?"

"I have an update on the Tohbi case. Do you have a minute?" I hated the polite, slightly upward inflection of my tone.

She pursed her lips and gestured absently to the seat across from her desk.

The chair pinched my ass as I sat down. I shifted my weight and crossed my legs, trying to get comfortable, and gave up within a millisecond. There was no way I'd ever find any comfort in the monster's den.

An annoyed look twisted her lips into a frown. "Yes? What is it already?"

I bit back a snarky retort.

Channeling my inner cool robot, I rattled off the facts. "It's about the police dog. The stomach contents were positive for cocaine. I strongly suspect that someone intentionally fed him sausage laced with the drug, and he died of an overdose within thirty minutes of eating it."

Her eyebrows jumped up in shock, and her frown disappeared.

I pressed on before she could say something stupid or irritating. "I wanted to let you know first. I'm going to call the detective next and give him a verbal. Once that is done, Sandy will release the toxicology results, and I will release the final report."

It was a statement, and I resisted the urge to add a question at the end, some way of asking if I was going about things the right way. The last thing I needed was Fran micromanaging this shit, and a question would only open that door for her.

She was probably still in shock over the bomb I'd dropped in the room, and all she managed was a "Yes, yes. You do that."

Before she could say anything else, I stood and said, "I'll get on it, then."

I turned and left her office without another word. I knew it was probably a bit rude, and it might bite me later after she had a moment to process everything, but at this point, I could give two fucks. Aunty's dog was dying, I was wrapped up in the murder of a police officer, and my boyfriend, whom I was desperately in love with, was leaving the country in less than a month.

I walked back to my office with purpose and was grateful that I didn't stumble across anyone on the way. I flopped into my chair and wiggled my mouse to wake my computer. The desk phone stared at me like a coiled snake. I didn't want to make this call, but I knew I had to.

I picked up the phone and punched in the numbers with a pen. As the phone rang, I twirled the pen nervously across my fingers.

Chuck answered, as he always seemed to, with a "Detective Pollard, here."

"Hello, Detective Pollard," I replied, unable to drop the honorifics. "This is Dr. Josie Harjo. I have an update for you."

"Glad to hear from you. What've you got?" he said, sounding a tad eager.

I licked my lips. "The stomach contents were positive for cocaine," I said matter-of-factly.

This was met with silence.

"My report will say that the cause of death was a cocaine overdose," I pressed on. "It'll include the positive results for blood and stomach contents. I can't come right out and say in writing that he was poisoned, because I have no way to prove intent. But I strongly suspect that someone laced sausage with cocaine and fed it to him. Or they stashed it somewhere for him to find."

A flat "Huh" was Chuck's only response.

"Dr. Bishop will finalize the toxicology results, and they should be headed your way shortly. I'll also be finalizing the pathology report within the next half an hour or so."

"Thank you for getting answers so fast," Chuck said. "I was trying to work out how he got access to enough cocaine to OD. Austin said there was no way anyone could get close enough to him to stick a needle in him. Offering a nice, tasty sausage makes sense."

"Did Austin notice him pick anything up while working the shipment? Did you see anything on the security camera footage?"

I knew it wasn't my place to ask, but I couldn't help but wonder how everything fit together.

Chuck was nice enough to answer and share what he could. "I've got someone going back through the video clips now. It'll help knowing exactly what we're looking for."

I nodded even though he couldn't see me. "Let me know if there is anything else you need from me."

"Just that final report," he said, not unkindly.

"Yes, sir," I answered reflexively.

"Oh, by the way," he said, tone shifting. "I gave Molly a call. It was nice talking with her. We're going to have lunch next week. Thanks for passing along the phone number."

My heart broke into a hundred pieces.

With everything happening with Chula, I knew Aunty was a mess. Reuniting with a long-lost high school friend was the furthest thing from her mind. I also wondered how she'd been able to hold a conversation with Chuck without crying over Chula. I'd certainly been walking a fine line all morning.

Maybe it'll be a distraction. Bring her some comfort, I thought.

I knew he was waiting for a reply, so I offered a simple "You're welcome. Glad to connect you two."

We said our goodbyes.

I hung up the phone and stared at it, feeling dazed.

After coordinating with Sandy to finalize our reports, time slowed to a crawl. Lunch came and went. I ate at my desk, unable to face the team despite the allure of laughs and treats. After lunch, there was a knock on the door.

"Come in," I called out dejectedly. I didn't want anyone to come in, but I didn't really have a choice.

Dustin slipped through the door, holding a couple of cookies on a napkin. "You doin' alright, Doc? Missed you at lunch." He laid the cookies on my table and stuffed his hands in his pockets.

I couldn't help but feel a surge of friendly affection for him. Dustin was a gruff dude. He'd seen some dark shit when he was a kid and now cleaned up stinky animal parts for a living. Here he was, one of my best friends, checking up on me, bringing me treats to cheer me up.

"I'm doing okay," I said, a part of me lying and another part of me meaning it. I'd get through this. I'd seen worse shit. It was just hard with everything coming all at once.

"Deep breaths. Little steps. Eyes on the prize and all that," I added.

His mustache twitched up in a slight smile as he studied me. "This too shall pass."

I nodded sadly. "Yep."

He didn't know the full extent of the shit I shouldered. But he knew I'd share when I was ready, and he was a good enough friend not to push it.

"Welp," he said, throwing a thumb over his shoulder. "You know where I'll be."

I gave another small nod, and my lips tipped in a small smile of appreciation.

With his hands stuffed in his pockets, he slipped back through the door.

I sat lamely for a good fifteen to twenty minutes, eyes shifting across the things in my office. The scope. The remaining cardboard flats filled with slides.

The cookies.

They were chocolate chews. The faint dusting of powdered sugar coated the spaces between the dark cracks. I picked one up, took a small bite, and paused to savor the deep chocolate flavor.

A deep breath in, and I started to refocus.

I laid the nibbled cookie on the napkin and swallowed. My mind was like TV static, and I knew I'd reached maximum capacity. I just needed to plow through, step by slow step. Life would keep grinding on. I knew it was going to be cloudy and gray for a while, but the sun would shine soon enough. I just needed to get there.

Deciding to make decaf mint tea to go with the rest of the cookies, I grabbed my mug and headed to the breakroom. I was distracted and had tuned out the normal hustle and bustle. Because of that, I'd completely missed the Gerald-ambush waiting for me as I rounded the corner on my way back.

"Dr. Harjo!" he called from his office as I passed his open door.

My shoulders tensed, and I flinched, almost spilling my tea. I stopped dead in my tracks, looking into his office.

He rose from his desk and came to the door. He looked immaculate as usual: button-up shirt and slacks clearly pressed. His hair was slicked back without a single strand daring to slip out of place. His sharp blue eyes pierced me.

"Yes, Gerald?" I said, trying not to cringe.

I had zero bandwidth to deal with Gerald today, even this new version of him that had emerged on the other side of the tiger drama.

A brief hint of worry crossed his features that he quickly tucked away.

"I saw the results on case 43518087. There was cocaine in the stomach contents," he said.

His statement was awkward, and I wasn't really sure how to respond, so I just said, "Yep."

He shifted uncomfortably, which was so unlike Gerald that I had to hide the flicker of surprise. "It is an interesting case," he continued. "Your investigation was superlative. Well done."

My jaw dropped. My cup of tea almost joined it.

Gerald had never given me a direct compliment. Ever. And the fact that it was something related to work was mind-blowing. I was stunned into silence.

His eyes narrowed, and I could only guess that he thought I was mocking him.

I quickly recovered, flashed a weak smile, and said, "It takes a village."

His shoulders relaxed slightly, even though a small thread of tension still coiled between us. He looked down at his feet and stood there uncomfortably.

Gerald had always been exceedingly socially awkward and sometimes downright nasty. I wasn't sure what had him paralyzed other than his own concern about fucking the conversation up.

"And Gerald..." I started, my words catching in my throat.

He looked up. A flash of worry furrowed his eyebrows for a millisecond before he regained control and smoothed his features out.

"Thanks for checking on me yesterday in the parking lot. I didn't mean to be rude. I just wanted to be alone."

A million half-expressions flittered across his face like he was trying on different features to find the right one. He landed on a small, worried smile, nodded his head once, and turned back into his office.

I stood there a moment in shock, trying to process what had just happened. Gerald had just *smiled* at me. It wasn't a leer. It wasn't smug. It wasn't the nasty smile of a villain. It was the smile of one human being who was worried about another human being and was trying to offer some reassurance.

My eyes followed him as he sat back at his desk, and I felt a thread of hope for our resident work troll. Maybe a Shrek-like, fairytale ending waited for him after all.

CHAPTER

TWENTY-SIX

Back at home, I nestled on the couch with Yersi curled in my lap, hoping the rest of the day would pass uneventfully. But the universe wasn't having any of that. There were two more cards left to play, and they hit one right after the other. The first was a text from Aunty that came in around six.

> Dr. Jones said that Chula's cancer is seedy three positive. What is that? Is that bad?

When I read the text, my heart clenched. As if all of the other bits of clinical information hadn't already sealed Chula's fate, that CD3-positive result was the nail in the coffin. It confirmed that Chula had hepatosplenic T-cell lymphoma. Most patients with that diagnosis didn't live more than a week.

My mind raced, trying to figure out the best way to tell Aunty. I knew it wasn't something that should be texted. I hit the call button.

"Hello, sweety," Aunty answered. Her voice was resigned, as if she already knew what I was going to say.

"Hello, Aunty," I said sadly. "Yeah. It's bad. CD3 positive means that it's a T-cell lymphoma. Chula has a type of cancer that isn't responsive to chemotherapy."

Aunty sighed deeply. "Oh, my dear, sweet Chula," she said, her voice almost a whisper. "Part of me didn't want to believe it was that bad, but I guess I should've known when Dr. Jones gave me the number for the euthanasia service."

A deep, brooding silence stretched between us.

"How's she doing today?" I asked. We were near the end, but I didn't know exactly how much longer we had.

"She's sleeping next to me," Aunty replied, her voice thick with tears. "She ate a few bites of bacon, but I think she did it to make me happy."

"You're doing right by her," I said, heartbroken. "Just be there for her. Make her comfortable. Give her lots of love."

"Yes," she replied.

"Tessa and I will be there tomorrow," I said. "We can all sit out on the porch together. Give her lots of love and attention."

"That would be nice," Aunty said.

"Want us to bring anything?" I offered.

"Just yourselves," she replied. After a beat, she added, "I think I'm going to go now, if that's okay."

"Of course, Aunty," I replied, and the tears pressed in. "Give Chula some scratches for me?"

"I will," she said. "Love you, sweety."

"Love you, too," I replied. I didn't feel ready to end the call, but I knew Aunty wanted some space.

After we hung up, a wave of deep, heart-wrenching sadness washed over me.

Yersi rolled over slightly, showing me his chin. A low purr rumbled from his chest when I scratched it. Even though he could be a huge pain in the ass sometimes, his relaxed purr anchored me, and I brushed the tears away.

A *bing* from my phone roused me, and the second ball dropped. It was a message from Zoe; she'd sent another Channel 4 News clip.

I chewed my cheek, unsure if I even wanted to watch it. I felt wrung out and wasn't confident I had enough emotional strength left to shoulder anything else. Another part of me knew that if I didn't watch it, curiosity would slowly eat at me.

I clicked the link.

Darryl's plastic, makeup-slathered face filled the screen. "Darryl Castor from Channel 4 News here with an update on the murdered police dog. Today, officials with the Oklahoma City Police Department announced the arrest of a suspect."

My breath caught.

The scene shifted to a clip with a bunch of men in suits in front of a podium. The police department logo blazed in the background. The name of the police chief flashed on the screen as a man stepped up to a cluster of microphones.

"At three forty-five today, we arrested a suspect in connection with the death of canine police officer, Ofi' Tohbi Ishto'. After reviewing footage, we believe that the suspect fed Tohbi meat laced with cocaine through the window of the police vehicle."

When he paused, a flurry of questions erupted from reporters. He held up his hand to quiet them and continued. "The suspect was an airport employee. Based on information obtained during questioning, we believe the suspect was paid to commit the murder as part of an alleged hit by the drug cartel."

Holy fuck.

The police chief made eye contact with the different cameras and said, "Ofi' Tohbi Ishto' was an outstanding canine officer, assisting with seizures of over five tons of illegal drugs during his tenure. As you can imagine...."

At that point, I tuned out, heart pounding in my chest.

A hit. Tohbi was killed in a hit.

After the shock of it all had flowed away, I felt completely and totally exhausted. The last piece had fallen into place. And even though I had all of the answers, I knew that the Tohbi case would stick with me forever.

CHAPTER
TWENTY-SEVEN

Despite everything churning in my mind, I fell asleep as soon as my head hit the pillow, and a long, dreamless sleep enveloped me.

The alarm blared at six. I reached for my phone, and Yersi's weight shifted off my lower back. After silencing the alarm, I set my phone back on the side table and rested my head down, relieved that I hadn't received any notifications overnight.

With a *merf*, little kitty paws tiptoed down the bed. There was a light *thud* as he hopped down. Even though I knew he'd take up his station and start mournfully calling for breakfast in about two seconds, the routine of it all was somehow comforting. Yersi was doing Yersi things, and it made my world complete. I needed that steady predictability when everything else outside my home felt so messy.

I went through the motions, feeding Yersi, caring for the chickens, brewing a cup of black tea, and eating a light breakfast. Even though I'd called out from work, today was going to be rough. I tried to take pleasure in the simple tasks.

I slipped on a comfy pair of jeans and a loose shirt. I brushed my long hair, taking time with each stroke and feeling the bristles tug slightly. Each divided lock twisted around my fingers as I folded them back and forth into a braid; the weight of it settled down my spine.

About an hour later, I curled up on the couch. Yersi sat in my lap, purring loudly and drooling like a fiend, his cute kitty loaf offering oodles of comfort. Even though he ruled Casa Harjo with an iron paw, he knew when it was necessary to soothe the souls of his minions. Either that, or he'd decided to take advantage of the free massage. I never knew with him.

We snuggled for an hour or so until Yersi perked up and leaped from the couch, making a beeline for the door. Within less than a minute, a soft knock sounded.

Tessa.

The enormity of what I had to do slammed into my chest, making my heart skitter.

Today might be the last time I ever see Chula.

When I opened the door, Tessa stood there, shoulders slumped and bags painted faintly below her eyes. Depression always stalked the perimeter of her mind like a tiger, and I could practically see the creature in there, tense and ready to pounce. Tessa had known the joy of Chula for less than a year, and the universe decided to yank the carpet out from under her.

Meow, Yersi chirped with a hint of worry. He whirled around Tessa's legs as I folded her into a hug.

It was a long, deep hug, and tears threatened.

When we let go, I took a good, long look into her eyes. "Ready?" I asked gently.

She nodded with her lips pressed into a firm line.

After a reassuring scratch for the fretful Yersi, I locked up the house, and we slipped into my car.

On any given Sunday, we'd be queuing up the tunes, chatting each other up about the week, and occasionally singing along at the top of our lungs to whatever old school song struck our fancy. Today, a veil of sadness had enveloped the tiny space within the Prius, and we were both solemn.

I put on our usual playlist of '90s hip hop out of habit more than anything, and backed out of the driveway.

As if we hadn't been kicked around enough already this week, the first randomized song was "It's So Hard To Say Goodbye To Yesterday." When the first hum of Boyz II Men swam from the speakers, I felt my hands clench on the steering wheel.

Tessa wasn't the prolific consumer of hip hop that I was, so it wasn't until the harmony group reached the chorus that the weight of the song really hit her. I watched her from the corner of my eye, expansive pastures of tall grasses streaking by behind her. She cupped her forehead in her hand and rubbed at the furrows, but she didn't move to switch songs.

I took one hand off the wheel to reach over and squeeze hers.

She sighed heavily. As she turned to look out the window, I caught a tear streaming down her cheek. The song ended and shifted to 2Pac's "Thugz Mansion," which was still pretty dark, but his voice was oddly reassuring, and the sadness in the car lifted slightly.

We rolled into Aunty's drive, the gravel crunching beneath the tires, and a small cloud of dust trailed after the car. The porch and yard were empty.

No scratching chickens. No Chula keeping watch.

That small little thing—the little shift from normal—slammed the last peg home. I swallowed back the tears.

The soft hum of the cicadas met us as we stepped from the car. A faint breeze rustled the leaves of the large oaks, bringing the smell of lavender. I wanted to shout at the merry expanse of turquoise sky and demand that it cover its cheerful face with gloomy clouds. The world had no right to be so beautiful today.

Tessa and I headed to the front door in silence, a heaviness pulling at our sneakers like we walked through mud.

The front door was wide open, and the gentle breeze flowed in through the metal screen. Chula hadn't been on the porch, she wasn't at the window, and she hadn't been at the screen door to greet us. Her absence tore at me like a knife.

I opened the screen door, holding it for Tessa. "Hey, Aunty," I called out. "It's us."

"I'm in the kitchen," Aunty replied from the other room. Her normally happy voice had a somber, downward inflection.

Tessa and I exchanged a worried look, still troubled by Chula's lack of greeting, and made our way to the kitchen.

We found Aunty at the stove, flipping pancakes, with her back turned to us.

Chula—dear, sweet Chula—was resting on her bed, which had been pulled next to the kitchen table. Her eyes traced our path as we entered, her tail thumping weakly on the floor. She didn't lift her head.

"Oh, Chula," Tessa whispered fretfully. She collapsed to her knees by Chula's bed, folding her arms around her neck. Silent tears started.

I bit the tender spot on the inside of my cheek, wanting to stay strong for all of us, and held back my own tears. I moved over to Aunty and placed a hand on her back, moving it in gentle circles.

She flipped the three pancakes over and laid the spatula on the counter. Her arms folded around me in a strong hug. "Hello, sweety."

After we released each other, I kept one arm around her shoulder. She held her hand to my back and fiddled with my braid.

"You didn't have to cook for us, you know," I said softly.

She flashed me a slightly playful, incredulous look. "Of course, I had to feed you."

A slight smile tipped my lips. "Can I help?"

"Will you make us all some tea?" she asked.

"Sure," I said, releasing her.

"Maybe some chamomile.... Yes, chamomile. With honey," she said, more to herself. She pulled out a jar of dried flowers from her yard.

I filled the kettle, set it on the stove, and leaned against the counter as I waited for it to boil. The soft sizzle of the pancakes and rumble of the warming kettle were the only sounds.

Tessa had shifted to sit on the floor, back against the wall. Chula's head rested in her lap, and Tessa gently stroked her ears. Tessa's back was bowed, face turned down to Chula, long black hair hiding her face. The cracks in my heart shattered into a million pieces at the sight of them.

At the whistle of the hot water, I added the dried flowers, watching the thin petals swell with the water, and let them steep before measuring out the tea into the three mugs. I stirred honey into each and set them around the table.

I joined Tessa and Chula on the floor. Chula lifted her head, giving me a single warm lick on the hand before returning her head to Tessa's lap. I gave her a scratch behind the ears, her soft brown hair swirling with the attention, and then folded my knees to my chest.

Soon, Aunty set the table, laying out a plate piled with pancakes, a bottle of whipping cream, and berry compote.

"Come on, ladies," she said lightly. "Let's eat before it gets cold."

I wasn't sure I *could* eat.

Most of my feelings of sadness, anger, and frustration could be temporarily consoled with ice cream or some other delectable treat. But food therapy only worked up to a point. Once I reached the edge of sadness, that point where it tipped over into inconsolable sorrow, the desire to eat was replaced by an emptiness that could never be filled.

Tessa and I took our seats at the table and courteously selected a couple of pancakes. I stared at mine, sipping on my tea to buy some time, hoping to calm my stomach. Tessa looked to be about the same. And then there was Aunty; she hadn't even served herself yet.

Realizing that I needed to be strong for the others, I reached over and filled my entire plate with whipped cream, the swishing sound echoing in the silence. I lifted my eyebrows and pressed my lips in a firm line. With determination, I spooned copious amounts of compote on top of the clouded piles of cream. I looked up to find Tessa and Aunty staring at me.

I arched an eyebrow in a mock challenge. Keeping my eyes locked on theirs, I grabbed a heaping forkful and stuffed it into my mouth, fully aware that I had smeared food around my lips. My cheeks puffed out as I chewed.

Aunty fought a smile. Tessa let out a snort.

"What?" I said, mouth still full.

Aunty shook her head knowingly. The skin around her eyes creased with pent-up laughter.

My eyes widened with mock innocence, and I shoved another huge bite in my mouth before I'd even finished the last. Though I knew I should've been declaring how wonderfully delicious every-thing was, the food tasted like ash in my mouth.

"Yum!" I grinned.

That seemed to break the ice. Aunty finally served herself, and Tessa spooned some of the berry mash onto her pancakes.

There was a comfortable lack of conversation as we ate our meals, each of us lost in our thoughts. The clinking of silverware on the plates and the occasional swish of the whipping cream can separated the stretches of silence. When we finished, there was an unspoken synchrony as we bussed our plates, rinsed them, and placed them in the washer.

"Let's go out on the porch," Aunty suggested.

We refilled our mugs and moved to follow her out.

Aunty patted her leg. "Come on, Chula, dear."

Chula lifted her head, trying to rise. She managed to get her front legs beneath her before she collapsed back onto her bed.

"Chula," Tessa cried softly.

We both moved forward. I took a knee and slipped my arms beneath Chula. "I'll carry her out. Can you grab her bed?"

Tessa nodded.

I lifted Chula in my arms, and she shifted weakly. "It's okay, girl. I've got you," I whispered to her.

A soft lick swept across my bare arm.

We moved outside. Tessa laid Chula's bed next to Aunty's spot on the porch. When I placed Chula gently down, she let out a sharp exhale of discomfort.

"Sorry," I whispered to her, stroking her ears.

"Thank you," Aunty said, taking the seat next to Chula, watching her with worry in her eyes.

Tessa sat on the floor of the porch on the other side of Chula, resting her hand on Chula's hip.

I sat crisscross in front of them, completing the circle around Chula.

The soft hum of the cicadas formed the background for the birds twittering in the trees. The smell of the chamomile from the tea mixed with the soft scent of lavender, sage, and jasmine that drifted from the plants surrounding the porch.

My eyes were locked on Chula. I knew she was dying, and it tore a chunk out of my spirit.

"Aunty," Tessa said softly, looking up at her with red, puffy eyes.

Aunty reached down and grabbed her hand. "Yes, sweety?"

"I don't think Chula has much longer..." she started.

"Yes, I know," Aunty said softly.

"If she didn't eat this morning and she can't walk, I...." Tessa trailed off again.

Tessa looked down at Chula and stroked her side.

"The end is never pretty," Tessa finally finished.

"I know," Aunty repeated.

Aunty had stood vigil for many as they lay dying. She'd been there for those last few, often agonized breaths, the startled looks, and the last bit of fight in even the sickest of creatures. Standing as the pillar of support as a loved one passed was one of the toughest roles to play.

Aunty had been by my mom's side in the hospital. I don't know how Aunty knew my mom was going to pass at the crack of dawn, but she did. And she'd somehow convinced the nurses to let her stay. Nowadays, hospice would let patients stay at home and pass there; I always thought there was dignity in that.

In a hesitant whisper, Tessa said, "If you want, I brought some stuff to help her pass."

My back stiffened slightly, and my eyes jumped to Aunty.

Aunty was one to embrace nature, inclusive of all of the beautiful and the terrible parts. She didn't want to see anything suffer, but she also wanted to be respectful of the spirit.

Aunty considered Tessa's offer in thoughtful silence.

I was afraid to move, worried that any motion might tip her decision one way or the other.

Aunty sighed heavily. "I know she will not last the weekend. It is selfish of me, but I don't want to see her go. I want to be there for every second, even though time is spinning by faster than I'd hoped."

Hot tears streamed down my cheeks, and I leaned over to rub Chula's soft ears. Her eyes stayed closed, her breaths coming out in short, almost painful huffs. I wanted more time with her, too.

"May I have this day? With both of you and my dear, sweet Chula?" Aunty said in a voice that was almost pleading.

My eyebrows crinkled, and I tried to smile reassuringly. "Of course, Aunty."

"Will you stay? And if she is still with us when the sun sets, will you release her spirit?" She looked at both of us, face wrinkled with anguish but eyes still dry.

"Yes. We'll stay," Tessa said, squeezing Aunty's hand once more.

This is our last day with Chula.

Grief washed over me.

The afternoon passed slowly, the weather just the right temperature for us to stay comfortably on the porch.

Aunty had let the chickens out, and they scratched in the yard. We sat on the porch, taking turns petting Chula and trying to make her comfortable. Trying to make sure she knew she was loved.

Chula was so weak. Her eyes would occasionally open, watching the chickens. And every once in a while, she'd get enough energy to give one of us a lick. But she didn't rise. She wouldn't take water, and we couldn't coax her to eat even the tastiest of treats.

And all around us, the world sang with life. Flower blossoms danced in the light breeze, bringing the smell of lavender and jasmine. Bees bobbed through the garden, and the chickens scratched in the yard. Birds sang in the trees, and the cicadas hummed.

Memories of Chula flowed through my mind. I saw Tessa—the first time she'd ever been to Aunty's—a time when her spirit still wasn't on the right path. She was throwing the ball for Chula. And Chula, seeing the good in her, bounded back to drop the ball at Tessa's feet, tongue hanging out. She'd been able to draw out one of the few smiles from Tessa during those first days.

There were images of Chula snuffling around on the floor of the kitchen, looking for any scraps on Sunday mornings. I remembered sneaking my fair share of bits of bacon and fry bread under the table to her. She would always take it delicately, never slobbering on my hands or brushing her teeth against my skin. I remembered all of the times walking along the path by the creek, Chula in the lead, snuffling in the bushes.

I realized we'd never do that again, and something inside of me broke.

As the sun began to set and the croak of the frogs joined the singing of the cicadas, there was an imperceptible shift in the world.

"It's time," Aunty said, voice hushed.

Tessa nodded and softly shifted Chula's head from her lap. "I'll be right back."

Charlie Anderson must've helped Tessa out and given her what she needed for today. I thought about how far Tessa had come, and I was honored that she was able to do this for our family.

I leaned over Chula, hugging her head. I dug my fingers in her thick brown hair and pressed my face against the soft velvet of her ears. The tears streamed down my face, and I licked my chapped lips.

"Thank you, Chula, for all of the love you have brought into this family," I whispered just to her. "I love you."

Chula shifted, and I felt a soft lick on my cheek.

Aunty shifted to sit next to me, grunting slightly as one of her knees popped. She pressed a hand to my back. "Her spirit will continue her journey. The memories of her will continue to bring us joy."

I shifted to the side so that Aunty could say her own goodbyes. Aunty put Chula's head on her lap, whispering to her softly.

When Tessa arrived, it was quick and mercifully peaceful.

We all knew the moment her spirit had left her, and that was when Aunty finally started to sob.

I leaned next to her, holding her shaking shoulders. Tessa sat quietly, lips folded in, with silent tears streaming down her face.

I slowly stood and tugged Tessa's arm. We moved silently to dig a grave beneath one of the sweeping oaks in the front yard. Aunty wanted her there, where she could always watch over the chickens.

When Aunty was ready, we buried Chula with her ball under the oak. We stood together in a line, our hands clasped, sweet memories swimming through our minds as the last of the light fled from the sky.

CHAPTER
TWENTY-EIGHT

Saturday morning arrived after a long, dreamless sleep. When I woke, my eyes were still puffy and red from all of the crying.

Sadness crouched on the edges of my thoughts. I tried to push it away and grieve later. Today, Tessa and all of her classmates would graduate. It was supposed to be a happy day, but it was so discordant from the day prior that the juxtaposition flung my emotions all over the place.

I hurried around the house, preparing for guests. The graduation was at two in the afternoon, and everyone was going to come over after for a dinner celebration. When I'd offered to host something at my place, Tessa had accepted, but she'd asked for a small affair.

The house was fairly clean. I gave the bathroom a once-over, made the bed, and swept the hardwood floors. I wiped down the surfaces in the kitchen, knowing Aunty would want a relatively clean place to make the fry bread.

I got everything ready for the tacos: took the ground beef out of the freezer to thaw, grated the cheese, and shredded the lettuce. I made a large pitcher of sweet tea. Last but not least, I made a chocolate cheesecake from scratch. Everything went back in the fridge until the afternoon.

Going through the motions of cooking helped distract me. It was a slow, almost meditative prep, during which I could zone out and complete small tasks to occupy my mind. Every so often, images of Chula would drift to the forefront, and a sob would escape.

I was determined to tuck everything deep in my heart to unpack later. Today was a day of new beginnings for the graduating class.

And Tessa, my sister-from-another-mother, had climbed mountains to make it here.

With the house good to go, I ate a quick lunch and changed out of my sweats. I slipped on a deep purple, fit-and-flare dress. Unsure of how to wear my hair, I decided to brush the dark waves and let them hang free below my shoulders, tickling the backs of my bare arms. I added long beaded earrings and a bracelet. I skipped any makeup.

Sitting on the couch, I brushed away Yersi's advances. I told myself it was because I didn't want to be picking black cat hairs off my dress for the next six hours. But deep inside, I knew any snuggles might open the floodgates.

At one, the doorbell rang. Armand stood there, dressed to the nines and smelling like absolute heaven.

"Hello," I breathed, feeling the tightness around my heart ease.

"Hello, *iubita mea*," he replied, and folded me into a gentle hug before I could even let him all the way in.

I pressed my cheek against his chest, inhaling the deep scent of his aftershave.

He stroked my hair tenderly. "I'm sorry about Chula."

I squeezed my eyes tight, fighting the emotions that threatened to bubble up. I forced myself to step back.

"Come in." I put my hand on the door handle and moved to the side to let him through.

His eyebrows crinkled slightly, but he didn't push it.

Closing the door behind him, I added, "Aunty should be here any minute."

There was an awkward moment as we both fumbled for something to do while we waited. Yersi saved us by letting out a plaintive *meow*. He rubbed against Armand's leg, begging for a lap. Armand moved to the couch and tapped his thighs. Yersi obliged, morphing into a drooling kitty loaf like a transformer. Black hair floofed all over Armand's tan khakis.

"Has she been neglecting you?" he cooed.

Yersi let out a small *merf* in reply, closed his eyes, and started purring.

"Oh, please," I said, rolling my eyes. A smile danced on my lips, and a small laugh escaped. I joined them on the couch.

To fill the empty space, I asked Armand about his work. I half-listened, mind swimming with pain but grateful for the buzz of normal conversation in the background.

Soon, there was a small knock at the door, and my chest tightened.

Aunty.

It wasn't often that Aunty made the trek up to Stillwater. Tessa had given Aunty a graceful way to bow out of the graduation ceremony, especially given the situation with Chula, but Aunty wasn't having any of that. "Life is precious and short. We must take the time to celebrate," she'd said.

When I opened the door, my teeth went right to the raw spot in my cheek. I hadn't seen Aunty look this rough-and-ready in forever. She'd made an effort and had even worn her dressy slacks and silk top. But her face was etched in sorrow, and there was a puffiness around her eyes that was impossible to hide.

Without a word, I folded her into a hug, taking a deep breath of the lavender and sage smell that was just so Aunty. I pecked her cheek before stepping back.

"Hello, Aunty," Armand said, as he shifted Yersi to the couch and stood. He looked like a cat bomb had exploded on his lap, and I admired the fact that he didn't even try to brush off the hair.

"Armand," she said, moving to him to give him a quick hug.

Reluctant to turn right back around and stuff Aunty back into a car, I offered, "Can I get you anything?"

"I'll just use the bathroom, and then we can go," she said and trundled down the hall.

Armand moved close to me and loosely clasped my fingers. "How is she?" he whispered.

Meeting his eyes, I pressed my lips together and shook my head slightly. I was having a hard enough time keeping the sadness at bay, and I figured it would be a million times more difficult for Aunty. We needed to be strong.

He seemed to get what I was putting down, because he stepped back with a slight nod, releasing my hand.

A quick flush was followed by the sound of water in the sink. Aunty appeared, swiping her hand over her braid, straightening any loose hairs that had escaped on the drive.

"Shall we?" I asked, trying to let myself enjoy the excitement of graduation and feel happiness for Tessa.

With nods all around, we bundled into my car to make the short drive to campus.

It took longer than expected to find a parking spot, but with some searching, we finally joined the flood of family and friends headed to the auditorium. The air was electric with giddy excitement. After eight or more years of school, the hundred or so veterinary students would now step into the world as doctors. The family and friends who had supported them were there, carrying bouquets and wearing huge, proud smiles. Chatter spilled over us from all directions.

The mood of the crowd was infectious, and I soon found myself smiling. Armand clasped my hand. He turned to me with his own smile and gave me a squeeze.

Once I'd gotten Armand and Aunty settled in with the families, I moved to sit with the veterinary school faculty, grabbing the seat Zoe had saved for me.

She grinned, happy tears pooling along her lower lids. "I just can't help it," she exclaimed. "Graduations get me every time!"

Before I knew it, the ceremony had kicked off. Speeches were made, and soon after, students walked across the stage one by one.

I knew some of them from rotations or pathology rounds and clapped for them all. Even Emma, the stuck-up snob I'd worked with back in September, received a half-hearted applause. I was surprised she'd made it and only hoped that she'd learned a lesson or two about being such a shitass. When Mackenzie crossed the stage, another student Zoe and I had both worked with, we cheered, excited to hear that she'd gotten an anatomic pathology residency.

And then came Tessa.

My heart swelled with pride as she walked across the stage, back straight and proud. She'd come so far, and it had been such a difficult journey. With that diploma in her hand, I knew she would be okay.

With the tassels flipped, the graduating class was officially announced, and a loud cheer echoed through the auditorium.

After graduation, the four of us gathered back home in my kitchen. Tessa sat at the counter, nursing a glass of iced tea. Armand stood to the left side of the stove, browning the ground beef under Aunty's watchful eye. Aunty dipped fry bread into the oil, waiting for each one to puff up, and flipping them before placing them on a plate adorned with a thick layer of paper towels. I stood on Aunty's other side, fingers sticky with fry-bread dough, as I pinched off small fist-sized pieces and shaped them into flattened circles.

"The graduation was beautiful," Aunty commented.

"Beautifully short," Tessa said, huffing a laugh. "Those speeches...." She rolled her eyes.

I was right there with her. Graduation speeches were just echoes of each other. There was nothing new said, nothing earth-shatteringly amazing. It was all just pomp and circumstance. It only made things worse when the speech was delivered by someone whose lived experience was miles off from that of the graduating class.

"Why did they play bagpipes?" Armand asked, all innocence.

I shrugged. "No clue. It's just a thing. I don't think there was anyone with a drop of Scottish blood in that room, including the bagpiper. It's just something Americans do, like at ceremonies, funerals, that kind of thing."

"Yeah, Go Pokes," Tessa said, flashing Pistol Pete's gun gesture.

That got a snort from Aunty.

"Huh," he replied, unimpressed.

He reached over. "I think the meat's done." He spooned the meat into a serving dish and set it on the table next to the other toppings before joining Tessa at the counter.

"You must be happy to be finished," Armand said to her.

She nodded, and her expression shifted between different emotions so quickly it was like playing cards flashing by in a shuffle. Relief sat at the forefront of it all. But there was a hint of pride, plenty of exhaustion, and a twinge of sadness.

"Yeah," she said. "It's been a long road. But after eight years, I can't wait to not be in a classroom anymore."

I remembered my own graduation, and how happy I'd been to start my residency. I thought about how grateful I'd felt to finally be practicing my craft.

They continued chatting about what the next week or so would look like for Tessa: moving out of the dorms, working full-time with Charlie, and all of the other bits and bobs that made up life after college.

Aunty and I finished up the fry bread, and we all tucked in at the table. Armand led the charge, holding the bowls out for Tessa to serve herself.

My head buzzed with so many different feelings. The routine of spooning toppings onto the fry bread and digging in made for a simple distraction.

The general mood was mixed. I could see the clouds of sadness behind Aunty's eyes. But I could also see a layer of happiness for Tessa. Human beings are such complicated creatures. The longer we live, the more baggage we carry, and the more difficult it is to boil everything down to a single emotion.

After several pieces of cheesecake had been consumed and the dishwasher hummed away, Aunty and Tessa bundled out of the door with hugs all around. Armand and I sat on the small couch, each snuggled into one end. We both cradled mugs of herbal tea. We were stuffed and had the glazed post-prandial look.

With some hesitation, he reached over and grabbed my hand. "Have you thought more about coming back to Romania with me?"

My chest constricted, and I felt like I was wearing a girdle laced so tight that I couldn't breathe. I knew the clock was running out on his visa. I'd been so distracted this week with the Tohbi case. And if losing Chula wasn't terrible enough, the last bit of my emotional bandwidth had been sucked up by Tessa's graduation. I just couldn't even think about it in that moment.

And yet, I knew I had to.

I gently squeezed his hand and rested my mug on the coffee table. I scooched into the crook of his arm and looked up at him. Beneath the pleasant smell of his aftershave was the light musk that was unique to him. It was a smell I'd grown to love. I couldn't imagine my life without him.

But there was so much to my life here that I would miss: meals and games with Laila, singing along to hip hop with Tessa like sisters, joking around on the necropsy floor with Dustin, sussing out the most difficult cases with Sandy. I'd miss my job at the lab—oh, how I'd miss it. The lunch crew was like a second family. A part of me might even miss Gerald, as weird and fucked up as that might sound.

And, the biggest piece of it all, I couldn't imagine my life without Sunday brunch with Aunty.

I had a life here: a life I loved. Even though Yersi could go with me and I knew I'd make a new home wherever I was in the world, I couldn't bring all of those people with me.

Armand must have seen all of this spin across my face. His smile slowly dropped, and his eyes grew sad. He brushed his fingers lightly through my hair.

He leaned his forehead against mine. "It's okay. I understand," he said as if I'd spoken my answer out loud. "I'll always love you, *iubita mea*."

CHAPTER
TWENTY-NINE

That night, alone in my bed, I dreamed of the white dog.

I sat on Aunty's porch, in my usual chair, a soft breeze tickling the hairs on my arms. My feet were bare, and I could feel the rough wood of the porch beneath them. The air was thick with moisture, but the sky was crystal blue for as far as I could see. A faint smell of sage drifted on a gentle breeze. The cicadas hummed the song of home.

Aunty sat next to me, looking out toward the creek and the path that we had walked so many times before. Her gray hair was pulled into a neat braid that draped down the front of her chest. She looked at peace.

At her feet, the white dog slept.

ACKNOWLEDGMENTS

It's bittersweet to end the Josie Harjo series. But like all life transitions, the closing of one door often leads to the opening of another.

When I first started writing this series, I channeled all of the evil shit I'd seen men do at work into a single character. But I believe that everyone has the ability to change for the better, and I knew from the start that I wanted Gerald to be set on a better path when I put the series down. Gerald isn't perfect—no one is—but Josie took a moment to try to understand him, helping him become a better person. Most people are assholes because they're hurting. Instead of locking them out, maybe think about passing them a lemon bar. It may be all they need to turn a corner.

The Josie series wouldn't be what it is without Derek Smith. He helped me build this story from the ground up, and he knew from the start where everything would need to land by book four. The story, especially Gerald's arc, is a product of our many conversations over breakfast. His empathy and desire to understand people can be felt in this book. Derek, I appreciate you.

Thanks to all of the talented women who polished everything up. My copy editor, Caryn Pine, and my proofreader, Yasmine Bonatch, worked on every Josie book and made the series what it is today. Angela Caldwell designed the cover, once again picking the perfect animal profile. Dr. Karyn Bischoff provided valuable toxicology input. Thank you, all.

And finally, to my partner, Justin. We've been through many of life's beginnings and endings together, and I'm glad you were there for every step. Thank you for supporting my retirement from veterinary medicine and the beginning of my writing career. You were on to something when you showed me the "fuck-you money" clip from *The Gambler*. We built our fortress of solitude, I shucked off the chains of corporate America, and here we are. A new beginning. Love you, babe!

ABOUT THE AUTHOR

Catherine Sequeira was born and raised in the Bay Area. She obtained her BS and DVM from UC Davis and completed an anatomic pathology residency at Cornell. Throughout her career, she has lived and worked in Switzerland, New York, Oklahoma, and Scotland before returning to California. With over twenty years as a veterinary anatomic pathologist under her belt, she now writes and teaches. In her spare time, she enjoys reading sci-fi and fantasy, playing tabletop games, and gardening. She lives in northern California with her partner, cat, and bearded dragon (the bearded kind, that is).

She can be found online at www.catherinesequeira.com.